CW01082402

ESCAPING WONDERLAND

TIFFANY ROBERTS

Cover Illustration by Gabriella Bujdoso

Portrait Art by Kataraqui

Chapter Illustration by Kaja A. McDonald (Averil the Artist)

Interior Illustrations by Donovan Boom

❀ Created with Vellum

ESCAPING WONDERLAND

He's deadly, seductive, and completely unhinged. He's also her only chance of escape.

Alice knows Wonderland is just a virtual world operated inside an asylum to which she's been wrongfully committed, but she can't find her way out—can't find her way back to the life she lived before she woke beneath titanic trees and towering flowers. With the terrifying Red King searching for her and chaos all around, her only hope of escape lies in Shadow, a tall, mysterious being with glowing eyes, sharp claws, and a haunting grin who may be the maddest of them all.

But even if Wonderland isn't real, her growing feelings for Shadow—and his desire for her—are. Can Alice and Shadow escape Wonderland together, or will she succumb to the madness like everyone else?

Contains dark elements and violence. Check the author's website for detailed content warnings.

DEDICATION

TO ANYONE WHO HAS EVER BEEN MADLY
IN LOVE.

CHAPTER 1

ALICE THRASHED like a rabbit caught in a trap, battling the cruel, strong hands of her captors. She had only one goal—escape. It didn't matter that there were at least four burly orderlies dragging her along, didn't matter that she was in an isolated, locked-down facility. She didn't belong here. This was a mistake.

This was a *crime*.

"Would you dose her before she kicks me in the balls?" one of the men said.

A man on her other side grunted. "Hold her still and I will!"

"No!" Alice swung her legs wildly until hands with viselike grips closed around her ankles and calves. "You can't *do* this. Let me go! I know the police chief, and he'd put a stop to this!"

"Why didn't you idiots sedate her while she was in transit?" asked a woman with a voice as cold and hard as granite. "Get her against the wall."

The orderlies turned and shoved Alice forward, slamming her face first into the wall. The impact jolted her, knocking the air out of her lungs; for an instant, her struggles ceased. Her captors took full advantage of the respite, forcing her arms

behind her back and pinning her against the wall with their bodies.

A large hand grasped her head and forced it to turn, pressing her cheek to the wall. Her breath heaved out of her, lifting the tangled strands of blonde hair that had fallen into her face. The men around her were made into featureless monsters in the dimly lit corridor. A smaller figure stepped forward—the woman—and raised an arm. The device in her hand looked like a gun.

The woman touched the gun to the side of Alice's neck. Before Alice could resume her struggles, there was a sharp click, followed by a stinging pain in her neck. The device hissed.

Alice flinched and tried to pull away as an icy sensation spread outward from her neck, but the men holding her only further tightened their grips. The chill raced through her veins to permeate her body. Against her will, her muscles relaxed.

"No," she cried, hot tears spilling down her face. "Don't do this. This isn't right. I...don't...I don't belong here."

Her strength faded as the coldness intensified, and, soon, she was held upright only by the unforgiving holds of the orderlies.

One of the men chuckled. "They all say that."

"But this one isn't like the rest," another man said. "This one's pretty. I wouldn't mind a taste."

A hand slipped between her chest and the wall to squeeze her breast.

Terror slithered through Alice, coiling tight around her lungs and heart. She strained to fight back, to shake out of the orderlies' restraining grasps, to move at all, but her efforts only produced a sluggish twitch of her fingers.

"This one isn't for you," the woman said. "She's here under the director's personal watch. Do you understand?"

"You spoil all the fun, Doc," the man grumbled.

Alice's vision blurred, making the forms of her captors even more indistinct; she didn't know if it was because of her tears or the drugs they'd injected her with.

The woman—little more than a shadowy mass slightly smaller than the rest—turned away. "Bring that gurney over here. She's to be put under immediately."

The corridor spun around Alice wildly as the orderlies pulled her away from the wall and turned her toward the hazy white object that must've been the gurney. Despite her limbs refusing to respond to her commands, her captors' fingers bit into her flesh with a surprising sting—as though the ice in her veins were real, leaving her skin hypersensitive to even the merest touch.

The men lifted her off the floor and laid her on the gurney. Their hands kept her arms and legs pinned atop it while they walked down the corridor. She stared up at the hazy, hypnotic lights, which wove strange, blurred patterns in her vision. The sounds around her—the grumbling orderlies, their heavy shoes thumping on the floor, the squeak of a wheel in need of oiling—echoed impossibly, growing louder and louder with each passing moment.

Her eyelids fluttered; she kept them open only by sheer force of will, though it made little difference—everything around her was a mess of gray and black shadows that merged with each other, separated, and retreated from the overhead lights in a nauseating cycle perpetuated by their motion.

The gurney swung around suddenly and came to an abrupt halt, making her stomach lurch. There was a beep behind Alice; she let her head loll back and looked up to see a dark door open. The orderlies wheeled the gurney through the doorway and into a room lit only by several cones of white light that wavered in her unreliable vision, each separated from its neighbors by patches of relative darkness.

The gurney turned again, granting her a view of several large objects along the wall. She blinked rapidly to clear her eyes for a moment; the long, box-like objects were all identical except for the numbers on their lids. The haze returned to her eyes.

Coffins. They're going to bury me alive in a coffin, just like my dad was put in a coffin, and I'll scream and scream but no one will hear me.

She blinked again, struggling to think clearly.

Coffins? No, that isn't right. This is...this is a psychiatric hospital.

There wouldn't be coffins in a psychiatric hospital. But then what were those boxes? What was this room?

Why was she here?

The gurney stopped.

"Strip her," the woman ordered.

The orderlies finally released Alice's limbs to instead grab at her clothing. They tugged off her shoes, her pants, her shirt, bra, and underwear, their predatory, invasive touches sparking fresh flares of discomfort across her too-cold skin and panic in her chest. Their fingers seemed to touch every inch of her body in the process. She screamed inside her mind, unable to move, unable to fight, unable to cry for help—not that anyone would come for her. Tears of anger and helplessness dripped from the corners of her eyes.

They left her naked and vulnerable atop the gurney. The air settled with odd weight over her bare skin, and she could *feel* the orderlies' gazes raking over her. At any moment, she expected their hands to return to her body—to her breasts, her thighs, and between her legs rather than her wrists and ankles.

"Get her in a gown. I want her under as quickly as possible. It's going to take a little time to build her profile. She is a rush job," the woman said.

"Come on, Doc. Just a little fun?" one of the men asked.

A shadowy figure moved beside the gurney, and a rough hand settled on Alice's upper thigh.

This isn't real. This isn't real. It's just a dream. I'll wake up and it'll all go away.

"She's not for you," another man said—a *new* man, his deep, smooth voice somehow even colder than the woman's.

"Shit! I mean, sorry! Sorry, Director Koenig," the first man replied, yanking his hand away from Alice and retreating.

Heavy footsteps approached the gurney. A moment later, Alice's vision was blocked by another dark figure looming over her. Director Koenig. Her eyes strained as she struggled to take in the newcomer's appearance, but all she could tell for sure was that he wore a dark, expensive suit.

"Alice," the director said as he brushed some of her hair back from her cheek. "You're as beautiful as they promised. And such *spirit.*"

Something about his touch was unsettling enough to help Alice find her voice.

"Please," she rasped. "Jon…athan. My…" Getting those few words out left her lungs burning with exertion.

The director leaned closed, placing his mouth next to her ear. "Who do you think sent you here, pretty girl?"

Her heart skipped a beat. "No… He wouldn't—"

"But he *did*. You're mine now, Alice."

No! Why would Jonathon do this? Why?

But he wouldn't *do this. I'm his sister, we grew up together. There's no way…*

Director Koenig chuckled. "How long will it take to get her loaded into the simulation, Doctor Kade?"

"As soon as she's under, sir, it should take two or three hours to construct her profile and spawn her in," the woman replied.

"Good. It's going to take me some time to finalize the adjustments to the simulation, anyway. Have her brought to Winters for her…*orientation.*"

"Are you sure, Victor?" the doctor asked. "As you said, she's…

spirited, and Winters has something of a temper. If you're making the proposed changes—"

"He knows better than to defy me," the director said firmly. "Finish up here, Doctor Kade. I expect her to be ready as soon as possible." He stroked the tip of his finger along Alice's lower lip. "Alice...I'll check on you soon to make sure you're assimilating."

Alice poured as much rage as she could into her eyes as she stared up at the director's shadowy visage.

The director chuckled and moved away from the gurney, his heavy footsteps sounding toward the door; they were quickly drowned out by Alice's pounding heart.

"Don't just stand there slack-jawed," Doctor Kade snapped. "Get her dressed. We don't have all day."

The dark forms of two orderlies appeared on the sides of the gurney. They were even less gentle than before as they took hold of Alice's upper arms and dragged her into a sitting position. Her head lolled forward and her hair fell into her face, fully obscuring her view, as the orderlies tugged a garment over her extended arms. She swayed helplessly while they pulled the fabric into place and tied it along her back.

"Now get her into the immersion chamber," the doctor said.

No, no, no!

One of the orderlies slipped his arms beneath Alice's from behind, looping them around her chest—brushing his fingers over her breasts and nipples in the process—and dragged her backward. Another man took hold of her legs. They lifted her off the gurney. Her head tipped back, and her hair fell to clear her vision. Her captors carried her toward one of the coffin-like pods along the wall.

This isn't real. This isn't real.

I'm still in my bed. I'm going to wake up any moment in my room, in my house...

The orderlies brought her to the open pod and lowered her onto the soft cushions within. Her body was impossibly heavy.

She felt herself sinking into the cushions, felt like they were going to swallow her up, and it sparked a fresh wave of panic in her—not that it was enough to get her body moving again. New tears fell from the corners of her eyes. The walls of the chamber rose over her on either side as dark blotches in her peripheral vision; they seemed to be getting higher and higher as the sinking feeling intensified.

This isn't real! This isn't real!

"Is she in position?" Doctor Kade asked.

One of the orderlies leaned over the pod and brushed his fingertips across Alice's cheek. He muttered, "Lucky the director's got his eye on you, or—"

"Is she in position?" the doctor repeated, a hard edge in her voice.

"Yeah," the orderly said, withdrawing his hand. He grinned, leaned down so his mouth was close enough to Alice's ear for her to feel his breath, and whispered, "Welcome to Wonderland, Alice."

The pod hummed to life around her, and Alice could only lie there, mentally screaming, as sharp, unseen objects pierced her skin from all around. There were too many of them to count, too much pain to fathom; they pumped fire into her blood that mixed with the iciness of her fear to become something that seared her very soul.

But the peak of her agony didn't come until something pushed up through the cushion beneath her, parting her hair to sink into the back of her neck. It felt like a knife slowly pushing into her flesh. The object clamped down on her spine, and she heard—*felt*—metal scraping her vertebrae.

The pod lid, which was hinged somewhere over her head, swung down. Darkness reigned in the pod, broken only by the dim, diffused bit of light trickling in through the small window directly over Alice's face.

No sounds existed in the pod except for those of her ragged

breaths and thundering heart. Her vision darkened and narrowed as the heat inside her grew. She focused on the little window, willing herself to keep her eyes open, to stay awake.

This wasn't real. The pain wasn't real. It was all a bad dream...

Despite her struggles, the light faded, and even the sounds of her body fell silent. The last thing she heard before darkness claimed her was a whispered voice rising from her memory.

Welcome to Wonderland, Alice.

CHAPTER 2

ALICE WAS first aware of darkness; it was wrapped around her like a funeral shroud, leaving her world empty and silent. But she wasn't alone—someone was with her, someone was *touching* her. The back of a finger, which felt like it was covered by a thin layer of velvet, trailed from her chin up toward her cheekbone. The hand—she couldn't see it, but she could sense it all the same —lifted away for a moment before gently smoothing back her hair.

She smiled. This mysterious touch was pleasant, and she leaned into it. Strange as it was, she preferred this dream to the last one; she was at peace now. There was an almost worshipful quality to the phantom touch. If she let it go just a little longer, it could erase the lingering memory of those other hands, those rough, cruel hands that had dragged her toward this darkness.

A gentle sound broke the silence—leaves rustling in a soft breeze.

"You're going to be mine," someone whispered, barely loud enough for her to hear.

Suddenly aware of her body and its weight, Alice had a brief but intense sensation of falling—her body jolted even though

she was already lying on the ground. Her eyes snapped open. She swallowed and turned her head to look around; whoever had spoken was nowhere to be seen. She was alone.

Or *was* she?

Pressing her lips together, she willed herself to sit up—expecting her body to be as unresponsive as it had been before she fell unconscious. To her surprise, her muscles obeyed.

The breeze picked up, and the sound of rustling leaves grew in volume. Alice looked up to see towering trees all around her, the canopy swaying in the wind, which carried upon it the night songs of unseen insects. It was at once soothing and deeply disturbing.

Something seemed wrong here, even though this was a perfectly natural setting.

I was in an asylum, *not the woods.*

Clenching her fists at her sides, she forced herself to study her surroundings.

Patches of a violet night sky were visible through the dark shadows of the leaves, which seemed impossibly high—a sense only enhanced by the immensity of the tree trunks from which their branches sprouted. Was she in a redwood forest? As far as she knew, those trees only grew on Earth—her home planet didn't have any—but she didn't know any other trees that grew so large...

Though her surroundings had been swathed in deep shadow at first glance, Alice's eyes quickly adjusted; she could see *everything*.

Clusters of foliage, much of which was twice as tall as Alice, took up most of the space between the huge trees. Giant, glowing green mushrooms grew in clusters along the bases of a few of the trees, and the massive leaves and flowers—the latter of which were so large they made sunflowers look miniscule—were scattered all over, many of them also glowing faintly. She couldn't tell if they were reflecting light from overhead or emitting their own. Where it wasn't cluttered with oversized plants, the ground was blanketed in thick, short grass. Most of the vegetation seemed familiar, but it was all too big, and it all looked a little...*off.*

A fearful chill crept through her body again. This didn't make sense, this wasn't right, but here it all was, right before her eyes.

This...this isn't real.

I was just standing in my father's office, thinking about...about starting to go through his personal belongings...about deciding what to...

She released a shaky breath.

It had taken her a few months after his passing to finally build enough courage to start the process of moving on, but she knew it was the right thing to do. Sorting his belongings didn't mean she was forgetting him or disrespecting him, it only meant she was getting on with *her* life...

And then those men came. They came right into the office, in the middle of my *house, and dragged me out.*

Everything had been so chaotic in those moments, so difficult to follow. She could recall her stepbrother, Jonathon, arguing with the men, while her stepmother, Tabitha, glared from the top of the stairs, but the men had said something about having a court-sanctioned obligation to take her. It had all happened so quick, she'd thought it was a dream, but...

I'm in an asylum. A...psychiatric hospital.

But this *is no asylum...*

Her memories from after they'd hauled her into their waiting vehicle outside her home were fuzzy. The events were jumbled and blurry, fraught with shadowy figures and echoing, unnatural sounds—and *pain.* Her skin prickled at the mere thought of the agony she'd endured.

Her eyes widened as she recalled the coffin the men had laid her in.

No, it hadn't been a coffin; the woman, the doctor, had called it an *immersion chamber,* had mentioned a simulation.

Was that what they'd done? Had they placed her in that pod and connected her to some sort of fully immersive simulation? She'd toyed with immersive virtual reality a few times with her friends; it was a popular form of entertainment, allowing people to go anywhere, to be anything. But commercial units usually had safety features—the sort that always kept you aware that you were in a simulation. Most sensations in those simulations were muted, more like distant *echoes* than the real thing.

This felt real. *Too* real.

She lifted a shaky hand to the back of her neck, slipping it under her hair, and found only unbroken skin—nothing clamped into the top of her spine.

Her trembling didn't ease.

She looked down at herself, and her breath hitched. She was wearing a pale green hospital gown. Lowering her hand, she took hold of the gown's hem and tugged it down, covering more of her bared thighs.

They undressed me. They touched *me.*

Alice grasped the gown in both hands and squeezed the fabric until her fingers ached. Gut-wrenching shame suffused her, but it was joined by a spark of fury in her belly.

They'll pay. As soon as I get out of here, I'll make them all pay for what they did. If my father knew—

Alice's throat tightened with that thought. Her father wasn't here. He wouldn't be able to help her. He'd never be able to help her again.

Don't think about that now, Alice. You need... You need to find a way out of this. Whatever this *is.*

She glanced around again. She was sitting in the middle of the woods, but these weren't normal woods by any measure. Everything was of exaggerated proportion, everything had just a touch of alienness to it. The hairs on her arms and the back of her neck rose, and that prickling sensation returned to her skin. The longer she sat here, the more certain she was that someone was out there, watching her. She could *feel* their gaze upon her.

"Hello?" Alice called shakily. "Is anyone there?"

Her echoing voice was the only answer to her question.

She released her gown and raised her hands, pressing the heels of her palms against her eyes.

"Wake up," she muttered, rocking back and forth. "Wake up, wake up, *wake up*! This isn't real. It's all a dream. I've just been really tired." She pressed harder on her eyes—hard enough for it to hurt. *"Just wake the hell up!"*

Tears stung her eyes.

You weren't supposed to feel pain in dreams. You weren't supposed to feel pain in simulations.

The foliage to her left rustled. Alice went silent, lowered her hands, and lifted her head, eyes darting toward the sound.

The vegetation shook again; the movement was closer than it had been the first time. Something was coming.

Alice scrambled to her feet and retreated several steps. The soft grass beneath her soles tickled as it brushed between her toes, but she was only passingly aware of the sensation. Her breath was ragged, and her heart pounded rapidly, but she couldn't tear her gaze away from the moving foliage, couldn't turn and flee.

A white figure leapt from the vegetation and halted a few feet away from Alice. Her eyes rounded.

The being standing before her was a praxian; she'd seen his kind often in her home city, Apex Reach. His skin was pale but had a faint, purplish undertone like an old bruise, and his hair was long and white, framing a sharp-featured face that was almost skeletal. Overly long, pointed ears stood out from his hair. His nose was a light shade of gray, wide and flat, and there was a patch of white hair on his chin that only enhanced the angularity of his face. The deep, dark hollows around his eyes contrasted his bright pink irises, making them nearly glow.

He was dressed in a white suit that was tailored to his lean frame, and the high-collared shirt beneath his jacket matched the color of his eyes. It was the sort of clothing she might have seen at one of her father's formal parties—a sleek combination of modern and traditional.

The praxian straightened the collar of his shirt, settled his gaze on her, scowled, and said in a reedy voice, "You're late—and in the wrong place, on top of that."

Alice's brows furrowed. "What?"

"You were supposed to get here an hour ago, and you should've arrived twenty yards *that* way." He pointed in the direction from which he'd come. "Now scurry along, he's waiting for you."

"Who is waiting for me?" Alice shook her head and took another step back as the praxian advanced. "I-I'm not supposed to be here. This…this isn't real. None of this is."

The alien huffed and closed the distance between them. His movements were quick and twitchy. His hand darted out and closed around her wrist, and he tugged her arm. "Come along. We mustn't delay any further; we have much to do to prepare you."

Alice gasped. "Wait. Stop! Who's waiting? Where are you taking me?"

She tried to yank her arm back, but his grip was too strong despite his thin frame. She had no choice save to stumble along behind him.

"No time to explain," he said, quickening his pace. "When the Red King calls, we all must answer! Hurry! Hurry, now. We're late, late, late."

They plunged through the foliage. Leaves and petals battered Alice's face and body; she raised an arm to shield herself, but it made little difference. She didn't know who this praxian was, where he was taking her, or who was waiting—didn't know whether she was safe.

Safe? None of this is real! This is a simulation, and the only chance I have of getting answers right now is by following this stranger.

The underbrush—not that the term seemed appropriate when most of the plants were taller than Alice—ended abruptly. She staggered when her feet slapped down on solid ground.

She was now standing on a meandering path, constructed of purple paving stones, that twisted its way through the woods all around. It seemed to start here, in the middle of the woods—though it was possible that this was also its end—and followed no logical trail, doubling back on itself in several places.

"Come on, come on!" the praxian urged, tugging on her arm again.

"I'm moving as fast as I can!" Alice said, breath ragged.

"Faster, faster." The praxian led her along the path, following it exactly around every unnecessary turn and nonsensical loop, even when two steps across the forest floor could've brought them to the next section and avoided dozens of yards of extra walking in the process.

Even if Alice had had any idea of where they were when they began their journey, she would've been lost after only a few minutes; the purple footpath obliterated her sense of direction and made it impossible to gauge travel distance, and every tree they passed looked both wholly unique and exactly like every other tree in the forest.

After what might've been a few hours or only a few minutes, Alice stopped paying attention to those details—she sensed that thinking too hard on such things was to court madness.

This isn't *reality. There's no logic behind any of this, so there's no point in trying to apply any.*

She found herself paying attention again, however, when they passed a house. It was a small building, oddly quaint despite its surreal surroundings—it was reminiscent of an old-fashioned country cottage, though there was something alien in the angles of its windows and the oval shape of its door. The windows were dark, and the building was quiet. The praxian didn't give the structure so much as a glance.

He seemed not to notice any of the houses that popped up with increasing frequency as they pressed onward. Each was different from the last, and each had a touch of familiarity in its design but possessed some strange feature that made it seem *wrong*. They were of wildly different shapes, sizes, and colors; the only commonality between all of them was that none were set more than six or seven feet off the path.

As the houses grew in number, the trees thinned, and all the plants gradually dwindled to a far more reasonable size.

"There it is," the praxian said, a mixture of relief and exasperation making his voice even higher than before. "Hurry, girl, hurry!"

Alice looked up to see what he was referring to, and her brows fell low.

The path they were following continued its winding trail despite there being no obstacles for it to avoid. About a hundred feet ahead, it met another path, and another a little farther on, and even more after that, creating a tangled web of walkways that came from every direction and led to every direction. A few even led up and down, though her mind could not perceive *how* they did so.

But it was the building amidst those confused pathways that commanded Alice's full attention. It stood on dozens of support stilts, none of which were quite straight and many of which looked far too thin and frail to support any weight. The purplestone paths wound between those supports and through the shadows beneath the structure.

The massive wooden platform at the building's base created a deck around it, and people milled about on that deck—humans and aliens together, dressed in clothing that must've represented a thousand years of history for at least ten different species, often with little rhyme or reason as to the combinations.

And the building itself…

It had at least six or seven floors, though it was difficult to tell because no single aspect of the structure lined up with anything else. The angles were all strange—some of them should've been *impossible*—and sections of it hung over the open air without any visible support. In the real world, such a building would've collapsed before even a fraction of it had been completed.

But none of that mattered here.

A wide, uneven set of steps led up to the deck, and a hand-painted sign stood on a tall, bent post beside them.

Hatter's Tea Party, it declared.

"Come, come!" the praxian said impatiently, tugging Alice's arm.

They raced up the steps and through the double doors leading into the building. The praxian stopped abruptly. Alice plowed into his back, causing them both to stumble forward. He waved his arms to the sides to keep himself balanced, and Alice grabbed his jacket to steady herself.

He turned his head and glared at her over his shoulder.

"Sorry," Alice muttered, releasing his jacket and taking a step back.

That was his own damn fault.

The praxian's glare only intensified as he meticulously straightened his jacket, moving his arms and tugging the cloth until not even the tiniest wrinkle remained. He turned away from her only when he was done.

Frowning, Alice looked up, and promptly forgot her collision with the praxian. They were standing in a large, circular room with a black and white checkered floor. The wide staircase ahead split in half partway up, the two pieces curving to lead to an open level that ran around the inside of the chamber. More stairs wound up the cylinder farther up. A massive crystal chandelier hung overhead—though she couldn't see any chains holding it in place. There were at least two dozen doors all around the chamber, each of which was a different size, color, and shape, and the walls were lined with paintings that varied wildly in their subjects—tea pots, dolls, nude males and females of several species engaged in lewd acts. Alice's cheeks heated.

Countless people—human and alien alike—milled about the space, many of them wearing masks or elaborate face paint. They wore dresses and gowns, suits and costumes, all somehow uniform despite being so wildly different.

But one figure stood out from the rest—a tall, lean man, his features shrouded in shadow save for his wide grin and vibrant, glowing teal eyes. Despite the people moving about all around, despite the myriad of distractions, those strange eyes met Alice's and held them for an instant. Then someone walked past Alice and the praxian, obscuring her view. The shadowy figure was gone when her line of sight cleared. Her brows furrowed. She scanned the room, searching for signs of the shadowy stranger, but he was nowhere to be seen.

She stepped forward, meaning to delve into the crowd to find the man—she wasn't sure why, but something about him called to her—when a sharp voice brought her to a halt.

"You're late, Miraxis!" A squat woman in a lacy red gown hurried toward Alice and the praxian. Her waist was cinched, exaggerating her wide hips and her large bosom, which was barely contained by her dress. She wore a mask with deep, dark eyeholes and a long, pointed beak, and her black hair surrounded her head in a mass of bouncing ringlets.

The woman shoved the praxian, Miraxis, aside and stopped in front of Alice, tilting her chin down. "And *what* is she *wearing?*"

Miraxis wrung his hands and bowed his head. "Hurried as

fast as I could, Madame Cecilia. *She* arrived late, no time to change anything."

"Then we'll need to prepare her ourselves—quickly—before we get her to the Hatter. The king means to collect her tomorrow, and he doesn't like to be kept waiting. That doesn't leave Hatter much time to work. I've kept my heart out of the king's collection so far, and I'd like to keep it that way."

A tall, barrel-chested man dressed in a black and white checkered suit with a matching domino mask approached, carrying a silver platter with several small, pretty bottles arranged atop it. Each bottle had a little tag on it that said *Drink Me*. He paused beside the red woman. "Madame."

"Yes, yes." Cecilia plucked a bottle from the tray, uncorked it, and offered it to Alice. "Drink this, girl."

Alice frowned as she took the bottle. She brought it to her nose and sniffed. The faint fruity smell wafting from the bottle couldn't disguise its sharp tang of alcohol.

Cecilia snapped, "We do not have time! Drink!"

Alice held the bottle out to the woman. "Thank you, but I don't want it."

Cecilia sighed heavily, took the bottle in one hand, and reached up to pinch the bridge of her beak with the other. "*Why* must you be so troublesome? Hold her."

Miraxis's hands were on Alice before she could react. He pulled her back against his chest, wrapped one arm around her middle, locking her arms down at her sides, and grabbed her jaw.

Alice's eyes widened as she struggled against him. "What — *No!*"

"No time for such nonsense," Miraxis said, squeezing her cheeks to force her mouth open. "When the king calls, we *all* must answer."

Alice jerked and wiggled, growled and stomped on his feet; Miraxis grunted but did not release her. Alice's struggles only seemed to make him more determined to restrain her, and he was far stronger than he looked.

Cecilia pinched Alice's nostrils shut and raised the bottle, tipping it to pour its contents into Alice's open mouth. The liquid was sweet—impossibly sweet. It sent Alice's taste buds into overdrive; electric tingles arced across her tongue.

Alice sputtered, but she couldn't spit; she choked the liquid down against her will. The cool liquid seemed to heat up as it flowed down her throat. By the time it reached her stomach, it was delightfully warm. She gasped for air, but Cecilia dumped the remainder of the drink into her mouth. Only when Alice had swallowed that last mouthful did Miraxis let go.

Lifting a hand to her burning throat, Alice stumbled forward. She needed to get away from these people, needed to get out of this place. Her entire body felt heavy again, and that set her heart to racing; this was too much like what the orderlies and that doctor had done to her. The entire room swirled and spun, the colors and people blending together. Voices and laughter echoed all around.

"What...did you...do to me?" she rasped, moving her hand to her head and squeezing her eyes shut. Though she could no longer see the room spinning, Alice now felt like *she* was twirling in place.

"Get her up to a dressing room," Cecilia said. "The Hatter will be livid if she's not looking her finest when we send her up."

Miraxis caught Alice's wrist and dragged her toward the stairs. Her stomach sank at the sudden motion, and she nearly fell; her limbs were delayed in obeying her mental commands to move, though they felt oddly light now despite the heaviness that had gathered in them a moment ago. The room continued to sway, but it wasn't quite so unpleasant anymore.

As she followed Miraxis up the stairs, Alice turned her head, searching the crowd for the grinning shadow man. All the colors around her seemed more vibrant; what would *his* eyes look like now? But she couldn't spot him; there were too many people, too many faces, too many masks, all of them drastically different and exactly the same.

Alice had no idea how far up they'd traveled when Miraxis turned into a long hallway. His pace increased as he led her along the hall, finally stopping near its end in front of a blue door. He opened the door without hesitation, stepped aside, and shoved Alice into the room ahead of him.

She stumbled forward and, as soon as she caught her balance, paused to study her new surroundings. There was a mirrored vanity against the wall, all its little shelves and compartments overflowing with a dizzying array of makeup and brushes. A tall standing mirror was in one corner with an open wardrobe nearby, the latter filled with bright swaths of fabric in all colors and more dresses than Alice could count.

Alice furrowed her brow. She knew what all these things were for individually, but her mind was too fuzzy to put it all together. Why was she here? And why did her hospital gown feel suddenly so…restrictive?

"Finally!"

Alice stepped back with a start, turning her attention to the person who'd spoken.

The woman standing beside the vanity was rail thin, wearing a plain brown dress and a white mask that was featureless save for its black eyeholes.

The faceless woman stepped forward, grabbed Alice's arm, and pulled her farther into the room, guiding Alice to sit on the cushioned bench in front of the vanity.

Alice swayed on her seat, feeling light, airy, and warm, and looked into the mirror. Her eyes were so vibrantly blue, her lips such a lovely pink, and her hair looked like strands of spun gold.

What…what's wrong with me?

Before she could answer her own thought, something in the mirror caught her attention—a thick shadow just behind

Miraxis, with two teal eyes glowing in the darkness. It was gone faster than she could blink. Alice turned her head toward the doorway, leaning far to one side to see around the praxian, but there was nothing there.

Miraxis cleared his throat. "She is to be collected by the king tomorrow, but the Hatter will be conditioning her until then. She must—"

"Shoo!" The thin woman waved Miraxis away. "I don't need *you* telling me how to do my work, especially when *you're* the one who brought her here late." Taking Alice's chin between long, cold fingers, the woman turned Alice's face toward her and sighed. "And there's much to be done."

Alice was only vaguely aware of Miraxis exiting the room and closing the door. She was sealed in here now, trapped in this building, and she needed to get out. She needed to go... where did she need to go? Why couldn't she think? Why couldn't she *remember*? Fear clawed up from her gut, but it was quickly swept aside by a wave of euphoria.

Gentle pulses of heat spread through her body, easing the tension that had begun to seize her muscles. This place, this room, was as good as any, wasn't it? Everything here was so wondrous—even the walls. They were blue. *So* blue. A pretty, robin's egg blue.

"Blue is my favorite color," Alice murmured.

"Is it now?" the woman said. "Well then, we'll have to find you something pretty and blue to wear for the Hatter tonight. It'll bring out those eyes of yours."

The woman set to work, selecting a brush from the vanity and sweeping it lightly over Alice's skin.

"What are you doing?" Alice asked.

"Making you the prettiest at the party, dear. You'll be my masterpiece. It's not going to stop him from doing what he means to do, but it might make him a little gentler. Now close your eyes."

Alice's eyelids fluttered closed, and she smiled; the soft motion of brushes over her skin was soothing, lulling her deeper into relaxation. It didn't matter where she was—she felt *good*.

Soon, the woman's fingers were no longer on Alice's face, but in her hair, brushing the strands, easing the tangles. Alice hummed appreciatively.

When those hands finally moved away, Alice felt bereft. Lonely. She wanted the hands back on her, massaging her scalp, brushing her hair, her face. Her skin tingled, and she longed for more attention.

"Lift your right foot," the woman said.

Alice obeyed, keeping her eyes closed; she'd not been told to open them.

A moment later, the backs of the thin woman's fingers brushed over Alice's skin from foot to thigh as the woman pulled something onto Alice's leg—it felt like a stocking. Alice caught her lower lip between her teeth; the feel of that stocking sliding on had been *exquisite* against her sensitive skin.

"Now the other," said the woman.

They repeated the process, and within a few seconds, Alice had a stocking on her left leg, as well. Her smile widened. She brushed her palm over her knee, thrilling in the smooth feel of the stocking against her skin.

"Stand," the woman instructed.

After reluctantly forcing her hand away from her leg, Alice stood up. She swayed like a blade of grass in the breeze, but didn't feel off-balance, didn't feel dizzy. There was nothing to worry over; she was free.

The woman deftly untied the fasteners on the back of the hospital gown. Alice spread her arms as the woman slid the garment off. Cool air caressed Alice's suddenly bare skin, hardening her nipples and sending a thrill directly to her core.

The sound of metal hangers clacking together told Alice that the thin woman had moved to the wardrobe. Alice hummed to herself as she waited, keeping her hands still at her sides even though they itched to run over her own skin.

When the woman spoke again, she was in front of Alice. "This should do nicely, I think. I'll help you get into it."

The woman guided Alice's feet up one at a time, slipping heeled shoes onto them, before pulling something up around Alice's legs—it felt like a dress. The fabric brushed along Alice's legs as the woman drew it higher. After helping Alice get her arms through the straps, the woman's hands settled on Alice's shoulders and turned her around. Within a few seconds, the woman had the dress's bodice pulled tight and tied securely.

Alice parted her lips; the heat in her body was only increasing now that she was dressed, as though it were rebelling against being contained, against being restricted. She wobbled unsteadily on the heeled shoes.

The woman clasped something around Alice's neck—it was snug, like a choker—and something looser around her wrist.

"Good! Good!" The woman took hold of Alice's hands and tugged her along a few steps before moving to stand behind Alice. "Now...open your eyes!"

Alice opened her eyes. She was in front of the tall standing mirror, staring at an unfamiliar woman.

No, that's not another woman. That's my reflection.

She wore a sleeveless sky-blue dress with a black and white corset, its skirt hanging midway down her thighs, and black and white striped stockings. Her hair hung in gentle waves around her shoulders, framing a face both familiar and foreign. Her skin was as pale as porcelain, combining with her dark eyeliner and lengthened eyelashes to make her blue eyes stand out like cornflowers in a green meadow. The natural pink of her lips was enhanced by subtle lipstick, and soft blue and violet eyeshadow completed the look.

"Oh, he will adore you tomorrow!" the woman said. "Not that his attention is something *any* woman should want."

"Who?" Alice asked; her voice sounded far-off even to her

own ears, as though it had come from another person entirely. Her brows lowered.

This...doesn't feel right. I don't feel right.

"Why, the Red King, of course!" The thin woman giggled, settled her hands on Alice's shoulders, and leaned forward until her masked face was beside Alice's ear. "You're perfect. You would've been the prettiest of the Hatter's dollies if the king hadn't set his eye on you. I suppose you can still be the prettiest, at least until the morning."

The growing sense of dread in Alice's gut battled the unnatural euphoria coursing through her veins as the thin woman stepped away.

"She's ready!" the woman called.

Ready? Ready for what? I'm... No...this... What's wrong *with me?*

Alice stared at her reflection with her brow creased. She lifted a hand to the choker, only then noticing the bracelet on her wrist. It had a little tag, just like the bottle they'd forced her to drink; this one said *Eat Me*.

Movement in the mirror caught Alice's attention; the door swung open. Two men wearing black and white checkered suits and domino masks entered the room. They moved to either side of Alice and looped their arms through hers.

"Oh, do enjoy what time you'll have with the Hatter at his party," the woman said, waving.

The men turned and escorted Alice out of the room.

CHAPTER 3

THE MASKED MEN took Alice up the stairs, which wound around the immensely tall, cylindrical space like the threads inside a nut. Hallways and doors lined those steps all along the way.

The building was big, but it hadn't looked nearly this large from the outside...had it? Alice pursed her lips and struggled to recall what the place had looked like when she'd first seen it, but the noise from below—the din of conversation, laughter, and music—combined with the feel of her new clothing on her overly sensitive skin was far too distracting for her to think straight. All she could remember was *Hatter's Tea Party*.

It had been so long since she'd been to a party!

She glanced down at her dress. It was a pale blue—the blue of the spring sky, the best blue of them all. Everything should've been that shade of blue. The whole *world* should've been blue.

"He's been waiting a long time," said someone in a deep, gruff voice.

Alice lifted her gaze to find herself at the very top of the stairs. A man—built like a brick wall with a flat, stony face—stood just in front of Alice and her escorts, his huge frame

almost large enough to completely block the door behind him from her view.

What a strange place for a wall. What a strange face *for a wall.*

A giggle escaped Alice; the sound startled her, making her jump. The chessboard-patterned escorts didn't ease their hold on her.

Why am I acting like this? Why am I feeling *like this?*

What was in that bottle? This...isn't supposed to be real. Why is it...why...

"Blame Miraxis," one of the escorts grumbled.

"Is...is this the party?" Alice asked.

"Take her in," said brick man, stepping aside.

The men walked her forward.

She turned her face toward the escort on her right. "Am I going to a party? The...the tea party?"

"All the good dollies go to the tea party," replied one of the guards.

"And you get to be a dolly until the king comes for you," said the other.

They brought her through the door, down a short hallway, and into the large, dimly lit room at its end. Simultaneously, the escorts released her and retreated. The sound of the door closing behind them was ominously loud, and only served to enhance the silence that engulfed her in its wake. Alice stepped deeper into the room and glanced around.

The chamber looked like an old-fashioned parlor, but—like everything else in this world—the angles were all *off*. Though the doors on each wall were perfectly lit, deep shadows lingered in the corners, apparently too strong for the light cast by the flickering electric candles scattered about the room. The carpet was a deep purple run through with golden, flourishing designs that created vaguely diamond-shaped patterns across the floor. Several upholstered chairs and a sofa, all in the style of furniture that might've been better suited to Victorian

England than whatever the hell this place was, sat around a long, low table in the center of the room, atop which was arranged an assortment of delicate, colorful bottles, cakes, and pastries.

Everything on the table was marked with either *Drink Me* or *Eat Me*, whether on little paper tags or written directly on the items themselves.

Alice moved to the table and reached for one of the pastries. Just before she picked it up, something inside her—something laced with that sense of dread still lingering in her belly—said *No*. She stilled.

The pleasant warmth in her intensified as if to fight back that mental voice of warning. She squeezed her eyes shut and focused hard. In her mind, she saw a little bottle, felt strong fingers clamped on her cheeks, smelled alcohol and fruit. She tasted cold but fiery liquid on her tongue.

Drink Me.

No.

Eat Me.

No!

Alice shook her head and stepped away from the table. This wasn't real. This was all…fake. It was a simulation, it was virtual reality. It wasn't supposed to affect her like this! All the sims she'd tried had muted the positive sensations and eliminated the bad.

*But why does this feel so real? Why do I feel pain? Why do I feel…*pleasure?

Why do I feel fear?

"Take one," a man said.

Alice started and lifted her gaze. There was a man seated in the chair at the far end of the table; she wasn't sure how she hadn't noticed him when she first entered the room. He wore a black and purple suit, and an old-fashioned black top hat was perched upon his head. Though the angle of his hat and shadows cast by the inconsistent lighting obscured his eyes, his wide smile was clearly visible.

This was the Hatter. This was…his tea party?

"Indulge yourself, little dolly," he continued. "Show me you are willing to join the celebrations."

Alice glanced at the cakes again. Her hand twitched; her urge to take a treat rose again, but she willed herself to remain in place. "I…I don't want one."

The Hatter's smile wavered. "They're here for you. Eat one."

His command compelled her a step closer to the table. She gathered the fabric of her skirt in her hands and stopped, squeezing until her knuckles were white. "No."

The Hatter's smile fell completely, warping into an angry grimace. He lifted an elegant hand, swept his hat off his head, and lowered it into his lap, fingers toying with the black silk ribbon wrapped around its base. His gaze, gleaming with menacing intensity, shifted up to her.

He was a human, with dark hair and what would've been a handsome face were it not for the unmasked malice in his expression and the furious light in his brown eyes.

"You arrived late," he said, voice darkening, "late for the party—*my* party. I only have so much time with you before *he* comes to take you. And now, when I've chosen to forgive your tardiness and grant you a chance to join the festivities, you refuse to partake in any of the refreshments I've offered you?"

The ceaseless movement of his fingers along the hat's band called Alice's attention down to it. Despite the room's dimness, she could see that the top of the hat was lighter than the rest, rust-colored instead of black—as though it had been stained.

Alice retreated a few steps, the unsteadiness of her legs heightened by the high heels she was wearing. Her unease spread, finally beginning to beat back the unnaturally euphoric sensation the drugging drink had caused. "I'm sorry. There's been a mistake. I…" She shook her head, trying to clear it, desperate to find the words. "I don't belong here."

"Come sit down," the Hatter said firmly, flicking his eyes toward the nearby couch.

She felt the pull of his command again, felt herself step forward; just as it had with the thin woman in the dressing room, her body seemed to move of its own accord, going toward the Hatter despite the warning signals blaring in her mind.

"That's it. Come, my pretty. Come," he beckoned, holding out a hand. "Even if you're meant for the king, you're my dolly for tonight. Have some sweets, and then we'll *play*."

Alice stopped at the table and looked down at the cakes and pastries again. She reached forward and picked up a small pink cake that was decorated with white-icing writing.

Eat Me.

"Yes. Eat it," the Hatter coaxed. "Enjoy it, and then I will enjoy you."

Alice raised the cake to her lips, opened her mouth, and hesitated.

Eat Me.

I don't *belong here.*

Calling upon every ounce of her willpower, Alice swung her arm and flung the cake across the room. "No! I don't want it!"

The cake struck one of the doors with a little *splat* made loud by the relative silence and stuck in place. Bits of icing oozed down around it.

The Hatter scowled, and his eyebrows slanted down sharply. He rose, shoving his chair back in the process. The hat tumbled from his lap, and his overcoat shifted, revealing a knife on his belt—the biggest knife Alice had ever seen.

"If you refuse to play nicely then so do I," he shouted.

Alice recoiled and spun around, stumbling in her heels as she ran for the door. Her frantic flight carried her directly into the door; she slammed into it hard, but she barely registered the pain against the immensity of her fear. She grabbed at the doorknob.

It was locked.

There was a huge crash behind her, and the sound of china shattering. She turned to see the table overturned with all the sweets scattered across the floor. The Hatter advanced through the space the table had occupied a moment before.

Heart pounding, breath ragged, Alice banged on the door. "Someone help! Let me out, please!"

The Hatter grabbed a fistful of Alice's hair and tugged her away from the door.

Alice screamed and reached up to grasp his hand, desperate to alleviate some of the pressure on her scalp.

"You are *my* plaything," he roared as he pulled her deeper into the parlor. "You leave only if I say you may leave. Perhaps if you'd been punctual, you might have had time to be schooled in basic etiquette before our playtime."

Tears blurred Alice's vision. "Please, just let me go. I don't belong here. This…this isn't real. None of this is real."

"That you've been a bad dolly is *quite* real, and you must be punished." The Hatter dragged her through the debris scattered on the floor—crushed pastries, shattered porcelain, and unidentifiable liquids that reeked of alcohol. "If you refuse to be compliant, compliance will be forced. You will learn your place, dolly. Best to learn it from me. I'm *far* more likeable than *him*."

They entered another dark room, this one with plush purple carpeting. Before she could get a look at her new surroundings, before she could even consider seeking another path of escape, the Hatter lifted Alice and threw her atop a large four-poster bed. She landed on violet satin sheets and a mountain of pillows. Without wasting a moment, Alice turned to roll off the bed. The Hatter caught her ankle and yanked her back toward him.

Alice screamed and kicked wildly. One of her heels caught him in the knee, and the other in his chest, but it wasn't enough to deter him. He snarled and threw himself upon her, settling between her legs. A brief metallic glint was her only warning before the cold blade of his knife was pressed to her throat. Chest heaving, Alice ceased her struggles and turned her wide, frightened eyes toward his.

"You have such lovely skin," the Hatter rasped. "So smooth, so pale, so perfect. Don't make me cut it to ribbons." He leaned his head down and extended his tongue, trailing it along her cheek.

She cringed and turned her face slightly away, terrified of moving too much and provoking the bite of his blade. "Please, don't."

"Dollies are meant to be played with. Some a little rougher than others." With his free hand, he grasped one of Alice's arms and forced it up toward the headboard. A moment later, something solid closed around her wrist with a pronounced click.

Alice's breath hitched as realization struck her. She wiggled beneath him, pulling on her arm, but it was caught fast by the manacle; its cold metal dug into her skin. "No. No, don't do this."

"Don't talk, don't move. A *good* dolly is seen and not heard." The Hatter grasped her other wrist and moved it up. When she resisted, he increased the pressure of the knife on her throat.

The prick of pain on Alice's neck forced her to still again. She stared up at the Hatter, trembling, as tears streamed from the corners of her eyes.

This is a vivid dream, nothing more. It's not real. It's not real. It's not real.

"You want to be good, don't you?" the Hatter asked, brushing his lips over her cheek and up to her temple, where he licked the trail of her tears. His breath was warm against her skin as he spoke. "You want to make me happy. Because if you can't make me happy, you won't make *him* happy…and he'll add your heart to his collection over and over and over again."

Alice released a shuddering breath and turned her gaze toward the dark ceiling. The Hatter's body was heavy atop hers, and she could feel his erection through his trousers, pressed against the bare juncture of her thighs. Horror and shame filled her as her nipples hardened and her body heated, tensing with need.

It's that drink. The drink is doing this to me. I don't want this.

"Good little dolly." He eased the knife away and fastened the manacle around her other wrist. Lifting his torso, he brought the knife to his mouth and licked a few drops of crimson—her blood—from its blade. "Mmm. I wish you had been nicer. I could've forgiven your tardiness and treated you so, so well. You're going to make it up to me though, aren't you?"

Blood?

This isn't real!

Alice pressed her lips together to keep them from quivering. She felt vulnerable, exposed, and weak. She'd never been placed in such a position, had never felt such terror. Alice looked past the Hatter, back toward the parlor, and saw something in the shadows—a flicker of movement, a flash of teal, there and gone in an instant.

The Hatter's lips spasmed as though he were uncertain of whether he wanted to smile or frown. He clamped his fingers on her jaw and forced her chin up, baring her neck to him, and lightly trailed the tip of his blade along her throat. Electric jolts arced across her too-sensitive skin.

"Ruining my special day," he muttered. "That calls for a special lesson. For special pain." He slipped the oversized knife into the sheath on his belt and reached up over his head, closing his fingers on empty air. The look of surprise that rounded his eyes and slackened his jaw might've been comical on any other face in any other situation.

The Hatter swept his hand through the air over his hair and then leveled a finger at her. "I'll be right back, dolly. Don't go anywhere." He chuckled, a deep, maniacal sound that bubbled from the depths of his gut. "Don't go anywhere," he repeated softly as he pushed away from her and climbed off the bed.

He walked to the doorway, where he touched a control beside the door. The bedroom lights dimmed drastically, lowering to a flickering orange glow that emanated from somewhere high on the headboard above her.

"Stay put, little dolly. Playtime starts soon." He slipped into the parlor, closing the door behind him.

Once she was alone, Alice released the gut-wrenching sob she'd been holding in, her body trembling as she let her tears flow unrestrained.

"This isn't real. This *can't* be real," she whispered.

CHAPTER 4

SHADOW LIFTED ONE LEG, settling his ankle over his opposite knee, and grasped his lower shin. His tail, which was draped over one of the arms of the chair, flicked slowly back and forth as his eyes roved around the Hatter's sitting room. Though he appreciated the Hatter's affinity for darkness—an affinity which Shadow shared—he was not a fan of his host's choice in décor. The best thing about this room currently was the overturned table; the mess gave the chamber exactly what it had been missing.

A touch of chaos.

Outwardly, the Hatter's Tea Party was glorious—it was all clashing angles, inconsistent colors, and floors and windows that never quite matched or lined up with one another. But inside, *especially* in this room, the place was a testament to what the Hatter craved above all else—control.

The very thought of it churned Shadow's stomach. Control was the strangler of life, the enemy of joy, the killer of freedom. Even after all this time, the Hatter hadn't learned that. Hadn't learned to *let go*. He'd only grown more exasperated with Shadow with each passing day, had only struggled harder to

take control. Why were some people so blind to the truth? How could they be so oblivious to the nature of the world, the nature of existence?

Movement at the bedroom doorway caught Shadow's attention. The Hatter slipped out of the room, closing the door behind him, and walked toward the overturned table. His lips were peeled back in a snarl, his eyes twitched, and his fists clenched and relaxed erratically.

"She's not going to ruin my party," the Hatter muttered as he stalked to the chair he'd been sitting in a few minutes earlier. When his dark eyes fell upon the mess on the floor—the mess *he* had created—he groaned. "Look at what she did, stupid girl. This is all her fault. Jor'calla said she was supposed to arrive *hours* ago..."

Shadow frowned. He'd already allowed the Hatter to go a little further with that *stupid girl* than he liked. The only thing that had held Shadow back was his understanding of the way the Hatter operated—he'd not do the woman any lasting harm without having his hat in his direct possession.

Letting the situation play out this far had been entertaining, but the heart of the issue remained unchanged; Shadow didn't care who else was interested in the new woman, because he'd decided she was his. She'd be leaving this place with Shadow, not the Red King—and that only made this more satisfying.

Still muttering, the Hatter stepped around the chair and scanned the mess with his eyes, toeing aside shards of porcelain and ruined sweets. "No, no, no. Where? Where is it? Should be right here, right where I left it."

Perhaps Shadow had always been naïve to think he could alter the Hatter's outlook through intervention; perhaps it was cruel to toy with such a damaged mind.

But it was *fun*, and that was justification enough.

"You look troubled, Edward," Shadow said gently. "The new girl giving you problems?"

The Hatter—or Edward Winters, according to Jor'calla, who was only ever wrong concerning matters of timing—started and drew his knife. His wide, wild eyes fell on Shadow.

Shadow reached up, grasped the brim of his hat—formerly the Hatter's hat—and tipped it in greeting.

"This is *my* place, not yours," the Hatter said. "Return that to me and you may leave alive."

Grinning, Shadow angled the hat to the side and leaned back in his chair. His tail perked, rising to sway a little faster. "Death is such a fleeting state, Edward. A minor annoyance at best. But I'm glad you're upping the stakes so quickly, regardless. We always seem to find ways to make our little games more exciting."

"This is no game, you faceless bastard. I'm going to slice you open from groin"—he jabbed the tip of his knife toward Shadow's crotch and angled it upward—"to chin. Slowly."

"Would you like some help cleaning up the mess you made first? I'm rather fond of the character it lends to this bland room, but I know it *must* bother you."

The Hatter adjusted his grip on the knife and lifted his free hand as though to reach for his hat. He stopped his arm before it reached the empty air over his head and curled his hand into a fist. The infuriated scowl that crossed his lips brought a surge of satisfaction to Shadow; angering the Hatter was never a dull undertaking.

"Before you make your next move"—Shadow brushed his palms over the chair's soft armrests—"allow me to counter your ultimatum with one of my own. Give me the female and *you* may leave alive."

Growling, the Hatter slashed his knife through the air and took a step forward. "She's mine until the king comes! My dolly! I'm taking the first taste. It's owed to me for taking her in while he's away. Her sweetness is not for the likes of you."

"I saw her before your little scurrier, Miraxis, did. That makes her *mine*." The blond-haired human had immediately intrigued Shadow. He'd seen many of her kind here, but none had caught his eye like this one. "She's better than you—or that red buffoon—deserves."

The wild light in the Hatter's gaze sparked brighter. Shadow took a moment to appreciate that gleam, priding himself in the fact that he'd ignited it.

Then the Hatter lunged at Shadow with a snarl. Porcelain shards cracked and crunched beneath his feet.

Laughing, Shadow lowered his foot and pushed the chair's front legs off the floor. In the same moment, he threw his weight backward, tipping the chair completely. He tumbled along with it, clutching the armrests to hold the chair against his back as he flipped.

With an audible tearing of fabric, the Hatter's knife punched through the back of the chair and grazed Shadow's ribs, producing a distant flare of pain. The sensation forced another laugh out of him. He couldn't recall the last time he'd been hurt without intending for it to happen.

My, he's agitated today. How thrilling!

The motion of the chair broke the Hatter's hold on the knife. The blade remained in place against Shadow's ribs as he used his momentum and strength to flip the chair the rest of the way. It landed right side up, with Shadow firmly in the seat, and teetered on its rear legs for a stomach-churning moment before coming down on all four legs.

"You're quicker than usual today, Edward," Shadow said.

The Hatter was on his knees two paces away, his cheeks stained a bright, furious red, his shallow breaths ragged. "Why won't you just *die?*"

"Well, it's certainly not for lack of trying." Shadow stood and reached behind the chair. He closed his fingers around the knife's grip and wrenched it free of the wooden frame in which it had been lodged.

The Hatter shoved himself up to his feet. "When I come back, I'm going to—"

"Yes. You'll try, and I'll be looking forward to it, Edward." Shadow stepped forward, raised a hand, and flicked the brim of the hat. "This is just *one* of the things you'll want to get back from me."

The Hatter charged. Shadow lunged to meet him, extending his arm. The Hatter's momentum drove the blade straight through his breastbone and deep into the center of his chest. The human halted with a choked grunt and glanced down at the hilt jutting from his sternum.

The Hatter weakly clawed at Shadow's shirt as his legs gave out. Shadow clamped a hand over the man's shoulder and eased him down slowly.

With his wide, bloodshot eyes staring up at Shadow, the Hatter pressed his fingers over the tear in Shadow's coat, which had been opened by the Hatter's initial attack. Shadow felt no pain now—not even a memory of pain.

"Why...don't you...bleed?" the Hatter rasped.

Shadow widened his grin. "Because I'm just a ghost."

The Hatter slumped, falling onto his side. His mouth moved, but no sound emerged. He looked like a fish stranded on land, gulping air he could not breathe. Shadow twisted the knife. The Hatter grunted. Dark blood poured from his chest, pooling on the carpet beneath him.

"Just to give you every advantage by making you as *angry* as possible," Shadow said, "I'm going to steal your signature move along with your hat and *my* new dolly. Bring all your rage when you come to find me."

Helpless, the Hatter watched as Shadow released the knife, took hold of the hat's brim, and lifted it off his head. Shadow flipped the hat upside down and lowered it. He held the Hatter's gaze as he dipped the top of the hat into the puddle of blood at his feet. Hatred gleamed in the Hatter's eyes. That light only faded—carried away on a final, rattling exhalation—after the hat was back in place atop Shadow's head.

Shadow tugged the knife free—producing another spurt of blood—and sprang to his feet. He stepped over the body and used the point of the blade to tip the hat to a jauntier angle. A lively tune, one the Hatter often played downstairs, drifted into his head. He hummed along with it, adding some flourish to his stride.

It was time to go meet his dolly—surely that was cause for celebration.

ALICE GRITTED her teeth and pulled down on her arms, keeping her fingers pressed together tight in the hopes of squeezing her hands through the manacles. She leaned to one side to put more of her weight into the effort. Tears stung her eyes as metal bit into her flesh. The pain helped clear her mind, speeding away the lingering effects of the drink they'd forced upon her.

The door was still closed, but she knew she didn't have much time. She looked up at the manacles and followed their chains up to the headboard with her eyes.

Leverage!

Twisting her body around to face the headboard, she planted her shoes against it as solidly as their spiky heels allowed. The chains were crossed now, one over the other, but the manacles were *just* loose enough for her to have turned her wrists. She hoped it would be enough to squeeze her hands through. Taking a deep breath, she clenched her straightened fingers together, trying to make her hands as narrow as possible.

One...two—

The door burst open, swinging hard enough to slam into the wall. Alice started, her heart nearly stopping, and her throat constricting in terror. She turned her head to look at the dark doorway; the shadows there seemed to have thickened significantly. A chill skittered up her spine.

Her eyes widened when she realized that some of the

shadows—darker than the rest—were *moving*. They seemed to solidify as she watched, taking the shape of a tall, lean man with a top hat on his head.

The dark figure slid through the doorway sideways, arms extended to either side. The light from over the headboard was too weak to reach the figure even as he approached the bed, leaving his features shrouded in darkness. But when he raised his head, his eyes—reflective, teal orbs—and his wide, fanged grin stood out starkly against the black.

Not real. This isn't real, he's not real...

The shadowy figure was humming a tune that was vaguely familiar to her as he danced around the edge of the room, each of his movements just slightly out of sync with the music— which itself was just slightly off key. Something glinted in his hand when he neared the bed.

Alice clenched her jaw to hold in a scream as she realized the shadow was holding the Hatter's oversized knife, its blade glistening with blood.

She didn't know what had happened, didn't know how the Hatter—who'd been frightening enough before—had become this grinning *thing*, but the nightmare before her was worse than anything she could've imagined. The concoction they'd forced upon her had dulled the worst of her fear, but she couldn't rely upon it now that its effects were fading.

The shadow Hatter twirled as his humming reached a high note, grasped his hat, and rolled it down his arm as he slid to the bedside.

Alice shut her eyes and turned her face away, clutching the chains as she chanted, "This isn't real. This isn't real. This isn't real."

Those words kept her grounded, they made her *remember* what had happened before she arrived here, and she had a horrible sense that if she stopped repeating those words—

whether in her head or aloud—she would start to perceive all this as real.

And that would break her mind.

She felt the bed dip beside her. It creaked beneath the shadow Hatter's weight, and though he didn't touch her, she could *feel* his presence, only inches from her skin. She shuddered.

"Not real, not real," she rasped, squeezing her eyes tighter closed.

"What isn't real?" he asked in a voice that was nothing like the one he'd used before. This voice was deep and rich, oddly leisurely, with just a hint of a rumble beneath it.

"You, this place," she said, barely able to keep her voice from quivering with fear. "Everything. None of this is real. I-I'm supposed to be clearing out my father's office...supposed to be—"

The bed creaked again, and there was a whisper of something across fabric. A moment later, the flat of the knife—now dry—slid along her forearm from the inside of her elbow toward her wrist. Alice flinched, unable to hold back a whimper.

"Do you feel that?" he asked.

"I-It's still not real."

"How is it not real if you can *feel* it?"

"It's a simulation. We're in an asylum. *None* of this is real, they just want us to believe it is."

Why is he acting so different? Why does he sound *so different?*

He took hold of her chin with his long, strong fingers and turned her face toward him. She swore she could feel the light press of *claws* against her skin. He tenderly stroked her cheek. His velvety touch was strangely familiar—but not from when he'd thrown her onto the bed and restrained her.

"Open your eyes," he coaxed. "They're far too pretty to keep them hidden from me for so long."

For one terrifying, gut-wrenching instant, Alice envisioned him gouging her eyes out with that blade. "What are you going to do to me?"

"I didn't really have any plans. Was there something specific you wanted done to you?"

"Let me go. Please, just let me go."

The flat of the blade trailed in the opposite direction. "Are you going to open your eyes or not? It's not helping me assess you as a rational person when you're sitting here with them squeezed shut ranting about how reality isn't real."

Steeling herself, Alice opened her eyes, and was completely caught off-guard by the face in front of hers.

"It's *you*," she breathed. She hadn't been insane, hadn't been seeing things.

She'd seen those eyes and that grin before—and not on the Hatter. This was the stranger who'd been in the crowd when she arrived here, the stranger with whom she'd briefly made eye contact. The stranger she'd been compelled to seek out afterward.

Though his face was human-like, he undoubtedly wasn't human. His jaw-length black hair was sprinkled with strands of gray, hanging in tousled locks from beneath the brim of the Hatter's top hat. Long, feline ears jutted from either side of his head, and his face was dominated by that wide, fanged grin. His intense eyes—intent upon her—were aglow in that vibrant teal. Despite his alien features, he was handsome.

That attractiveness, however, didn't take away from how unsettling he was.

"What a silly thing to say," he replied.

Alice's brows lowered. "W-What? What's silly?"

"Of course I'm me. Who else would I be? Are you not yourself?"

"I...I thought you were the Hatter." Her eyes flared as she stole a glance at the open doorway. "The Hatter! Where is he?"

The stranger's grin tilted to one side as he lifted the knife away from her and spun it between his long, dexterous fingers. He raised his other hand and tipped his hat forward, hiding his eyes behind the brim.

Alice's heart skipped a beat when she realized that the top of the hat was glistening with *blood*.

"You don't need to worry about him for now," the stranger said. "Though, perhaps, you can take some satisfaction in knowing that he's going to be late for his own party this evening."

"Who are you?"

He arched a brow. "I thought we've already established that I am me. Really, are you paying *any* attention?"

"You never…you never told me your name."

"Well that's a little more complicated than simply asking who I am, isn't it?" He leaned forward slightly. "What's *your* name? I'm fairly certain it's not Little Dolly."

"Alice. My name is Alice."

"Alice," he said, putting more gravel into her name than she'd thought possible. Were his voice not quite so deep, she might've considered it a purr. His eyes drifted toward the ceiling, and his brow furrowed as though in contemplation. Then he nodded. "It suits you. I approve."

Alice tightened her grip on the chains. "What should I call you?"

"That depends on what you would like to call me." He leaned back, propping himself up on one arm, and continued twirling that big knife with impossible speed and steadiness. "People call me all sorts of things. Shadow is what I usually go by. I'm not sure if that means anything to a woman who disbelieves reality, though."

Alice glanced down Shadow's body. His clothing was as rich and old-fashioned as the Hatter's had been, but it was even fancier. He wore a long, crimson velvet coat with black cuffs. A black button-down shirt with a high collar was beneath his satiny crimson vest, which was adorned with shimmery patterns that almost looked like plants and flowers. His long legs were clad in straight black pants, and his black leather boots looked freshly polished. He appeared as though he'd just stepped out of nineteenth century London. But none of that caught her attention nearly as much as the long, black-furred tail swishing lazily behind him.

He suddenly tossed the knife aside, swung his legs off the bed, and lay on his belly with hands—which did indeed include dark claws—beneath his chin. "I like your clothes, too." As though to prove it, he raked his eyes over her body. *Slowly*.

A blush stained her cheeks. Sitting the way she was, with her heels against the headboard and knees bent, her skirt had fallen down to her lap, exposing her thighs above the striped stockings. And she *felt* his eyes on her. Alice's body warmed beneath his gaze, and her skin tingled as though craving his touch; it was like the concoction's effects weren't fading at all.

"Are you going to hurt me, Shadow?" she asked.

"No. I rather like you. I'd hoped we might get to know one another better, Alice." His eyes flicked toward the chains binding her to the headboard. "Seems you've nowhere better to be at the moment."

Alice shifted her wrists toward him. "Could you…free me?"

Shadow pushed himself up on his arms and swung his legs up again, folding them beneath him. His tail fell on the bed beside him, its tip flicking back and forth with subdued excitement. The position, given his height and leanness, appeared almost comical—but the blood drying on his hat eliminated the humor from the situation. It reminded her that for all his carefree, strange ways, he was still dangerous.

He settled his hands on his knees and said, "Absolutely."

"Do you know where the key is?"

Suddenly, his grin eased into something subtler, something

smoldering, and his hypnotic eyes were half-lidded. "I've found that such bindings can often make things more interesting. If it makes you feel better, I can take a turn in them afterward."

Alice's breath hitched. Heat coalesced low in her belly, and her sex clenched in sudden arousal. Her reaction to him was so swift, so shocking, that she reared away from him. "No. No. I-I would prefer to be out of them. Now."

"If they aren't real, how are they still holding you?" He leaned his face closer to her. "That must mean you want to be here, at least a little."

Alice stared into his eyes. "That's not...that's not how it works. They want us to feel that this is real, but it's not."

"Oh, you're the most delightful sort of mad, aren't you?" Shadow nimbly leapt backward off the bed, landing lightly on his feet, and tipped the bloody hat. "Grant me but a moment, sweet Alice, and I will fetch the key for you."

Relief eased some of the tension from her limbs. "Thank you."

His features—save for his eyes and his grin—faded into obscurity when he reentered the shadows around the edge of the room. As he neared the doorway, he turned his back to her, becoming little more than another black shape in the darkness before disappearing entirely.

Alice forced herself to breathe slowly, listening for any sign of him, but only silence came from the room beyond.

His gentle humming was the first indication that he was returning, followed shortly after by the gleam of his piercing eyes. He hopped onto the foot of the bed and walked across it to drop into a crouch beside Alice. She'd never seen anyone move so gracefully.

Shadow raised one hand. A set of remarkably mundane keys dangled from between his forefinger and thumb, their metal smeared with crimson.

"Sorry. They were in his coat pocket, and, well...his knife *is* rather large, don't you think?" He flicked his arm. Several droplets of blood spattered the headboard.

Alice felt the color drain from her face. "A-And you won't... use that knife on me, will you, Shadow?"

Shadow arched a brow, staring at her as he slipped a key into the manacles' keyhole. "When I said I wanted to know you better, I didn't mean from the inside."

"That's...reassuring." And it was, despite knowing that he'd killed the Hatter.

Shadow's grin widened as he lightly ran the back of a claw along her outer thigh from her knee toward her hip. "Well, I mean, I *would* very much like to get to know you from the inside, but not in a way that has *anything* to do with a knife."

A shiver stole through Alice, and her flesh broke out in goosebumps. The farther his claw traveled, the more aroused she became. Something was definitely wrong with her to be reacting this way when she knew the hand touching her was covered in blood, when she knew the man Shadow had killed was likely lying on the floor in the next room.

Or perhaps it was him—Shadow. His hypnotic eyes, with their glimmer of madness, enthralled her, promising wicked delights.

I'm going crazy. This is absolutely insane! It...it has to be the drugs still in my system.

Thankfully, the click of the lock saved her. The manacle on her right wrist opened and fell away, hitting the bed with a dulled thump, and Shadow turned his attention toward the remaining manacle, taking it delicately in his left hand while inserting the key with his right. As soon as Alice was fully free, Shadow wrapped his unnaturally long fingers around her forearms and guided her hands closer to him. He leaned forward to examine the chafed, bruised skin around her wrists.

"That damned fool," he muttered. He brushed a thumb over

the red skin; despite the wicked claw at its tip, his touch was whisper-soft.

Alice watched Shadow in silence. From what she'd seen of him so far, he was unpredictable, unfocused, and absolutely mad. She had the sense that he was...*untethered*, like his presence had no grounding in this virtual world, like he'd just float away at any second. But for a moment he seemed almost sane; as he examined the damage on her wrists, he looked like he actually...cared.

I can work with this. I can use this to my advantage.

"Shadow?"

He lifted his eyes, and his grin widened as he purred, "Hmm?"

"Would you help me escape this place?"

His thumb continued its gentle caress. "Escape? That seems a bit overly dramatic, doesn't it?"

Alice's brow lowered as she struggled to focus on the conversation, on the situation, and not on the way his tender ministrations made her skin tingle and warm—or how his other hand was moist and sticky with blood. She reminded herself for the thousandth time that this was *not real*.

"What do you mean?" she asked.

"*Escape* is such a strong word, Alice. I was just going to walk out the front door." He looked away for a moment. "At least I think it's the front. Sort of hard to tell by looking at the outside of this place, isn't it?"

Without thinking, Alice lifted her hand and placed it on his cheek, turning his face back toward her. He didn't relinquish his hold on her. "No, I don't mean just *this* place, I mean the simulation."

He stared into her eyes as though searching for something. Then his brow smoothed, his eyes lit up, and his grin—which she *should* have found deeply disturbing rather than intriguing

—only grew. "I've met a lot of crazy people in my time, Alice, but you may be the maddest of all."

Alice dropped her hand from his face. "I'm not crazy, Shadow."

Holding her gaze, he tilted his head to the side. "That's exactly what a crazy person would say."

Frowning, Alice turned away from him.

"And because that makes you the most interesting person here, I'll help you, Alice."

She looked back at him as hope sparked inside her. "You will?"

"Let's see it through to whatever end we reach. It sounds *exciting*." He leaned closer to her, his expression falling into that eyes-half-lidded smolder. "And it should give us some valuable *alone* time."

Alice's heart fluttered, and she blushed. "I'm not a...dolly, Shadow."

Shadow moved closer still—close enough that she could feel the tickle of his warm breath against her skin. "No, you're not a dolly, Alice. But you're mine all the same."

CHAPTER 5

ALICE'S delectable pink lips parted as she sucked in a sharp breath. Her vibrant blue eyes flared, and her cheeks flushed beneath her pale makeup.

She and Shadow stared at each other for what seemed a long while, her lips occasionally moving as though she meant to speak—but she didn't utter a single word. And Shadow was content to stare. He'd not seen anyone as beautiful as her in all his time here, and he suspected she was even more beautiful without the makeup the Hatter's people had caked on her face.

This Alice was a strange creature, an intriguing creature, and she heated his blood in a way he'd never experienced. Many of the people who came to Wonderland were confused and disoriented, sometimes for a great while, but she was different. She was unique. No one, in all his time here, had so adamantly and confidently proclaimed reality unreal. It only piqued his curiosity further.

He had the sense—nearly overwhelming in its surety—that spending time with her would be far more entertaining than his games with the Hatter and the Red King. His time with her would be far more...*fulfilling*.

Alice's eyes shied away from him as she cleared her throat. "Are we...leaving, then?"

Shadow blinked. "Oh. You meant you wanted to leave *now*?"

She looked at him again, and the corners of her lips twitched as a hint of humor entered her gaze. "Yes. I'd rather not stay here any longer than necessary."

"All for the best," he replied with a resigned sigh, taking her hand as he slipped off the bed. "As you're currently not interested in deepening our relationship, I suppose this peace and quiet would've eventually grown stifling, especially after my eighth or ninth hour of staring at you."

"Eight or nine hours..." She arched a brow. "You'd stare at me for that long?"

Shadow helped her off the bed and onto her feet. "I don't mean to be insulting. I'd gladly stare at you for longer, but I would think you'd be quite ready for a break by that point. I don't want to assume your endurance."

"My...endurance? From staring?"

"I can only imagine that constantly looking as beautiful as you do is a tiring affair, and I don't want to overburden you." He led her through the door and into the Hatter's parlor, where the cakes and the carpet alike had soaked up much of the blood. The carpet made little squelching sounds as he stepped over the body.

Alice gasped behind him, and her arm stiffened, suddenly resisting his lead.

Shadow paused and glanced back to find her staring down at the Hatter, her face paling beneath her already ghostly white makeup. "You were in such a hurry a moment ago, and now you want to dawdle? Do you really want to be here when he gets back?"

She looked up at him, startled. "When he gets *back*? What do you mean? He's...dead."

"For now." A flicker of silver caught his eyes. Shadow turned his attention to the bracelet on Alice's wrist. *Eat Me* was written upon the charm attached to it. He grinned. With quick, nimble movements of his fingers, he unlatched the bracelet and held it up between forefinger and thumb. "I'll have to make good on *this* later."

Her gaze caught on the bracelet and a delectable blush stained her cheeks. "What?"

Shadow chuckled, pocketed the trinket, and took her hand again. He tugged on her arm gently. "Come along. This building is far more pleasant from outside."

Her hold on his hand tightened, but she came without resistance. The small, simple action—her clutching his hand—made him feel warm inside. She was taking comfort in his presence.

He liked that feeling. He liked it *very* much.

When he reached the door leading out of the Hatter's quarters, Shadow produced the keys he'd taken from the Hatter once again. He slipped the appropriate key into the lock, unlocked it, and left the keys dangling in the door as he pulled it open.

The Hatter's door guard, a broadly built human who was roughly the size of a small house, turned to glance at Shadow and Alice as they emerged from the darkened chamber. His eyes widened.

Without missing a step, Shadow led Alice past the guard, giving the man a hardy slap on the shoulder.

"Hey, stop!" the man called, seeming to snap out of his shock as he hurried after them.

Shadow turned, slipped an arm around Alice's waist, and swept her onto his lap as he sat on the sloped, curving bannister. He curled his tail around her middle.

Alice threw her arms around his neck. "What are you *doing*? We'll fall!"

"That *would* be a more direct way down," Shadow replied. Wrapping her securely in his arms, he kicked off one of the steps just as the guard lunged toward him.

He and Alice slid down, leaving the guard's hands to close on empty air. Their speed rapidly increased, and Shadow's stomach flipped; he laughed in delight as they passed doors, hallways, and startled patrons on their way down, everything soon becoming a blur.

Alice shrieked and buried her face against his neck, clinging to him. Her lips brushed his throat as she muttered quietly but frantically to herself.

"Enjoy yourself, Alice. It's not real, after all!"

She only clung to him tighter.

Shadow grinned.

Guards shouted on the levels above him, patrons gasped as he sped past them, and the hypnotic music from below grew steadily in volume as he wound lower and lower around the cylindrical chamber. His heart raced, adding to his giddiness; its speed was almost matched by the heavy footsteps thumping on the stairs overhead.

When they finally neared the place where the staircase met its twin and merged into one, Shadow unwound one arm from around Alice and thrust himself off the bannister. His momentum carried him and Alice through the air for a few yards. He swept an arm beneath her legs, cradling her against his chest, until his feet came down on the central landing.

The people around him cried out in startlement; for a moment, all eyes were upon Shadow and Alice.

Shadow unwound his tail from Alice and settled her on her feet, keeping an arm around her waist as he dipped into a low bow and swept the hat off his head with his free hand. "Good evening, ladies and gentlemen. Please, do not allow me to interrupt your debaucheries."

"You!" A woman in a red gown and a beaked mask broke from the thick crowd below—the Tea Party's madame, Cecilia. "You don't belong here!"

Shadow laughed as he straightened. "None of us do. None of this is real!"

Alice turned her face toward him, and he could feel the question in her eyes. But she had no opportunity to ask it aloud; Shadow swept her off her feet, clutching her against his hip, and bounded down the steps three at a time. She released a startled squeak and clung to him, her fingers digging into the fabric of his clothing. His ears perked in unexpected satisfaction; suddenly, he was quite interested to learn what her blunt little nails would feel like against his chest or his back without any clothing in the way.

At the edges of his vision, guards were shoving through the crowd, forcing their way toward him, and he knew more were hurrying down the stairs in pursuit.

He'd not been sure how any of this would turn out when he'd followed Miraxis and Alice inside earlier. Though he always *hoped* for excitement, those hopes were rarely fulfilled—but this was thrilling on so many levels.

And the Hatter would be *livid* when he came back.

Shadow darted through the crowd, carrying Alice as he dodged and wove between patrons and dollies.

"Stop," Madame Cecilia shouted. "Release her, or you will bring the wrath of the Red King upon us all, you cowardly wretch!"

Shadow spun around and met the woman's gaze. "You'll have to catch me first!"

A guard shoved toward him, reaching out with one large hand. Shadow swayed backward. The guard's fingertips brushed over the fabric of Alice's dress, but the man was unable to get hold of it. Shadow turned toward the exit; he reached it in a few quick strides and tugged the door open, darting through.

He ran for the railing ahead, stooping slightly to lift Alice fully into his arms again.

She looped her arms around his neck, her wide blue eyes meeting his. "We're too high!"

"Maybe," he replied. He leapt into the air. His leading foot came down atop the railing, and he used it to launch himself forward. That fluttery feeling returned to his stomach, and, for a few wonderful moments, he and Alice were weightless, soaring at least fifteen or twenty feet above the ground.

Alice made a frightened sound and closed her eyes. She squeezed him, holding his head against her breasts in a viselike grip as though she were facing her impending demise. The hat tipped back and fell off his head. He caught it on the tip of his tail. The fabric of their clothing fluttered, and her hair streamed around them.

Once again, he couldn't help but notice how much he enjoyed the feel of her clinging to him—especially the way her soft breasts yielded to him. Her scent filled his nose, almost overpowered by whatever spicy floral perfume they'd sprayed on her when they dolled her up, but unmistakable—warm honey and vanilla, so subtle and pure. There was no one who smelled quite like she did, no one whose scent could make him feel intoxicated.

His feet came down on one of the paved pathways that formed a convoluted web around the Hatter's Tea Party. The impact jolted up his legs; his knees bent, but he remained upright, stumbling a few steps before resuming his run. The pain caused by his landing was fleeting, like most pain was for him—there for an instant and then gone, carried away on an unseen wind never to be felt again.

"This is insane," Alice whispered. She lifted her face from the top of his head. "They're running down the stairs."

Shadow shifted his gaze to the nearby woods. He had an urge to slow his pace, to give up his lead, so the guards would chase him into the forest. He could keep just ahead of them for hours, leading them deeper and deeper in. Most people couldn't find their way anywhere in those woods without the aid of a path. The thought of the Hatter's goons lost and wandering for days amidst the towering trees was an appealing one.

But he found himself far more tempted by the thought of having time alone with Alice; he couldn't have a very meaningful conversation with her while they were fleeing, not while she was in the clutches of fear. She needed some time in relative safety to learn that she had nothing to be frightened of—at least not while she was at Shadow's side.

He wouldn't allow any harm to come to what was his.

Shadow ran his tongue across his teeth, held Alice a little closer, and increased his speed.

Perhaps her madness is rubbing off on me.

The shouting behind them faded as the surrounding vegetation gradually thickened. By the time Shadow and Alice had entered the forest proper, the guards were little more than a memory. Shadow shoved aside his pang of disappointment. He had the greater prize right here, in his arms.

Ignoring the purple-stone path, he sprinted between massive trunks, bounded past towering flowers and giant mushrooms, and carried his female deep into the woods. Eventually, he slowed. Alice's grip on him—to his regret—eased. In retaliation, he tightened his hold on her.

"I think they're gone," she said.

"Quite easy to shake pursuit when you're lost," he replied.

Alice leaned back to meet his eyes. "We're lost?"

Shadow arched a brow. "Obviously. Isn't that the best way to avoid capture? If you can't find yourself, how is anyone else meant to find you?"

Her features were strained with worry. Even wearing that expression, she really was an exquisite thing—especially because of her revealing, vibrant eyes. His hands, one of which was on her bare thigh, flexed. Were he to slide that hand up, he'd feel the intimate heat between her legs. It was a tempting thought.

"You look worried, Alice," he said huskily, barely resisting the desire to shift his hand.

"Why wouldn't I be?" Her gaze flicked behind them. Her fingers idly twirled and brushed through the hair at the back of Shadow's neck, sending delicious pulses of pleasure down his spine. "Everything here is…different. Strange. The things I've experienced here, all the fear, pain, the um…" Her cheeks reddened. "It all feels so real even though I know it's not."

Shadow continued onward in a casual stroll, paying no mind to direction. He was more focused on her; she'd not tried to get down yet, and he wouldn't relinquish his hold on her voluntarily. "Ah, so we're back to that again. Have you ever stopped to consider that this *is* real?"

Her eyes locked with his. "But it's *not*, Shadow. I *saw* them. The coffins. The…pods they put us in. There were wires and tubes and needles. They're keeping us asleep, keeping us in this simulation like prisoners."

He raised his tail and delicately settled the hat over his head again, tipping it to a sideways angle. He drew in a deep breath; the air was scented with *life*, with the smells of earth and growing things, with the perfume of at least a dozen different species of flower—and with her sweet, mouthwatering aroma, which only grew stronger as time passed. "You can see all this, smell it, hear the wind in the leaves and the wood creaking, touch it, *taste* it, if you were so inclined. This, my dear Alice, is as real as it gets."

"Drugs can make you feel that way, and they're pumping us full of them."

"I don't partake," he replied. "They make me feel unbalanced."

She frowned, appearing to be in deep thought before her eyes widened. "The Hatter!"

"What about him? He'll be furious, but we've no need for concern."

"You said he'd come back, right? But he's supposed to be dead. If this was a real world, he would stay dead. He wouldn't come back. So how does that make sense?"

"Because that's how things work." Shadow shook his head and chuckled. "Really, just saying people ought to stay dead doesn't make it reality. And how dull would that be, anyway?"

"Because that is how the real world works, Shadow. People die."

"Yes. In the real world, people die. And then they come back—usually angry that they were killed to begin with."

Alice stared at him, searching his face. "You really believe that." She sighed, and her body sagged. "You can set me down now, Shadow. I can walk."

He lifted his chin slightly. "I rather prefer carrying you, Alice. I enjoy the way you cling to me."

"But I'm not—" She hurriedly loosened her hold on him. "I wasn't clinging."

With a heavy sigh of his own, Shadow halted and stooped to set her on her feet. She did, in fact, *cling* to him as she found her balance.

"You've a strange way of looking at things, sweet Alice."

"I could say the same about you," she replied, glancing up at him before stepping away and looking around. "So...you really have no idea where we are?"

He felt oddly incomplete without her in his arms. He ran his palms down his coat, smoothing the fabric, and tossed the feeling aside. Things between him and Alice had only just begun; there was plenty of time for her to warm up to him. He spun in a slow circle, studying their surroundings. "We're in the woods, of course."

She chuckled. "Aside from the obvious, I mean."

Shadow turned to face her, arching a brow and tilting his head. A soft smile lingered on her face. He couldn't recall anyone reacting to him like this, with genuine humor, with *warmth.* He'd been an outsider here for as long as he could remember—and even if he couldn't quantify his time in Wonderland, he knew it had been a great, great while.

"We'll find our way to wherever it is we're going," he said.

"I suppose if we keep walking one way, we'll end up *somewhere.*"

"That makes more sense than anything you've said so far, Alice." He folded one arm across his chest, leaned his opposite elbow on the back of his hand, and took his chin between forefinger and thumb. "So, we need to find a way to return you to unreality, correct?"

"To reality, yes. I need to find some way to...wake up, I guess. There have to be others like me here—people who know all this isn't real."

"Hmm…" Shadow tapped his chin. "I suppose we just need to find other crazy people, then."

"I don't think they're the—" She shook her head. "Never mind."

A sudden thought occurred to Shadow. His eyes widened, and he raised a finger into the air. "We'll go talk to Jor'calla. He's the maddest person in Wonderland. The two of you should get on well." He narrowed his eyes on her. "But not *too* well, mind you."

A crease formed between her eyebrows. "What do you mean?"

He stepped closer to her and slipped his tail around her waist, tugging her against him. Before she could pull away, he cupped her face in his hands and looked into her lovely eyes. "Have you forgotten already, Alice? You're *mine.*"

ALICE FLATTENED her hands on Shadow's chest, eyes rounding at his declaration.

You're mine.

He'd said the same in the Hatter's bedroom. She'd thought little of it at the time—she'd been preoccupied with more pressing matters and had dismissed the words as those of a madman. But hearing them again now—while looking into his eyes—she had a feeling that he truly *meant* them.

The tips of his claws were settled lightly against her skin, his warm, hard body—including one particular *hard* part against her belly—was flush with hers, and his tail was wrapped possessively around her waist. She should've been frightened—she should've found *him* frightening. Shadow was an unsettling individual, and she should've been running from him as fast as her legs could carry her. Fleeing was logical. Fleeing was *smart*.

But Alice didn't want to run; she only wanted to get *closer* to him. He was compelling, but more than that, she felt safe with him. And, for some inexplicable reason, her body reacted to him fiercely. She wanted to feel him, *all* of him—his lean muscles, his strong, long-fingered hands, his lips. Everything.

Maybe I am crazy?

She didn't know who Shadow was or what he was capable of —apart from *murder*. What would he do if she angered him, or if he grew tired of her? They were in an asylum. People would be unpredictable here, and she had a feeling he was even more unpredictable than most.

No, we're not just in an asylum. We're in a simulation in an asylum. None of this is real. Even if I feel pain...he can't actually hurt me.

Can he?

Alice cleared her throat and looked away from him. Though his hold was by no means painful, she could sense his dormant strength—he made Miraxis seem weak in comparison. If he didn't want to let her go, she'd never escape his grasp. She needed to distract him if she wanted to open some space between them. "So where is this Jor'calla?"

His thumbs trailed over her cheekbones, and he shrugged. "In a house somewhere, I imagine."

For a moment, she leaned into his touch, nearly letting her eyes drift shut. His caress shouldn't have felt so good.

Focus, Alice.

She met his gaze, reached up, and took hold of his wrists, guiding his hands away from her face. "And you can find him, right?"

He didn't resist, but neither did he remove his tail from Alice's waist. "I always wind up where I intend to be eventually."

"We should go now then, just in case the guards are still behind us."

Shadow turned his head, glancing first over one shoulder and then the other. "Behind or in front. They're *somewhere*, that's for certain. I doubt they've followed us into the woods, though. Only a mad person would wander off the path."

Alice pointedly looked at the grass-covered ground—there was no path in sight—before returning her eyes to his with one brow arched.

He raised an eyebrow in response. "Is something wrong?"

"*We're* not on a path."

"I *did* already mention I always make it to wherever it is I intend to be, didn't I? I'm not the crazy one here."

"Do you not realize how ridiculous that is? How you're... contradicting yourself?"

"I do prefer to keep things interesting," he said before turning away. His tail finally fell from her waist as he put his hands on his hips and scanned their surroundings, facing a different direction every few seconds. He hummed thoughtfully, his catlike ears drooping, and muttered, "If I were Jor'calla, where would I be?"

Alice watched him, unable to keep the smile from her face. There was something charming about him, something almost childlike.

But he's a killer, Alice. Don't forget that.

His ears perked. "Silly question, simple answer. I'd be exactly wherever I was. Let's go, Alice!"

Shadow started off in a seemingly random direction, his long legs carrying him a great distance rather quickly.

Startled, Alice hurried after him. "Shadow! Wait! Slow dow—ouch!" She cursed as she stumbled and her foot bent to the side, sending a jolt of pain through her ankle. Gritting her teeth, she hopped on her other foot until she regained her balance before bending forward.

Something soft brushed down her arm.

"Are you all right, Alice?" Shadow asked from immediately beside her.

Alice blinked and glanced at the tail stroking her arm. She tipped her head back, brows high. How he'd get to her so fast? He'd been at least fifty feet ahead of her a second ago. She hadn't even heard him approach.

"I'm fine. Just need to get rid of these." She tugged one shoe off, lowered her leg, and kicked away the other. Her stockinged feet sank into the soft grass as she stood up straight.

"Now you're even smaller than before," he said, leaning closer to her.

She looked up at him. "Or you're just very…tall."

And he was. He towered over her, standing at *least* a foot taller—likely more.

"I'm exactly the size I'm meant to be. You, on the other hand, have changed sizes. It's quite inconsiderate."

"In…considerate…" she said slowly. "Well, don't you think it's inconsiderate that *you* took off and forced me to run after you in heels?"

He pursed his lips and furrowed his brow, making another thoughtful humming sound. He sank into a crouch, extending an arm and settling his palm on her bare thigh just beneath the hem of her skirt and above the top of her striped stocking. She sucked in a sharp breath. His hand was so warm, so soft, and yet also so solid and strong, that she found herself unable to immediately react; it felt *good*.

Shadow slid his palm down her leg, catching the stocking and drawing it down, too. He brushed his thumb over her knee, and his fingertips grazed the sensitive flesh behind her knee before moving lower. His hand cupped her calf. A shiver stole through her, and warmth pooled between her legs.

"What are you doing?" She couldn't muster the willpower to pull away from him.

His hand finally stopped at her foot, which looked tiny compared to his long fingers.

"Your legs *are* rather shorter than mine. Though I must say, they are"—his tongue slipped out and ran over his lips—"*perfect*." With his other hand, he lifted her foot and peeled the stocking off completely, his fingers trailing over her sole.

His touch, combined with his words, sent a bolt of desire straight to her core. She couldn't tell based on the hungry look in his eyes and the flash of his fangs whether he intended to bite her or *taste* her, but she found both options oddly thrilling.

Eat me.

Did I seriously just think that?

The thought—combined with her sudden mental image of him leaning closer and pressing his mouth between her legs—was as startling as it was arousing.

I'll just have to make good on this later, he'd said as he pocketed her bracelet at the Hatter's. She found herself suddenly wishing he'd do so *now*.

"Um, Shadow," she said, a bit breathlessly. "Shouldn't we...go?"

He tucked her bunched-up stocking into his coat. "Why are you in such a hurry? Our destination isn't likely to get up and move somewhere else—at least not anytime soon."

Why *was* she in such a hurry? Why not just let him touch her? Why not lie upon the grass, spread her legs, and let him devour her with his tongue and lips just like she craved?

Because this isn't real.

But wasn't that only more reason to immerse herself in this fantasy?

It would be so easy to forget that this was all a simulation, so easy to just live in this make-believe world and embrace the madness. So easy to let go of all the things she was desperate to remember. Somehow, she knew this place would take *everything* from her if she submitted to it.

The thought shook her.

Reaching down, Alice cupped Shadow's chin and tilted his face toward hers. "Please, Shadow. I…I feel like *I* am running out of time, like I'll just…"

His stunning, teal eyes searched her face, and his features smoothed; even his grin faded. "Lose yourself?"

Alice nodded. "Yeah."

Shadow covered her hands with his own, squeezing them gently. "I won't let you get lost, Alice."

For a moment, there was clarity in his eyes, and Alice saw the man—the *real* man—behind the grinning mask, a man who was just as lost, just as vulnerable—if not more so—as her.

She smiled down at him. "Thank you."

He smiled back, but his smile spread slowly until it was that huge grin again. Unsettling cheer sparked in his eyes. Just like that, his moment of lucidity had passed.

He leapt to his feet, simultaneously lowering her hands from his face, and tugged her into a spin that would've been well-received in a dance competition. The forest was a blur around her; when she finally came to a stop, he was holding her in a low dip, one arm around her lower back and the other still holding one of her hands.

"Let's away to Jor'calla, my dear. I'm sure we'll find some fun during our journey."

Clinging to Shadow, Alice stared up at him with wide eyes. Her heart fluttered; she couldn't tell if it was with startlement or anticipation.

He stood straight, lifting her with him and twirling her away along his arm. His firm hold on her hand stopped her with both their arms extended. She turned her head to look back at him.

How different would things have been if she'd gone into the Hatter's on Shadow's arm, if he'd led her through dances like these? Would his confidence, agility, and grace have forced everything else to fade away until only Shadow—only his eyes, only his mischievous grin—remained?

"No need to look so confused, Alice," he said. "We've a long way to go, and little time. Or a short way to go, and more time than we think. Either way, we'd best be off."

He brought her hand to his lips and kissed her knuckles before releasing her. He turned and started walking—in what she believed was an entirely different direction than he'd gone the first time—but now kept his pace easy.

Glancing down at her knuckles—she still felt the phantom touch of his lips on her skin—Alice sighed and started after him.

CHAPTER 6

ALICE COULDN'T BE sure whether it was a lingering effect of the drugs she'd been given by Madame Cecilia or some aspect of the simulation, but she had great difficulty determining how long they walked. Minutes, hours, *days*; it all seemed the same, one way or another. Despite being barefoot—with only one stocking on thanks to Shadow—she never once stepped on anything rough or painful, and she felt surprisingly good even though her brain told her she should've succumbed to exhaustion long ago.

The trees and other plants remained mostly uniform throughout the journey, though a few different varieties popped up here and there. All of it was massive, all of it was a little alien, and Alice might've paid it more attention were it not for Shadow.

Her eyes drifted to him frequently. Though he never strayed too far, it was always difficult to say just where he'd be at any moment. He could be walking five feet ahead of her only to appear beside her in an instant without ever having moved. A few times, he roved a little farther ahead—twenty or thirty feet, maybe—only to suddenly walk past her from behind as though he'd been lagging the entire time. Whenever she saw him from

the corner of her eye, his features were shadowy and indistinct —just like they'd been when she first glimpsed him at the Hatter's. It was like he really was a walking shadow and not a man—an *alien* man—at all.

Even stranger was his size. Again, she couldn't be certain of anything, couldn't tell if it was a strange trick of the inconsistent lighting, an effect of her odd surroundings, something to do with Shadow himself, or her own delusion, but his size seemed to...fluctuate.

Whenever he was near, he towered over her—she guessed he stood around seven feet tall. But when he was farther away, she found it increasingly difficult to judge his size. Sometimes, he walked beneath branches—without ducking—and had room to spare above the top hat, and when she walked beneath the same spot a moment later, the branch brushed the top of her hair. Other times, his hat bumped into foliage that she swore she wouldn't have been able to reach if she climbed an eight-foot ladder.

To say it was disorienting would've been an understatement, especially when he always seemed a consistent size while he was close. Her mind insisted there was a rational explanation—dips and rises that she couldn't see but which he was adept at traversing—but she knew that applying logic to anything in this place was a likely path to madness.

Nothing here made sense, and she would never be able to *force* it to make sense.

Despite the matter of his possible size-changing, she found herself captivated by his body and the way he moved. He was tall and lean, with long limbs, but he wasn't gangly or awkward; his movements flowed with preternatural grace, so smoothly that she sometimes had the impression he was more *floating* than walking. For much of the time, he hummed softly, occasionally demonstrating dance moves directly out of an old Earth musical. His tunes were sometimes familiar, and sometimes seemed to be inspired by the various alien bird songs from the boughs around them—though she'd yet to spot a single bird.

An alien in Victorian clothing who phases around like a ghost and has the grin of a madman, but I'm *the crazy one?*

She *was* the one seeing it…maybe she was crazy, after all.

Alice was suddenly aware of the darkness that had settled over the forest. She came to a halt and frowned, surveying her surroundings. When had it grown so dark? She hadn't even noticed the sun setting, hadn't noticed the light fading, hadn't noticed the sky changing color through the gaps in the leaves high overhead. She'd arrived in Wonderland at night and had emerged from the Hatter's during the day—though she had no idea how long she'd been at Hatter's Tea Party, no idea how long she'd been following Shadow through the woods.

Surely an entire day couldn't have passed already.

She turned in place. A cool, gentle breeze brushed over her skin. The birds had ceased their singing, and unseen insects had begun their night music. Tiny glowing specks drifted through the air nearby, looking like little lightning bugs, but as one drew near, Alice realized they weren't bugs at all—they were free-floating orbs of yellow light. She reached out her hand, fingers outstretched, to touch the orb.

The light passed *through* her fingers, creating a faintly tingling warmth as it did so.

"Curious…" she whispered.

It was like magic.

The orb's light bathed Shadow's face as he leaned in close. Alice started; he hadn't been in front of her a moment ago, but there he was now, grinning, with that soft yellow glow high-lighting his features.

"Curious indeed," he said. "What do you suppose they taste like?"

"Um, nothing, I would guess. They're just light."

"*Just light*, Alice? One touch and you think you know everything about it?" He cupped his hand around the orb and swept it into his mouth.

It had been insubstantial when she touched it!

The light shone briefly through the tiny spaces between his fangs before he swallowed. His brow creased in a thoughtful expression as he smacked his lips. "A bit more sunshiney than I'd have liked, but I should've known."

"They taste like sunshine?"

"To *me*. I can't account for *your* tastes." He reached up and curled his hand around another orb, guiding it toward her. "You try it and tell me how it tastes to you."

Alice frowned. "But it's just light, Shadow. Light doesn't have a taste. It...it can't even be held."

And yet, here he was, holding one out to her.

"You keep going on about how none of this is real, Alice. *Why* are you holding yourself to such rules if you don't believe in any of this, anyway?" He held the glowing orb closer; it hovered in the air just above his palm, flickering. "If this is all fake, like you say, embrace it for a little while. It can't hurt, can it?"

Alice stared at the light.

Why not embrace it? Why not enjoy herself? She'd always been so proper, had always been so worried about the rules, so worried about what others thought of her, about what they whispered behind her back. Why not let go and have a little fun?

She cupped her hands over his, easing her face just a little closer.

Indulge yourself, little dolly.

The Hatter's voice echoed through her mind, and she recoiled from Shadow; for an instant, he *was* the Hatter in her imagination, poised over her with a knife at her throat.

"No! No, no, no, no!" Alice turned away from Shadow, plunging her fingers into her hair as she clutched her head between her hands. She dropped to her knees and squeezed her eyes shut. "I don't belong here. This isn't right. This isn't *real*."

Alice heard a gentle rustling of cloth but did not open her eyes; she sensed Shadow was crouched in front of her, and felt that strange, intense energy radiating from him. His hands, warm and gentle, settled on her shoulders.

"Whether or not you belong, you're here, Alice. If it's not real...why not use that to become whatever you want to be while you're here? Become a queen, if you wish it. You can't do any worse than the one who calls himself the king."

"How can you just accept this, Shadow?" She opened her eyes and looked at him, brows drawn low. "We're prisoners here! This is a simulation. Nothing is real. Not the grass we're standing on, not the clothes we're wearing, or even...even your *touch*. It's all fake. A...a shadow of reality, driven by memories of feelings, smells, and tastes. While we're inside this make-believe world, our real bodies are out there dying!"

Shadow frowned, tilted his head slightly, and curled forward. He settled an elbow on his knee and propped his chin on his palm. "Okay."

"That's really *all* you have to say? *Okay?*"

He shrugged a shoulder. "If none of it is real, my words don't matter. I can say or not say anything I want, and it will have no effect. I'm not telling you to embrace this as your reality. Only as your...*present*. You're here for now, aren't you? Play the game a while. Enjoy yourself while you're here."

His words reminded her of what awaited in reality, beyond the asylum—the loneliness, isolation, and pain that had consumed her after the death of her father, the people who'd called her *friend* and acted devastated after learning that she'd inherited his fortune, the bleakness of not knowing what to do with herself now that there was such a huge hole in her heart. None of those so-called friends had ever cared about her— they'd only cared about her money. They'd been the same people who whispered behind her back in school, the same people who'd been nice only when it suited them, the same people who'd deemed her not good enough because of the rumors about her mother.

And their *support* after her loss had only intensified her sense of being lost and alone.

"You don't understand, do you? You don't understand how tempting that is," she said quietly. "Do you know how tempted I was to eat the cakes the Hatter offered me? To forget everything and just feel *good*, like that drug they forced upon me made me feel? To *play the game*, as you say? Should I have let him do whatever he wanted with me?"

Shadow's features darkened. He lifted his index finger and said in a guttural tone, "You do *not* eat his cakes, and he does *not* get to touch you."

"Why not, Shadow? You're asking the same of me. Weren't you just telling me to do what I want? To enjoy myself while I'm here? I could have done that with him, couldn't I have?"

"No"—he flattened his palms on his knees and leaned closer to her, his eyes burning like teal flames—"you *couldn't* have. People like the Hatter are not concerned with the pleasure of others. He would only take from you."

"But none of this is real. So why not play anyway?"

"*You* are the one who doesn't understand, Alice. You don't understand what I mean. The game is not about submitting to this world. If none of this is real and you know that, then *you* have the power to make your own rules. You do not have to bend to this place, make it bend to you!"

"Is that what you did, Shadow?" Alice asked. "Or did you let it consume you?"

He pulled back, expression strained for an instant. "I have no idea what you're talking about."

Alice stood up. "I think you do. There must've been a reason you were brought here, a *terrible* reason, a reason you might've wanted to forget. Why go back to the real world when you have this one, where you have nothing to worry about? No rules, no consequences. Why wouldn't you embrace it? To you, this *is* reality because it's easier."

Shadow shoved himself to his feet and spread his arms wide. "Yes, Alice, this *is* my reality. The only one I've ever known. Why wouldn't I make the most of it? Why wouldn't I do as I please here?

"But it's not the only reality you've ever known. You just chose to forget the other one."

"There *is* no other one." He waved a hand dismissively, turned away, and sat down.

To Alice's surprise, he simply lay down on his back, stretching his long legs out and sliding the hat forward to cover his eyes.

She glanced through the canopy above, letting her gaze linger on the dark sky for a few moments, before looking in the direction in which they'd been traveling—or at least in which she *thought* they'd been traveling. The darkness between the trees was deepening at an impossible rate. She sighed.

"Since we're having such a *logical* conversation, it only stands to reason that we rest for the night," he said. "It will be full dark soon."

"Isn't it already full dark?"

He settled a single finger on the brim of the hat, tipping it back just enough for his glowing eyes to meet hers. "Can you still see the things around you?"

Since she could, she had to assume that *full dark* meant exactly what it implied.

With another soft sigh, Alice lowered herself onto the grass a few feet away from Shadow and lay on her side, facing away from him. She curled up and bent one arm, using it as a pillow.

This place wasn't real, after all, so why not just lie down and sleep in the middle of the woods? It wasn't like they'd come across signs of any predators during their journey. She hadn't even seen a single animal, bird, or insect—she'd only *heard* them.

But if it wasn't real, why was her exposed skin so chilled by the night air?

Too much had seemed real since she'd woken up in the woods. She touched her fingers to her neck, where she'd felt the bite of the Hatter's blade.

A shiver coursed through her, and she curled up a little tighter. Tears filled her eyes. She sniffled; in that moment, she felt incredibly, wholly alone.

There was a whisper of moving fabric behind her. A second later, something warm and soft settled over her—Shadow's coat. In her position, it was large enough to cover her entire body.

She lifted her head and looked over her shoulder. He was laid out just as he'd been when she last saw him—on his back with the hat covering his eyes—but he was no longer wearing his coat, and he was a foot or two closer to her.

"Thank you," she said.

"Mmhmm," he purred.

Alice laid her head down and clutched the coat, drawing it tight around her and burying her face in the fabric. She inhaled. It smelled of damp earth and springtime air, but beneath that was another scent, a scent belonging only to Shadow—oakmoss and amber.

Snuggling into the coat, she closed her eyes and slowly exhaled. The tension in her muscles gradually faded.

As she was drifting to sleep, she was distantly aware of a solid body pressing against her back and long, strong arms wrapping around her, drawing Alice into the shelter of a warm, hard body.

"Whether you believe or not, I will keep you safe, Alice," Shadow whispered.

CHAPTER 7

ALICE WOKE AS THOUGH ONLY a second had passed since she'd closed her eyes. Despite having spent the night on the forest floor, she'd suffered no restlessness or discomfort; her sleep had been deep and dreamless. If it weren't for the golden morning sunlight streaming through the leaves, she wouldn't have believed she'd slept at all.

She was wide awake without a hint of grogginess.

She sat up, and something slid off her chest to pool on her lap—Shadow's jacket. She recalled him covering her up with it, and even vaguely remembered the warm, hard press of his body as he'd pulled her against him.

Curling her fingers into the coat's velvety material, she scanned her surroundings, searching for Shadow, but he was nowhere to be found. Alice frowned. Where was he? Had he gone with a purpose, or simply wandered off?

He wouldn't just leave her, would he?

"Shadow?" she called.

The only answer she received was a gentle rustling of leaves and the soft creaking of massive tree trunks in the breeze. Even while Shadow was walking beside her, head and shoulders

above her, she'd never felt quite as small as she did in that moment, alone and surrounded by these massive, almost-familiar plants.

Alice drew in a deep breath and shook her head. It was okay. None of this was real. She had nothing to worry about.

If only she could believe that.

She looked around again only to realize that everything was *different*. Not that any individual plant *looked* different, but they all seemed to be in different places—like the whole forest had picked itself up and shuffled around during the night. Even in the dark, she'd been able to make out the vegetation that had been around her; none of it was in the same position now as it had been before she went to sleep.

Maybe I just got turned around while I slept?

It wasn't like she'd have known which direction they were heading to begin with—Shadow had said they were lost, and he seemed to wander without any set course. She'd likely have to do the same, at least until she found a path. Surely there had to be one *somewhere*.

"Shadow?" she called again, louder this time.

Again, there was no answer except for sweet bird songs and the faint echo of her own voice between the trees. She wrung the jacket in her hands.

She was alone.

Alice should've felt relieved—Shadow was completely mad, and it was foolish to believe she was safe with him around. Despite how he'd acted around her thus far—friendly and oddly gentle—he was still a dangerous, unpredictable male.

So why was her gut heavy with building disappointment and fear? Why was she so anxious to hear his voice, to catch even a tiny glimpse of him among the trees?

Whether you believe or not, I will keep you safe, Alice.

She'd heard him say those words as she'd fallen asleep; she remembered them as if he'd spoken only moments ago.

If he was going to keep her safe, where *was* he?

A faint tingling sensation crept across her skin, sending a shudder along her spine, and the little hairs on her arms stood on end. Just like when she'd first woken in Wonderland, she felt like she was being watched...but she found herself oddly unalarmed by the sensation.

Alice pushed herself onto her feet, swung the jacket to her back, and slipped her arms through the sleeves. She had to roll those sleeves up to free her hands, and the jacket's hem fell past her knees, but once she drew it closed around herself, it warded off the morning chill.

"Well...any direction is as good as the rest," she said, brows creased as she turned in place. She stopped at random and began walking. The grass was laden with cool dew that dampened her single stocking. Sighing, Alice stopped to lift her left foot, tug off her remaining stocking, and tuck it into one of the pockets in Shadow's jacket.

She took in a deep breath and resumed walking. Hints of his scent wafted off his jacket, stoking a strange sense of longing in her. Though she didn't have any idea how it was possible—as they'd only just met—she *missed* Shadow. She couldn't deny it. She missed his presence, his voice, his glowing eyes, and his disturbing but oddly charming grin.

With all her senses contradicting what she thought to be true, it was already a struggle to keep herself convinced that this world was a simulation, and Shadow made that struggle even more difficult—because even if this world wasn't real, *he* was. He was somewhere in the asylum, hooked up to a mess of tubes, wires, and needles in one of those pods just like she was. Even if he didn't realize it, he was as much a prisoner as Alice.

Whether it had to do with a quirk of this virtual world or something within Alice herself, her body had reacted strongly every time Shadow touched her. If she continued traveling with him, how long would she be able to resist him? How long would it be before desire overwhelmed her good sense and she gave in?

His words from the night before drifted to the forefront of her mind.

Play the game a while. Enjoy yourself while you're here.

Was it wrong to seek out the good in a bad situation? She'd never indulged such urges in the real world—she had loved her father, and she'd always avoided anything that would've caused him scandal, that would've tainted their family name any more than her mother already had. But *here*...

Whatever happened in this simulation would have no consequences, no impact on the world outside. No one would ever know. There'd be no repercussions if she—

Alice shook her head sharply.

I need to find a way out of here. Before I give in to temptation.

And oh, she was sorely tempted when it came to Shadow, despite his alienness.

Her trek through the forest was a lonely, quiet one. The giant leaves and flowers occasionally rustled as though something were moving through them, but Alice never saw any wildlife—even though the sense that she was being watched persisted.

She passed countless trees; before long, they all looked the same. Her worry that she was walking in circles was assuaged only by the varying colors of the flowers—they were much easier to distinguish from one another than the trees, just different enough to tell her she wasn't wandering in an endless loop.

The forest presented conflicting airs of unease and serenity. The light filtering through the oversized leaves high overhead, paired with the smell of living, thriving plants and the high, carefree bird songs created a peaceful environment, but like everything else in this simulation, it was all *off*.

She couldn't help but wonder whether this place was

designed to ease the mental illnesses of its patients or feed into them.

After what felt like a long time—during which it also seemed like she'd only traveled a few hundred feet from her starting point—she realized that mist was forming between the trees. The golden sunlight had been replaced by uniform gray, and her unease intensified, tinged with an inexplicable sense of loss and sorrow.

It's not real, she reminded herself as she continued forward.

Now, tufts of sagging moss hung from the trees, and the oversized flowers and undergrowth that had dominated the rest of the forest gave way to clinging vines. The trees were steadily thinner, many of them standing almost perfectly straight and branchless for their lowest twenty or thirty feet, their bark dulled and gray beneath the moss.

Her visibility diminished as the mist thickened. Slow-moving wisps of fog connected larger, impenetrable pockets, giving Alice the sense that she was walking amidst the clouds—at least until her leading foot came down in knee-deep water and plunged into soft, hungry mud up to the ankle. The cold, squishy mud certainly *felt* real for being a simulation.

She wrinkled her nose and was tugging her foot out of the mud when she glanced up and noticed something within the fog —the dark form of a person.

"Shadow?" Alice's voice sounded broken and weak. Fear coiled within her, colder than the mist caressing her skin and the water at her feet.

The figure didn't move.

It's probably an odd stump or tree, its silhouette warped by the fog.

Pressing her lips together, Alice continued forward, her gaze shifting constantly between the figure ahead and the water below. The mist recoiled from her as she moved, leaving a tiny barrier of clear air around her that was only barely enough to see the mucky water through which she waded; the bottom wasn't visible through all the sediment she was kicking up. She moved slowly, using her toes to feel out a path that wouldn't see her sink to her waist in mud or submerged up to her eyeballs.

As Alice neared the figure, its shape solidified—it was a woman, a human woman, facing away and standing utterly motionless.

Alice nearly breathed a sigh of relief when she finally reached solid ground. She splashed the muck off her legs as she stepped out of the water and walked toward the woman.

The woman was wearing a pale green hospital gown with ties on its back, the material surprisingly clean despite the muddy swamp in which she stood.

Alice's memory flashed back to her arrival at the asylum; though the images were blurry, she remembered them dressing her in something very similar to this woman's hospital gown.

I was wearing the same thing when I woke up.

She'd nearly forgotten about her hospital gown, and that triggered a wave of panic. What else had she forgotten since she'd come here? What else would she forget while she was trapped in this simulation?

"Hello?" Alice said softly. "I...I'm lost. Could you maybe... point me in the right direction?"

The woman remained silent and unmoving. Her hair—short and brown—was messy and unkempt, a surprising contrast to her pristine hospital gown.

Alice swallowed and walked around the woman, keeping several feet of distance between them.

"Miss?" she asked as she stepped in front of the stranger. Alice stopped when the woman's face came into view. Alice's brow furrowed; she wasn't sure what she was looking at.

The woman couldn't be more than a few years older than Alice. She had a pretty face, but her expression was slack, and her eyes were closed. Her skin was pale enough that it was almost translucent—as though it hadn't been touched by sunlight in years. Now that Alice was close, she could tell that the woman was, in fact, moving. The woman's chest expanded and contracted with her breathing, which was so shallow that it was nearly imperceptible, and her eyes rapidly flicked back and forth behind her eyelids.

She's dreaming.

Alice twisted around, suddenly aware of more figures looming nearby in the mist, all of them as still and as silent as this woman.

The blood drained from Alice's face. She continued walking, keeping as much distance between herself and the silent figures as she could without plunging back into the swampy water. Everything was so still, so quiet, so eerie; she felt like she was walking through a graveyard in the middle of the night. All the figures—humans and aliens alike—were dressed in similar gowns, and all of them appeared to be sleeping on their feet.

She kept her eyes in constant motion as she traveled, unable to shake the feeling that she shouldn't have been here, that she didn't belong here, that this place wasn't meant for the awake, for the aware.

Her gaze caught on one of the figures up ahead, which was separated from her by a fallen tree and strings of moss; there was something familiar about the tall, lean frame. Drawing in a steadying breath, she moved toward the figure. The figure's details materialized out of the mist—the male was standing with his back toward her, but she could clearly make out his black and gray tousled hair, his long, feline ears, his gray skin.

Was that...*Shadow?*

Alice approached the fallen log and settled her hand on it. The bark bit into her palm as she lifted her leg to climb over.

The male was dressed in one of the hospital gowns like everyone else. A long, black-furred tail dangled from beneath it.

"Shadow?"

"This is no place for you to be wandering, Alice," Shadow said—from directly behind her.

Alice shrieked, lost her balance, and fell forward over the log. Its bark scraped her shins and knees.

Shadow's strong hand clasped around her right bicep, halting her fall, and he carefully tugged her back toward him. He drew her against his chest, spinning her away from the mysterious figure, and she flattened her hands on the soft, silky fabric of his vest.

Heart racing, breath ragged, Alice tipped her head back and looked up at Shadow's mirthful face. The Hatter's hat was perched upon the top of his head, tilted down roguishly.

"You scared me, Shadow!"

His grin tilted up at one corner. "You seemed frightened well before I spoke."

She shoved at his chest, but he held her firmly in place. "You *also* left me."

"No, I didn't."

"You did. I've been alone since I woke up."

"I've been with you the entire time, Alice."

"Are you saying…you've been *following* me?"

"Well it would've been foolish to let you wander off on your own, wouldn't it have?"

Alice didn't consider the potential consequences, didn't pause to consider how he'd react or how strong he was, she simply succumbed to the flare of anger in her chest; she clenched her fist and punched him in the shoulder as hard as she could.

Shadow grunted softly and swayed back a bit; she moved with him, thanks to his unrelenting hold on her.

She glared up at him. "I called for you, and you just ignored me! You let me think you abandoned me."

"I hardly see how I'm responsible for what you do or do not think. What goes on in your head is no fault of mine."

94

Alice pressed her lips together as tears of fury and hurt welled in her eyes. She pushed against his chest again, struggling to break his hold. "Let me go."

His grin broadened. "Now you *want* to be alone?"

Alarm fluttered in Alice's stomach; this was the turn. He wouldn't let go, and then he'd do something to her, something bad, he'd hurt her...

But Shadow *did* release her, backing away and keeping his hand on her arm only until she'd regained her balance before breaking physical contact with her completely. He sank into a deep bow and swept the hat off his head. "My deepest apologies, dear Alice. Though I must say, your beauty takes on a unique cast when you are angry. I find it hopelessly alluring."

Alice stared at him, dumbstruck for a moment. As soon as she regained her wits, she yanked off his jacket and threw it in his face. "You are such an ass. You're not in the least bit sorry."

His free hand caught the jacket before it fell. To her disappointment, he was still smiling when he lowered the garment. He straightened and tossed the hat in the air. It flipped end-over-end several times; Shadow swayed to the side, and it landed right-side up atop his head. "I just like to keep things interesting. No harm done, is there?"

He pulled on the jacket as he stepped closer to her, but Alice spun away and folded her arms across her chest. Her gaze fell on the nearby male who bore such a striking resemblance to Shadow. If she crossed the fallen log, it would only take a few more steps to get around the man and see his face...

Shadow's arms wrapped around her from behind, and he leaned his chin on her shoulder, resting his cheek against her ear. He was warm, and solid, and his hold on her was so gentle, so secure, so *sheltering*, that she couldn't help it when some of her anger dissipated and she eased against him.

"Did you miss me, then?" he asked.

Alice stiffened. "No."

He chuckled; the sound vibrated into her from his chest. His fingertips brushed along the backs of her arms, tickling the skin just above her elbows. "I think you *did* miss me, Alice. You can tell me. It's all right."

It irritated her that she really *had* missed him, especially after the stunt he'd pulled, but she wasn't going to give him any satisfaction by admitting that.

"Why did you follow me? Why didn't you just come out when I called?" she asked.

"I wanted to see what you would do. What fun is there in spoiling it right away?"

"You find it fun to scare me?"

"I find it fun to be near you. Even when you don't know I'm there." He turned his head toward her slightly, and his breath was feather-light on her cheek. "I've been with you since you came here, you know."

Alice turned her face toward him, her lips nearly brushing his. "What?"

"I found you while you were asleep"—he gestured to the figure standing just on the other side of the log—"just like them. You looked so beautiful, so peaceful, and I wanted to know what you were like when you were awake. You were so confused when you first woke, yet there was such determination in your eyes... I had to see what you would do, but the Hatter's little scurrier showed up before you could act."

He'd found her while she was asleep? Alice frowned, but now that he'd mentioned it... She recalled the light touch of velvety fingers on her face and a whispered voice from just before she'd woken fully.

You're going to be mine.

That had been Shadow, even then? Though she'd first glimpsed him when she'd entered the Hatter's place, that apparently hadn't been his first look at her—and it *must've* been him she'd seen in the mirror while she was being dolled up. Her memories after the drink was forced down her throat were hazy, but she *knew* the shadow she'd seen in the mirror had been more than a trick of the light.

He'd been there, too, in the Hatter's parlor—and the guard posted at the only entrance she knew of had been unaware of Shadow's presence until he led her out.

She lowered her eyebrows. "How did you get into the Hatter's room?"

Shadow shrugged. "Like I said, I always end up where I want to be eventually."

Suddenly, his arms were no longer around her, his body no longer against her—he was sitting on the fallen tree in front of her, one leg up with his knee slightly bent, reclining on one elbow. Alice jumped back with a startled gasp.

She stopped when her back bumped into something solid and familiar—Shadow's chest. She spun to find him behind her again.

"Don't be frightened," he said, sweeping off his hat and tucking it away behind his back. "This is all perfectly natural."

Alice swept her gaze over him as though her eyes could somehow stop him from disappearing again. "B-Because none of it is real. It's…like a dream."

He shrugged again and took her hand in his, drawing it to his mouth. He pressed his lips to her knuckles; she was too stunned to react.

"And it has been the sweetest of dreams since you arrived," he said.

Heat blossomed on her cheeks, and a pleasant warmth swirled low in her belly. "How do you do that? Why does no one else?"

His gaze flicked past her for an instant. She turned her head to look—had the figure behind her moved?—but he released her hand and caught her chin with his fingers first, guiding her face back toward him.

"I just do it, Alice. It's likely because I'm the only sane one in this entire world," he said with such genuine solemnity that she wasn't sure how to take the statement.

If this simulation had its own particular laws of physics, he was clearly not beholden to them.

No wonder he'd been all over the place while they were traveling through the woods yesterday.

"You said you found me while I was asleep?" she asked.

"Mmhmm," he purred.

Alice waved a hand toward the sleeping figures in the mist around them. "Like them?"

He turned his head and scanned their surroundings slowly, his persistent grin making his expression largely unreadable. "More or less. But these are the ones that never woke."

"Why didn't they wake? And how did they all get here?"

Shadow lowered his hand from her chin and turned to face one of the indistinct figures off to the side—as though he couldn't see the one directly behind Alice. The one that looked like him.

He shrugged again. "Maybe they're still tired?"

"And that one?" Alice asked, pointing behind her.

He turned his head slowly to look past her. "What about that one? Same as all the others, I imagine."

Alice tilted her head and narrowed her eyes. "He bears a bit of a resemblance to someone I know."

Shadow lowered his gaze to meet hers. "Are you saying his back looks like *my* back?"

She stepped backward. "Do you think his front looks like your front, too?"

His grin changed; Alice didn't quite have the words to encompass what was different, but somehow it shifted from an expression of unhinged but mostly harmless glee to one of an exasperated parent trying hard to maintain calm while dealing with a petulant child.

"These are the sleepers, Alice. I don't know who brings them here, but they're in this place so they are left in peace. Even *I* know better than to play with them." He vanished again—like an afterimage that had been cast by intense light fading suddenly out of her view—and slipped one of his arms around her waist from the side a moment later.

Alice turned her head to see him standing beside her, the hat in place atop his head once more.

"We're wasting daylight," he said, guiding her along as he walked forward. "If you still want to find a way out of this unreality, we really should be on our way, shouldn't we? This place isn't meant for those of us who are awake."

"Then why did you let me wander here in the first place? You could've stopped me at any time." Another thought suddenly occurred to her; she tensed, digging her heels into the soft ground, and glared at him. "Why didn't you stop the Hatter sooner?"

"Because I knew he wouldn't do anything without his hat." Shadow lifted a hand and flicked the underside of the hat's brim, tipping it back slightly. "He is a woefully predictable fellow. I've tried to break him of his habits, but he's quite stubborn."

"What do you mean he wouldn't do anything without his hat? He only lost his hat because I got him angry! What if I had eaten his cakes like he wanted me to? What if I had complied and went along with his commands like a good *little dolly*?" She pressed her hands against his chest and shoved away from him. "He had a knife to my throat, Shadow! He was going to-to…"

"Yes, Alice, he *was* going to. But he didn't."

"Even though he didn't, do you understand how terrifying that was?"

Shadow shook his head and sighed heavily, scratching his cheek with the tips of his claws. "No. I don't."

She'd never heard his voice so small, so solemn; he'd spoken with his eyes averted, his signature grin nowhere to be seen.

His brow furrowed, and the carefree glee that so often sparkled in his gaze was replaced by confusion and worry when he looked at her again. "But I stopped him. I stopped him before he did anything more, and...isn't that good?"

Alice searched his eyes, and all the heat went out of her. This was the second time she'd seen a more vulnerable side of him. Who was this man who called himself Shadow? Who had he been before he was committed to this awful place?

Whatever Shadow's reasons for not stopping the Hatter sooner, it didn't matter now. What mattered was that Shadow *had* stopped him. In truth, Shadow hadn't been obligated to do anything at all. He could have looked the other way and moved on without a backward glance.

She stepped closer to him and cupped his face with one hand, stroking his cheek with her thumb. "It was. Thank you, Shadow. And...I'm sorry. I am more grateful for what you did for me than you know."

Because he'd done more than simply delay the Hatter; Shadow had *killed* the man.

He'd killed the man for Alice.

Shadow raised his hand, brushed the pads of his fingers over her cheek, and frowned. Reaching into his coat with his free hand, he removed one of her wadded-up stockings and crouched. He dipped the stocking into a crystal-clear puddle and stood up again. With surprising gentleness, he used the cool, wet stocking to wash her face; the stocking was soon stained with the white, black, and blue makeup that had been caked on her skin.

When he was done, he tucked the stocking away and studied her face. A soft smile settled on his lips as he placed his hand on her cheek and ran the pad of his thumb over her cheekbone. "*There* you are, my sweet."

Alice's heart swelled; for the first time in a long while, she felt *seen*. She closed her eyes and leaned into his touch. She'd had so little human contact, so little comfort since her father died, and Shadow's simple gesture was almost her undoing. She wanted more, she *needed* more.

"I don't know if you're right or wrong about this world, Alice, but the way you make me feel...it's new to me," he whispered. "And I would be lying if I said I didn't want to keep feeling it forever."

Alice opened her eyes in surprise. His words were completely unexpected—and too heartfelt and lucid to be untrue. "What do I make you feel?"

He lowered his gaze, eyes shifting back and forth as he stared at the ground between them. "You make me feel...*full*."

"Full?"

"Yes, like..." He looked at her again, and his lips slowly curled into a wide grin; crazy Shadow was back that quickly. "Trying to pry all my secrets out of me, Alice?"

Once more, Alice wondered what had happened to make him this way—the man beneath his mask was confused, broken, and sorrowful. She couldn't help but be drawn to him. Mad Shadow intrigued her, aroused her, and set her alight with anticipation despite the danger he represented, but Vulnerable Shadow called to her in an entirely different way. She wanted to wrap her arms around that side of him and draw him close, wanted to help him piece himself back together, wanted to hold him until he gave her not the grin of a madman, but the tender smile of someone finally at peace.

Alice lowered her hand from his face. "It's not prying if you were giving them willingly."

Shadow kept his hand on Alice's face. "Since you've taken from me, I think it's only fair I take something from you. That way we're even."

She furrowed her brow. "I didn't take any—"

He silenced her in a way she would never have expected—he slipped his hand to the back of her head to draw her closer, leaned forward, and slanted his mouth over hers. Her heart jolted, and her pulse pounded. His lips were firm and demanding, and they sent a thrilling shockwave straight to her core.

Alice's eyes widened, and she raised her hands to grasp his vest. Instead of pushing him away, she found herself pulling him closer. Her eyelids fluttered and closed as she gave in to the kiss; when his tongue brushed along the crease of her mouth, she opened her lips to him.

Shadow groaned and looped his other arm around her middle, tugging her against him. Alice didn't resist. She slid her hands up and buried her fingers in his hair, clutching the thick strands. His hand settled on her lower back, and the prick of his claws through her dress sent tingles of delight across her skin.

His tongue swept past her parted lips. Alice met it with her own, flicking and caressing it; his tongue was rougher than a human's, and that knowledge brought to mind delicious imaginings of where else his tongue might delve, where else it might stimulate and pleasure.

She moaned as he took her mouth with a reckless abandon. His lips caressed, his tongue stroked, and his fangs grazed—and Alice submitted. She'd never felt so intensely as she did in that moment, wrapped in his arms with his mouth against hers. She'd never been so *alive*. Her sex clenched in desire, slickening with liquid heat. Her clothing felt suddenly burdensome and restrictive as it scraped against her sensitive flesh and hardened nipples.

I want him.

Shadow's chest swelled with a deep inhalation, and he released a rumbling purr as he murmured against her mouth, "You smell even more delicious now."

Alice gasped.

What am I doing?

Play the game a while. Enjoy yourself while you're here.

And in playing that game, she risked losing herself completely to this place—to *him*.

Alice wrenched herself away from him. There was a sharp prick of pain on her bottom lip as she stumbled back on unsteady legs. Her heart thundered, and her breath was harsh as she stared at Shadow.

He stared back at her dazedly; his pupils were dilated, his ears perked, and the hat had fallen off his head. The hand that had been cupping the back of her head lingered in the air for another second or two before he lowered his arm and curled his fingers into loose fists. His tail flicked restlessly behind him.

"I believe you've taken enough," Alice said.

"It's not *taking* if you give it willingly," he rasped.

She narrowed her eyes, brows falling low; it wasn't pleasant having her words thrown back at her, especially because they were true. She *had* given in willingly. *Too* willingly.

Something tickled her lip, and she lifted the back of her hand to wipe it away. She stilled when she saw the streak of blood on her skin. Slipping her tongue out, she lightly dabbed the tiny cut and licked away the remaining blood.

Shadow's eyes were focused on her mouth, his pupils narrowed to tiny points of black. The heat in his gaze only intensified.

Alice swallowed thickly and squeezed her legs together as though that could quell the desire raging through her veins. Her thighs were slick with her arousal. "Don't we need to find Jor'calla?"

"Yes... I suppose that *is* where we were going." He slid his foot to the side, calling her attention down to the hat. She watched as he deftly kicked it into the air, caught it in one hand, and brushed the dirt and mud off it with the other. His eyes never left her throughout his movements. When the hat was in place atop his head again, he extended a hand to her. "Shall we, dearest?"

"I-I think it would be best to keep our hands to ourselves."

His grin returned. He shrugged, flipping his palms skyward, before lowering his arm and turning away from her. He started walking without hesitation. "Keep close, Alice. I'd rather not see your lovely legs covered unnecessarily in muck again."

CHAPTER 8

ALICE STAYED AS close to Shadow as she could without touching him; sometimes, the fog was so thick that only five or six feet of separation seemed enough for her to lose sight of him, and she didn't want to find herself alone in this place again. It wasn't that it was frightening—okay, so maybe it was a *little* creepy—but it was a sad place. She couldn't help but again liken it to a graveyard, even though the people here were alive. She had no idea why the sleepers had never woken, had no idea who any of them were, but there were so many of them here in this misty limbo that she couldn't help but mourn the lives they were missing out on.

It felt like she and Shadow walked forever, picking their way across narrow patches of relatively solid land that stood above the water. They were forced to cross the water in several places. Alice was left shivering after the first such crossing—the water was colder than seemed reasonable—and Shadow took to carrying her across those spots afterward, ignoring her protests.

And, despite those protests, she wrapped her arms around his neck and clung to him every time, silently appreciating his caring and thoughtfulness.

Still, it seemed like the swamp would never end, like she'd already spent a lifetime traversing it with those dark, motionless figures always nearby in the mist.

Shadow stopped when they came to another stretch of deeper water. She didn't bother complaining as he scooped her up; it had become routine by now, and the body heat radiating through his clothes was too comforting to forego.

"It feels like we're never going to get out of here," she said as he trudged into the water.

He was up to his waist after a few strides. "Do you mean the swamp or the *simulation?* Either way, I'm content—it gives me an excuse to hold you."

When Alice met his gaze, he grinned and waggled his eyebrows.

She laughed and rolled her eyes. "You're impossible."

"I suppose it's easier to be impossible when nothing is real, isn't it?"

Her laughter faded, and her smile eased. "You are real, Shadow."

His expression took on an uncharacteristically solemn cast. "I believe that's the nicest thing anyone's ever said to me, Alice."

"People must not say nice things to you often, then."

"Usually its things like *get the hell out of here* or *I'm going to gut you when I get my hands on you.* I assume they mean it all in good spirits, as most everyone says something along those lines when they encounter me."

"I...don't think they do, Shadow."

His grin returned, and he moved his face into her hair, brushing his nose along her neck and behind her ear. "But *you* say nice things. You smell nice, too."

Delightful shivers swept through her. Alice gasped and flinched away, her hands tightening around his jacket as her skin tingled in the places he'd touched. "Shadow!"

He chuckled huskily and held her closer. "You smell even better when *I'm* nice to you."

Heat suffused her cheeks. She couldn't believe how swiftly he'd caught scent of *that*. Of course, it didn't help that she was wearing nothing beneath her dress, but still! To actually *smell* her desire while they were kissing? It was as embarrassing as it was arousing.

"Are we almost there?" Alice asked.

"Oddly enough, we are there. Or here, rather."

Her brow furrowed. "What?"

She looked away from him, and her eyes widened when she realized they were no longer in the swamp, trudging through water and muck—they were back in the woods, and Shadow's feet were planted on solid ground.

She scanned their surroundings; there was no sign of the swamp anywhere behind them, not even a wisp of fog or a single dangling strand of moss. Afternoon light streamed through the forest canopy, which granted glimpses of a pure blue sky just a shade or two darker than her dress. It was as though they'd somehow teleported while he'd been talking to her.

Alice turned her attention forward. The purple-stone path— or at least *a* purple-stone path—meandered past directly ahead of them, and on the other side of it, no more than ten feet away from the paving stones, stood a strange house.

The structure looked like it was made of some sort of pale gray, hardened material—stucco or clay, perhaps. Its lower portion was a wide, squat cylinder with a small round window to either side of its comically wide front door, and the tiled roof swept outward from the central point high overhead and hung at least five feet past the exterior wall to give the entire structure a decidedly mushroom-like appearance.

"How did we— Never mind," Alice said. She should've known by now not to question this place. "This is him?"

"No. That's his *home.* Jor'calla is a *person*, not a building."

She chuckled. "I know that. I wasn't asking if this was literally him."

"But that's exactly what you asked." He shook his head. "And people call *me* mad."

Alice glared at him. "You can set me down now."

"And if I don't want to?"

"You should."

"Well, when you put it that way, it all makes sense," he said without a hint of irony before gently setting Alice on her feet.

Alice brushed her hands down her skirt, tugging the hem a little lower on her thighs, and started toward Jor'calla's house. Shadow fell into step beside her.

"So, you think he can help?" she asked as they approached the door.

Shadow shrugged nonchalantly. "Probably not. He's a strange one. Doesn't usually make much sense when he talks. It often seems like he's never truly where he is."

"I thought you said he could help us."

"Hmm." Shadow lifted a hand and tapped his chin with the tip of his finger. "I believe I said you'd get on well with him, as he's one of the maddest people in Wonderland. I never mentioned anything about *help* specifically."

Alice made a mental note to *very* carefully choose her words when asking Shadow questions in the future—and to pay extremely close attention to the way he worded his answers. She shook her head and reached forward to knock on the door. Before her knuckles made contact, Shadow grasped the latch, pushed open the door, and stepped through.

Her eyes widened. "Shadow! What are you doing?"

He paused and twisted to look back at her, brows knitted. "Visiting Jor'calla, of course. That's why we came."

"Yeah, but you don't just walk into someone else's house uninvited."

"Perhaps *you* don't." He turned and continued inside, adding over his shoulder, "Besides, he already knows you're here. Why waste time knocking?"

Already knows I'm here?

Alice glanced up at the sky and sighed. "That's not the point." Reluctantly, she followed Shadow across the threshold.

The interior of the house was dimly lit, but once Alice's eyes had adjusted to the gloom, she came to an abrupt halt and glanced behind her to make sure she'd actually entered a building—the inside of Jor'calla's home looked exactly like the forest outside, with lush vegetation and huge tree trunks. But in here, it was relatively dark—the only light was provided by those little orbs floating around like tiny, faint suns.

She didn't know if it was the result of expert paintings, holographic projectors, or simply another quirk of the simulation, and she supposed it really didn't matter. If she had to journey through this world to find a way out, she'd have to learn to shrug off things like this no matter how disorienting they were.

Alice hurried to catch up with Shadow, who was several paces ahead. Everything was closer together in here, giving the sense of walls and a ceiling around her even if she couldn't see them, and the air was hazy with sweet-smelling smoke that thickened as she advanced.

They followed a path between the trees and thick clumps of foliage, curving ever to the right, as though they were winding steadily toward the center of the building—but it seemed to go on and on, much farther than could've been possible given the size of the home from the outside.

Finally, Shadow stopped. Alice peered around him to see a door in front of him—not a door on a wall, but a door on the forest floor, standing without any apparent support. Like the door through which they'd entered, this one was oddly shaped and overly wide, as though it hadn't been designed with humans —or humanoids—in mind.

Alice placed her hands on Shadow's back, instinctively pressing against him. "Is it...safe?"

Shadow twisted to glance down at her; his eyes and grin were bright despite the poor lighting. "As safe as anything we've done so far."

Before she could reply, he took hold of Alice's wrist, reached forward, and opened the door.

A cloud of smoke billowed around them. Alice coughed, squeezed her eyes shut, and waved a hand in front of her face to clear the air. The smoke filled her nostrils and stung her eyes, and its sweetness was overpowering. Shadow pulled her forward.

"No, no, no!" someone cried in a thin, warbling voice. "You're not supposed to be here, not you, not now."

With a final, sputtering cough, Alice opened her eyes.

Though a faint haze lingered in the air, the worst of the smoke had cleared. Her eyes rounded; she was now standing inside a circular room, its walls made of the same material as the outside of the home. The light in here was stronger than in the fake forest—or was it technically a *fake-fake* forest?—they'd just come from, cast by electric bulbs in several lantern-shaped light fixtures along the wall.

Large pieces of fabric in various colors hung from the wall and ceiling, and an overly wide bed was positioned directly ahead, covered in what Alice could only describe as a nest of blankets and pillows. Sticks of incense—the source of the smoke —glowed orange as they slowly burned on a table positioned on the right side of the room. The lantern light, which was somehow white and gray at the same time, dulled all the colors and made the entire room seem...*muted*. It was reminiscent of the lighting in an old underground bunker.

That thought didn't provide Alice any comfort.

She glanced behind her to see a closed door identical to the one Shadow had just led her through.

Her attention finally fell on the individual who'd spoken. She'd seen many aliens during her lifetime—though she'd seen few of them in person—but none of them had been quite like Jor'calla. From head to toe, he couldn't have stood more than four and a half feet tall, but he was at least just as wide thanks to his long, spindly arms—*six* long, spindly arms. His legs were comparatively short and thin, and he seemed to support his hunched upper body on his knuckles. Each of his hands had two long, thin fingers and a thumb of nearly equal length.

He had large, black eyes that gleamed with reflected light from the lanterns, and long, yellow protrusions sweeping back from his head. His mouth was a set of insect-like mandibles, which seemed odd given that he had skin rather than a rigid exoskeleton. He was primarily green, but there were splashes of yellow around his mouth and along his forearms, and a deep, rich purple at his shoulders, fingertips, and around his neck, with another swatch of it bisecting his face.

To Alice, he seemed almost a cross between a spider—an oddly *cute* spider—and a caterpillar.

Jor'calla lifted one of his arms—Alice guessed it was at least as long as he was tall—and pointed a finger at Shadow. "Ill omen, harbinger of doom! You *should not* be here."

Shadow lifted the hat off his head and dipped into a bow. "Pleasure to see you as well, Jor'calla. It's been too long."

Jor'calla turned and paced away—primarily using his arms to move—shaking his head; the gesture seemed more like he was simply thrashing his chin from side to side, as he seemed not to have much of a neck. "Never too long with such as you. Grinning Ghost, Slinking Shadow, Faceless One."

Alice frowned as she glanced between the two of them. "What does he mean we shouldn't be here?"

"Not you," Jor'calla said, "*him.*"

Shadow smiled at her as he replaced his hat. "He's quite mad, Alice. Best not try to make sense of everything he says."

"Why did he call you all those names?" she asked.

"Because he has a tendency to be rude, I suppose." Shadow stepped to the center of the room—causing Jor'calla to back away farther—and sat on the floor with his legs folded beneath him. "We have some questions for you, Jor. Feel up to giving answers?"

Jor'calla retreated onto his bed, still shaking his head. "Away, away! Do not speak in steel, Wandering Void. Death has returned to Wonderland, and now it will not go."

Shadow glanced at Alice over his shoulder. "See? Stark raving mad."

Alice slowly approached Jor'calla, placing herself between him and Shadow. "He looks like he's scared. What did you do, Shadow?"

Shadow crossed his arms over his chest. "I didn't do *anything*, Alice, and I don't appreciate your accusatory tone."

"The Hatter is no more," Jor'calla whispered hoarsely.

Shadow scoffed. "I only stabbed him a little. He's come back from worse. No need to be so dramatic about it."

"No, no," Jor'calla whined. "No coming back now. No one coming back—none but the Red King. He rides with his faceless army, and his touch is forever-death. The Hatter is gone, and the Red King hunts."

Alice stopped once her thighs hit the bed and reached toward Jor'calla. She lightly patted one of his arms. "Hey, it's okay. We're not here to hurt you, I promise." She glanced point-edly at Shadow, who put on an offended pout. "We're here to see if you could help me."

Jor'calla looked from Shadow to Alice, his mandibles twitching. He shifted the arm that she'd touched, gently wrapping his long, spindly fingers around her wrist, and his eyes—though still impenetrably black—seemed to clear. "You...you are differ-ent, Alice Claybourne. Not like the others. You *know*. Do not let yourself forget, never forget. Remember how you came here—it is how we all came here, but the rest released their memories."

"How…did you know my name? How do you know all this?"

"I hear you. I hear *them*. All of them, all the time." He lifted two hands and clamped them on the sides of his head.

Alice's eyes widened. "You can hear thoughts, can't you? Even the ones out there, where we're sleeping?"

Jor'calla nodded. "Never quiet, never silent. All but *him*. All but the ghost."

She frowned and turned her face toward Shadow. "Why is he different?"

"He is *empty*. Dangerous. Chaos that walks."

"He is also sitting right here," Shadow said in an exasperated singsong. "We didn't come to listen to how much you don't like me despite my obvious charm and charisma, Jor. She wants a way out. Is there one?"

But Jor'calla was staring at Alice; if he'd heard Shadow, he made no indication. "The Red King is from beyond. He did not come like us. Wonderland is too full, too many, and death rides to collect hearts. Cull the people, cull the city… What is dead is dead. Flee, Alice, flee far and pray you never meet the king again."

"Again?" she asked, brow creasing.

Jor'calla dropped his hands and clutched the bedding in his fists. His mandibles moved rapidly as he muttered; the words were too jumbled, too indistinct for Alice to decipher. He shook his head throughout.

He was a broken being who'd been horribly mistreated; Alice guessed many of the people in this asylum were just like him.

She leaned closer and gently placed her hands on his arms. "Jor'calla, how do we get out of here? How do we leave Wonderland?"

"*Remember*," he replied. "Remember, and wake."

"*How* do we wake up?"

Jor'calla released a distressed, chittering sound and leapt back suddenly, pressing himself against the wall behind the bed. "He comes! He comes, he comes for me."

"Who, Jor'calla?"

"Red Death, Red King, King of Hearts." Trembling, Jor'calla tipped his head back. "Too much noise. Couldn't hear...and now *he* has come, now he is here."

"Finally, something that makes sense," Shadow said.

Alice glanced back to see Shadow push himself to his feet, his lips curling into a grin.

He met her gaze. "I think I'll have a look."

Before she could say anything, Shadow was gone—vanished like a ghost.

Grinning Ghost.

Unease filled Alice as she stepped to the spot in which Shadow had been standing a moment before. The air was thick with foreboding and tension, which mixed with the wisps of smoke to press in around her.

"Shadow?" she called shakily.

"He has come! He is here!" Jor'calla cried out.

The door burst open and banged against the wall, startling Alice. She spun around, eyes wide, to see at least six tall, black figures march into the room. They were clad in armor and roughly human in size and shape, but the exposed metal at their joints and necks revealed their true nature—they were robots. The only color on them came from their glowing red eyes and the X's on their chests, the latter of which were painted in dripping crimson over the place where a human's heart would've been.

Several of the robots fanned out around the room, aiming their guns at Alice and Jor'calla, as four more filed inside. These four wasted no time in grabbing hold of Alice and the alien.

Their fingers were impossibly strong and solid as they hauled her toward the door. Terror seized her.

Rapid flashes of memory assailed Alice—cruel hands and rough fingers, mocking laughter, searing pain, a dim corridor.

"No! No! Not again," Alice screamed, only vaguely aware of Jor'calla's voice in the background; he was speaking too frantically for her to understand. She thrashed against her captors' holds, kicking and clawing, seeking any means of escape.

They held firm, unfazed by her struggles. Her shoulders burned with the exertion, one of her nails broke, and pain radiated up from her toes as they struck solid metal, but she didn't stop as they dragged her along the spiraling trail through the interior forest.

When they emerged from Jor'calla's home, the woods were gloomy with approaching twilight. More of the robotic soldiers stood on either side of the purple cobblestone path, lined up in neat, mirrored rows that ignored the way the path meandered and curved.

The robots holding Alice dragged her between the lines of their fellows, toward the man standing at the end of the formation. He was tall and broad-shouldered, dressed in a long, red, double-breasted leather overcoat that had polished silver armor pieces on the shoulders and arms. The belt around his waist held a holstered gun on one hip and a sheathed sword on the other. His coat's collar was upturned, wrapping around the back of his neck and framing his cheeks. Like the robots, he had a mark over his heart, but his *was* a heart—or at least the shape of one, depicted in the deepest black. It matched the black hair that hung past his shoulders in waves.

The man's dark eyes fell on Alice as she neared.

Breath heavy and ragged, she bared her teeth and stared up at the man through the mess of her hair. His lips were curled in a self-satisfied smirk, and smugness gleamed in his eyes. He exuded the air of a powerful man—but more than that, he exuded the air of a man utterly confident in his power.

"Alice"—his smirk shifted into an unsettling grin—"I've finally found you."

CHAPTER 9

ALICE TREMBLED in the grasp of her robotic captors as icy fear crept through her veins and dread pooled in her stomach.

She knew the king's voice—it was familiar, it was horrible, and she'd heard it *somewhere* before. The answer danced along the edges of her consciousness, but she just couldn't figure it out. Why couldn't she place that voice?

Oh God, why can't I remember?

She swept her gaze around, searching for Shadow, for even a hint of him, but he was nowhere to be found.

Another pair of robots dragged Jor'calla up beside Alice. They had their arms looped around his, keeping his long, thin limbs pinned together. His legs kicked and scrabbled for purchase beneath him in vain; they were too weak to resist his captors.

"If I'd known she was here, I would've paid you a visit sooner, Jor'calla," said the Red King. "I hope you didn't run your mouth too much. Wouldn't want you spoiling the fun."

"Who are you?" Alice asked, barely keeping her voice steady.

"Here, I'm the king. Act accordingly."

One of the robots placed a hand on the back of her neck and

forced her to her knees with her head bowed. Alice gritted her teeth and pushed back against the robot's hold, but it was useless.

"Perfect. Before long, you'll learn to do it on your own." He placed a finger beneath her chin and tipped it up once the robot removed its hand from the back of her neck. "And you'll get on your knees often—any time I want my cock between those pretty lips."

From somewhere nearby, there was a faint, nearly inaudible growl; Alice heard it only as a low rumbling, but it was somehow reminiscent of an agitated lion.

Pulling her chin away, Alice snapped her teeth at the king's finger.

The king yanked his hand back, narrowly avoiding her chomping jaw. His features contorted in fury, eyebrows angling down and nostrils flaring. With a snarl, he grasped her hair and jerked her head back, brandishing that finger in front of her nose. "You're going to pay for that, Alice. I'm not going to kill you, not right away. You're going to suffer for a long, long time. People can survive a lot of punishment here, but they feel"—he trailed the back of his finger down her cheek—"*everything.*

"Winters failed to condition you as I instructed, but that's all right. I think I'll enjoy breaking you. I'll enjoy making you learn."

Alice glared at him with her teeth clenched and lips pressed tightly together. Anger overrode her fear, and she didn't bother to hide it.

The king yanked her head back farther, tugging hard on her hair, and she hissed at the flare of pain on her scalp.

"Like I said, girl, you'll learn. One way or another. I guess if you don't…you'll just have to be part of the culling, won't you? Just like our friend here."

Releasing her, the king stepped back and turned toward Jor'-calla, who was squirming in his captors' restraining arms.

"You've always been a nuisance, bug. Always caused issues. Because you knew there wasn't anything we could really do about it. What do you know now, Jor'calla? What do you see?"

"The mandate," Jor'calla rasped. "The culling. *Death*."

"*True* death." The king reached forward and patted the side of Jor'calla's face. "True death for any I choose. And you…well, time's come for you to stop being a problem." He swept aside his coat, revealing a knife strapped to his thigh, and wrapped his fingers around the grip.

Alice's eyes widened, and she threw her weight forward. "Don't! Leave him alone!"

The robots holding her didn't move so much as an inch.

Jor'calla twisted his head to look at Alice. "He is deathless in Wonderland! End him beyond, only beyond!"

"Pull his head back," the king spat.

The robots complied, forcing Jor'calla's head up to expose the soft-looking skin of his throat. The alien's mandibles twitched and writhed.

"The Red King knows the way," Jor'calla cried. "He travels between worlds! He—"

The king plunged his knife into Jor'calla's throat, cutting off the alien's words.

"No!" Alice's stomach churned; she was sickened and horrified but unable to look away.

Settling his free hand over the butt of the knife, the king dragged the blade downward, opening a huge gash down Jor'calla's chest. Thick, blue blood gushed from the wound, bathing the king's hands.

Jor'calla spasmed, his mandibles flaring wide, and Alice watched in silent horror as the alien's entrails spilled from the gaping wound.

The king pulled the knife free and plunged a hand into Jor'calla's chest. He tugged on something inside; there was a wet, squelching sound, followed by a long, slowly fading hiss from Jor'calla. The alien sagged in the robots' hold.

Stepping back, the king pulled something out of Jor'calla's chest—a *heart*. He raised it high, like a grisly trophy, and grinned. "One less problem for the future."

One of the robots walked forward, holding an open sack, the bottom of which was glistening and dripping with dark liquid that could only be blood. The king tossed the heart into the sack as if it were nothing more than a measly pebble and flicked droplets of blue blood off his fingertips.

Numbly, Alice turned her face back toward Jor'calla. Though she'd only just met him, she mourned his death. He must've suffered so much—both here and in reality—but, rather than beg for his life, he'd used his final breaths to try to tell her something. He'd been trying to *help* her. He hadn't deserved this. She doubted any of the king's victims deserved this.

The king stepped back over to Alice and took firm hold of her jaw, smearing warm, blue blood over her skin. He wagged the knife toward the robots, and they released her. The king took hold of her in their stead, wrapping his arm around her and drawing her close with seemingly as much strength as his mechanized minions. He pressed the flat of his blade along her spine.

Alice stiffened and forced herself to meet his gaze, narrowing her eyes as disgust, hatred, and anger rose in her throat like bile.

"Now that I've concluded my business with Jor'calla, I have some time to spare for you," he said, brushing his finger over her bottom lip in a way that, like his voice, was frustratingly familiar and unsettling—but which she could not place. "Shall we begin your lessons?"

His mouth descended upon hers.

. . .

THOUGH THE RED King was not nearly as predictable as the Hatter, he had certain habits that Shadow had learned to recognize and exploit—the most interesting of which was, perhaps, his tendency to make unnecessary displays of force.

No one was quite sure where the king's army of automatons had come from; nobody was quite sure where anything in Wonderland came from, in fact, but there was nothing else in the whole world quite like the king's minions. There'd always been something familiar about the faceless, unfeeling soldiers that Shadow couldn't place, but he never let himself dwell upon that notion for long.

All that mattered was that he knew how to take advantage of their weaknesses.

He'd gone outside ahead of Alice and Jor'calla to deal with the black-armored machines, knowing they'd pose the greatest threat in this situation—the king alone was easy enough for Shadow to handle. The automatons' eyes—or sensors, or whatever it was they were called—had always had difficulty detecting Shadow, especially when he didn't want to be seen; that allowed him more than enough space to work.

True to form, the king had arranged his guards along both sides of the path, ten in each line, with ten more having marched into Jor'calla's home.

Nothing sounded more entertaining to Shadow in that moment than the thought of the king ordering his soldiers to attack only for all of them to simultaneously malfunction. The king's face would turn a shade of red that by itself would've been enough to justify his most commonly used moniker.

All it would take was a few disconnected wires where each automaton's neck met its head…

Shadow had only made it through the first line when the other automatons emerged from the building, dragging Alice and Jor'calla along with them.

Alice struggled against her captors like a cornered animal,

displaying a ferocity that Shadow hadn't yet seen from her—he was equal parts proud and aroused. But those feelings quickly vanished when he realized *why* she was struggling.

The Red King had no intention of being nice to her. The Red King wasn't nice to *anyone*. He wanted something from Alice—likely wanted Alice herself—and he wasn't the sort to stop before getting what he desired.

Neither was Shadow.

Shadow hurried along the second line of automatons, working as quickly as he could. Leaving the machines fully functional would only complicate his escape with Alice; even if they couldn't do much to harm him, they could certainly harm her.

But his frantic pace wasn't enough to keep him from hearing what the king said to Alice—about making her take him with her mouth. Jealousy and rage roared to life within Shadow. He clenched his fists, digging his claws into his palms, and involuntarily released a low growl that nearly revealed him to his foe.

When the king sliced open Jor'calla—a decent person, even if he was sometimes quite rude—only a minute later, Shadow knew he was out of time. There was no more room for elaborate plans, no matter how entertaining they'd be.

The threat to Alice was too great.

Shadow was creeping around the machine soldiers, meaning to sneak up behind his foe, when the king pulled Alice against him and kissed her.

Kissed her.

He kissed *her!*

Shadow's rage grew into something powerful and primal, sweeping through him from head to toe to the tip of his tail. It was heavy; it was fiery; it was *raw*. For as long as he could remember, he'd played his games with the denizens of Wonderland because those games were *fun*. And those people had looked at him like he was a freak, had called him the Grinning

Ghost, the Faceless One, the Slinking Shadow. And he'd never hated any of them—not even the ones who'd been angry at him, who'd tried to kill him. It had all been too amusing.

But there was nothing amusing about this. There was no fun to be had here.

Even after witnessing the Red King's cruelty over an unfathomable length of time, even after countless games—most of which culminated in violence—between Shadow and this man who called himself the ruler of Wonderland, Shadow had never hated the king.

Until now.

Shadow had planned to toy with the king for a little while before escaping with Alice. He'd planned to taunt and tease, and he'd been in a good enough mood that he probably wouldn't have killed the man before going.

That was no longer the case.

Because the Red King had kissed Alice. *Shadow's* Alice.

Snarling, he darted behind the king, sank his claws into the man's scalp, yanked the man's head back, and drew the gun from the king's hip.

"Fuck!" The king released Alice and lifted his arm as though to reach back and stab Shadow.

"No more games," Shadow growled as he jabbed the barrel of the gun just behind the king's ear and pulled the trigger.

The boom of the gunshot echoed through the trees, followed a moment later by the light, splattering sounds of chunks of the king's brain and skull raining on the forest floor nearby. Using his grip on the king's hair, Shadow thrust the limp corpse backward.

"Shadow," Alice rasped, her big blue eyes bright against her pale skin. An instant later, she lunged toward him, throwing herself into his arms.

He caught her in an embrace, but his attention was focused on the automatons beyond her.

The machines along the sides of the road snapped their heads toward him. Sparks flew from their necks, and small explosions blasted their heads apart in rapid, irregular succession. But the ten on the path—the ones who'd captured Alice and Jor'calla—just stared at Shadow with their glowing red eyes and lifted their weapons.

"Didn't get them all, we'll talk soon," Shadow said quickly, lifting Alice off her feet and spinning her around so he was shielding her from the robots with his body.

She released a startled cry; when she repeated his name, it was with alarm.

Shadow darted forward, willing himself somewhere, *anywhere*, but right here.

At least half a dozen guns boomed behind him.

His foot came down on…*nothing.*

CHAPTER 10

VICTOR DREW in a strained breath as his eyes snapped open. For several seconds, he could not release that breath; it burned in his lungs like a cloud of fire, exacerbating the dull throbbing in his head. His discomfort only began to fade after he finally exhaled.

"That fucking shadow," he growled through his teeth.

Clutching the arms of his chair, he sat forward. The small, dimly lit room spun around him. He squeezed his eyes shut and reached behind his head to press the release on his sim-needle. The device detached from the connection port implanted at the base of his skull and fell away.

That damned faceless glitch had been a thorn in Victor's side for *years*, constantly disrupting his leisure time. But now he was also disrupting Victor's business. That was unacceptable. This situation, this *shadow*, needed to finally come to an end.

Victor shoved himself out of the chair and walked toward the door. His legs felt rubbery and unsteady, and his stomach churned; being jolted out of such an immersive simulation almost always brought on sim-sickness, but he refused to be

placed in a temporary comatose state after a forced despawn. That was for the patients, for the *worms*.

Victor Koenig was the director of this facility. He wouldn't be stopped by a little nausea.

"That was the last time." He threw open the door and strode into his office, his sim-sickness recoiling from his growing anger.

He'd been despawned by the shadow more times than he cared to count, but years of hunting—and many, many programmers and simulation specialists being hired and fired— had turned up *nothing*. That faceless, always changing shadow was a ghost in the system, totally untraceable.

Victor tugged the tablet from his belt and activated it, synching its display to the holoscreen on his desk as he sat down there. For what must've been the millionth time, he pulled up the patient records list and scrolled through it, scrutinizing every one of the pictures it displayed in a search for any features he could attribute to the anomaly that had plagued him for so long.

He *knew* the shadow was one of the patients. But which one?

"Going to find you," he muttered. "You won't escape this time."

Victor paused when a familiar face appeared on the list—a young woman with blonde hair and bright blue eyes. Alice Claybourne.

He'd had her in his grasp despite Winters's ineptitude, despite the shadow having taken an apparent interest in her. She was the point where business and pleasure overlapped. There were far more attractive patients in the facility, many of whom were far more willing, but where was the fun without a little challenge? Conquest with no struggle seemed meaningless. At the same time...she did need to die. The financial gain he'd see through her demise was far greater—and more personal— than the government subsidy the facility would receive by bringing another new patient into her soon-to-be vacant immersion chamber.

He *would* take care of her—but he was going to enjoy her a little first. Something about the thought of breaking Alice was particularly appealing to him, especially if it would upset the shadow.

Fulfilling those goals, however, would be complicated so long as the shadow kept close to her.

"I'm going to take my time with you, little Alice."

An insistent, chiming tone shattered Victor's thoughts. Gritting his teeth, he tapped the tablet screen to answer the incoming call.

The holoscreen on his desk displayed a video feed with Doctor Kade's face on it. She wore her usual expression—a little cold and largely unreadable. One day, Victor would get *her* into the simulation, just to see if he could make her face change. It'd be worth the effort to see her features contorted in fear.

"What is it, Olivia?" he asked.

"You're out early, Victor," she said in a dispassionate but subtly judgmental voice. "Have you seen the reports?"

"No. I haven't checked my messages. I'm well aware of Accounting's assessments, regardless."

She shook her head. "No, the reports from Operations. Fourteen deaths since the change was implemented."

"Good." Perhaps he'd not been set back by the shadow quite so much as he'd assumed. "Causes?"

The doctor raised a hand and slid up her glasses to pinch the bridge of her nose. "Cardiac arrest induced by total overload of their nervous systems."

Victor smiled; the news was good enough to make him forget about the shadow, if only a little. "Just as you predicted."

"Don't you think it's a bit much, Victor? *Fourteen?*"

"They're just the beginning—and only seven were by my hand."

"It's been less than five days."

"And?"

"Twelve dead of identical causes in five days, Victor, with more to come?" Doctor Kade sighed heavily and lowered her hand. "You're going to attract outside attention."

"Perhaps. But these are the dregs of society, the unwanted. No one cares about them. And *you* are going to work with Operations and Engineering to ensure our explanations of these deaths don't draw any suspicion."

"Victor, this is—"

Victor leaned forward and slammed his hand on the desk, silencing her. "Don't you *dare* tell me how to run this facility. We are nearly at full capacity, but we need new patients coming in to boost our revenue stream. *I* am solving a problem."

She pressed her lips into a tight line, and the set of her eyebrows hardened. "You're indulging yourself."

"And you, *doctor*, are already complicit in all this," Victor snapped. "I expect you'll handle the situation accordingly." He terminated the call before she could respond.

The video window closed, returning Alice's picture to its former place of prominence.

No more games, the shadow had said.

Victor agreed. Too much was on the line now to let the shadow put it all at risk. The time had come to stomp out this problem, to grind it to dust beneath his boots, to make it clear to everyone both within and outside Wonderland—Victor Koenig was the fucking *king*.

And Alice had a role to play in this beyond his desire to conquer her, beyond his urge to take her apart piece by piece, beyond the money he stood to gain in silencing her forever. She would be the key to finding the shadow.

Victor leaned back in his chair, drumming the fingers of one hand on the armrest while he resumed scrolling through the patient list with the other. He absently ground his teeth as he perused the faces, unable to shake his irritation and impatience —at least until he stopped on a picture of a patient with unsettling, reptilian eyes.

Victor grinned. The shadow wasn't the only anomaly in the system—just the only one they'd failed to identify and contain. Perhaps all it would take to erase the glitch was another glitch.

His grin remained in place as he made a call.

CHAPTER 11

FOR A MOMENT, Shadow fought to regain his balance, extending his tail behind him as he teetered precariously on the edge of a small rise, but he'd already shifted too much weight forward. Clutching Alice against him, he fell, twisting to ensure he hit the ground first.

His shoulder took the brunt of the initial impact, and then he and Alice were tumbling down a steep hill. Shadow stiffened his arms in a desperate attempt to shield her as they crashed over grass and thick vegetation.

Finally, they came to the bottom of the decline. Shadow landed on his back, and Alice came down atop him, straddling his hips with her hair in his face. Her body was light, soft, and warm, and fit perfectly over his. The fires of hatred in his veins suddenly gave way to a different sort of heat.

"Hardly seems an appropriate time," Shadow said, "but I'm willing if you are."

Alice lifted her head and met his gaze. She searched his face for a moment before she scooted up his body, caught his cheeks between her hands, and kissed him.

It was a desperate kiss, demanding everything from him whether he was willing or not—and he *was*.

Electric tingles spread across his skin, arcing outward from his lips, and the intensifying heat inside him rushed to his cock. Closing his eyes, he slid one of his hands up and twined his fingers in her hair to cradle the back of her head as he enthusiastically returned the kiss. His other hand dropped to her bare thigh, fingers flexing as he warred with his urge to pull her pelvis against his hardening cock. Her mouth was sweet, sweeter than any cake or ambrosial drink, and Shadow gladly gave himself over to the intoxicating haze her taste induced.

When she broke the kiss and rested her forehead against his, she was breathing heavily. Shadow, though tempted to resume the kiss, was content to hold her, to feel her against him, to be engulfed by her heady fragrance.

Something fell upon his cheek, something warm, wet, and smelling of salt. He opened his eyes and looked up to see tears trickling from hers.

The sight didn't make sense to him; was she crying because the kiss had been so good, or the opposite? Was she crying because of what happened with the king, or because she'd been hurt?

"What is it, Alice?" he asked softly, moving his hand to her cheek to brush away her tears.

"He's dead. He was only trying to help us, and the king killed him." She sat up and turned her face away, wiping her eyes with the back of her hand. Her tears continued falling. "And it was s-so *awful.*"

Shadow didn't immediately understand who Alice was talking about; it was ultimately the blue blood smeared on her chin that triggered his realization. *Jor'calla.*

"I've seen the king do worse," he said. "Jor'calla will be back soon, and it'll be like it never happened. He'll be okay."

She turned her eyes back to his, and a crease formed between her brows. "Did you not hear what Jor'calla told us? What the *king* said?"

"I *heard,* but I suppose I wasn't really *listening.*"

"The Hatter is dead. Jor'calla is dead! It's *true* death, Shadow. They are *not* coming back!"

Something in the back of Shadow's mind shifted. He wasn't sure what it was or what it meant, but it created a dreadful, sinking feeling in his stomach that he certainly didn't like—especially in the wake of the passion he'd felt only moments before. "They're not dead, Alice. Death is just a...a transitory state. The Hatter is probably already back, playing with his dollies, and Jor'calla will be back soon, just as healthy and insane as always."

Alice stared at him. "If you're so confident in that, then kill me. I'll come back." She laughed and raised her arms, waving vaguely at their surroundings. "None of this is real, right? It's only a dream. I can't die here."

Shadow frowned. The pit of dread in his gut deepened, threatening to swallow him up from within. "I would never hurt you, Alice. But...that's the way it works here. You die and you come back. *That's* reality. That's the truth."

She lowered her arms and placed her palms upon his chest. "Then there's nothing to fear, right? You can make it quick."

His throat constricted, and his breath was suddenly ragged. "What are you doing? Why...why are you saying these things? You're being..."

Crazy?

But is she, really?

What if I could've lost her back there? What if I had lost her forever?

It couldn't be right. The rules didn't just *change* like that. Reality couldn't just suddenly be different, could it? He *could* kill her, and she *would* come back.

But it was much more than the notion of doing her harm—which was nauseating by itself—that kept him from acting. The mere thought of there being *any* chance, no matter how infinitesimal, of her *not* coming back was too much to bear.

The Hatter is no more.

That couldn't be true. He couldn't accept that the Hatter was dead for good, because that would mean Alice was more vulnerable than ever.

Alice slid off him, lay on her side next to him, facing away, and curled into herself. "I've seen a dead person before I ever came here, but I've never seen someone *killed*. There was so much blood, so much…" She shuddered. "He didn't deserve that. Maybe he will come back. If he does, I hope he doesn't remember that…that awful death."

Shadow rolled toward her onto his side and stared at her hair, uncertain of what to do. He didn't know what she was going through, didn't understand what she was feeling; violence had been a part of his life for as long as he could remember, and such sights had never affected him much, even in the beginning. He'd always been…detached from it all. But he didn't like some of the things she'd said. He didn't like her tone—didn't like her sounding so sorrowful and troubled.

He reached out and ran his clawed fingers through her hair, gently combing out the snarls and tangles and removing bits of grass, leaves, and twigs. She had such pretty hair. Golden in the sunlight, and pale silver by moonlight—and it was that pale silver now that made him realize night had fallen. They had a little time still; full dark hadn't yet set in.

"We should try to find a more comfortable spot to sleep," he said softly. "Before it's too dark to see anything."

"Okay," she replied.

He slowly pushed himself to his feet. He'd dropped the gun sometime after taking hold of Alice, but he wasn't concerned about that; he had other, more reliable means of defending her. It was only when he reached up to adjust his hat that he paused —his hand found only empty air over his head.

Shadow spun in place, searching the ground for sign of the hat and finding nothing. When had it fallen off? Where was it?

For a few seconds, his legs itched with the urge to climb up the hill and retrace the path of their fall. His heart pounded, and panic tightened his chest.

Why am I getting so worked up over a stolen hat?

The answer came to him immediately, but he didn't want to acknowledge it—some part of Shadow, deep inside, said the missing hat was a confirmation of what Alice had told him. Death was permanent, and the Hatter was *gone*.

If anything happened to her, *she* would be gone, too.

Don't need it. Just need her. Just need to keep her safe.

Shadow turned to look at Alice. She had stood up while he'd searched for the hat, and was now a few steps in front of him, looking out across the land with her arms folded in front of her chest. He tilted his head and narrowed his eyes slightly; it was difficult to see, but she was trembling.

He shrugged off his jacket and shook off the leaves and twigs clinging to it before stepping behind her and settling the garment over her shoulders.

She placed one hand over his before he could pull away, turned her head, and smiled up at him. "Thank you."

Her smile was so genuine, so grateful, so *tired*, that it struck his heart directly, making his chest ache.

"I'm sorry, Alice. I only wanted you to have some fun with me. Not...all this."

She tilted her head, her smile fading. "It's not your fault." She turned toward him fully and lightly ran her fingers over his vest. "You've saved me—more than once. And despite them, despite all this, I enjoy my time with you. You make me laugh."

He smiled; it wasn't his usual grin, not nearly as large, but it felt *good*. "At least *someone* laughs. Everyone else gets so angry."

She grinned. "They don't know you like I do."

Shadow tilted his head and couldn't help running his eyes over her body. Even though her pale skin was smudged with dirt and blood, she was beautiful. "I get the sense I don't know me like you do, either."

"No, I don't think you do." She flattened her palm over his heart. "But you're still there."

He furrowed his brow. He wasn't entirely sure what she meant by that, but her words somehow felt...right.

"Come along, dearest," he said, slipping his arm around her shoulders and drawing her against his side. His tail coiled around her hips. "Let's find a place where we can rest and get to know each other even better."

She ducked her head, but not before he caught sight of her shy little smile and darkening cheeks.

They walked together, beneath the boughs of towering trees and the petals of huge flowers that glowed in the moonlight. Shadow had no destination in mind; he didn't know where they were and didn't particularly care. All that mattered was that they seemed to be far away from the king's soldiers.

If death is permanent, I hope it took him.

But something else Jor'calla had said drifted up from his memory to quash his hopes.

He is deathless in Wonderland! End him beyond, only beyond!

Shadow knew, somehow, that those words were true—even if permanent death had come to this world. It made no difference that everyone else would simply cease to be when they died; the king would come back. He would *always* come back.

The night seemed to hold its breath, as it was sometimes wont to do; the moon didn't move, the darkness didn't deepen, and even the usual rustling of leaves and night songs of insects seemed muted. It was impossible to tell how long or far Shadow and Alice walked—not that he often paid attention to such things to begin with. Time worked however it pleased, wherever it pleased, and who was Shadow to question it?

"Are there animals and birds here?" Alice asked, her voice breaking the silence.

"There must be, mustn't there?"

"I've heard them, but I haven't seen any."

Shadow shrugged. "Neither have I. I supposed they simply don't want to be seen."

"Are they like you, then?"

He inadvertently slowed his pace as he contemplated her question, which was more difficult to answer than he might've imagined. The train of thought it sparked led him to a question of his own well before he could provide a satisfactory answer to hers. "What *do* you see when you look at me, Alice?"

Alice stopped, and Shadow did the same. She moved to stand in front of him and gazed up at his face. Raising her hand, she brushed her fingers along one of his ears before tracing them slowly over his other features. "I see a face. I see you. Not a shadow, not a ghost, just *you*."

Warmth blossomed in his chest. "No one else sees me. No one but you." He knew his words were layered with meaning, knew she might not be able to decipher all that meaning, but it was the truth. For the first time in his existence, he had a companion, a friend, and he longed for her to become more.

She returned to his side, and they resumed their journey.

When they finally reached one of the many purple-cobblestone paths—which, like the flowers, seemed to glow with its own soft light—that wound aimlessly through the forest, Shadow stepped onto it without hesitation.

It seemed they'd followed the path for only a few paces when they rounded a bend to find a house—a white, two-story structure with four dark windows on its front. A low white fence surrounded the little patch of land it was nestled upon, butting up against the edge of the cobblestones.

"This looks like a good place to rest for the night," Shadow said, leading Alice toward the waist-high gate.

"Whose house is this?" she asked.

Shadow bent forward and opened the gate. "Miraxis's."

Alice had taken one step toward the open gate before halting, her eyes rounded. "What?"

He paused beside her, arching a brow. "It's Miraxis's house. I would say he won't mind if we see ourselves in, but it really doesn't matter. He usually stays at the Hatter's."

"He…won't come back and find us here, will he? He won't… take me back there?"

Shadow tightened his hold on her. "No one is going to take you anywhere, unless that someone is *me* taking you somewhere."

No one would touch *his* Alice ever again.

The tension drained from her, and a relieved gleam sparked in her eyes. She nodded. "Okay."

Her trust in him only strengthened the warmth in Shadow's chest. When he continued forward, Alice walked with him, no longer hesitant.

The front door was locked, but locks had always seemed to have a difficult time denying Shadow; it clicked open after he rattled the handle a bit, and he preceded Alice inside, holding the door open for her. Once she was in the foyer, he closed the door behind her.

Some fumbling in the dark resulted in Alice locating a light switch. She flipped it on, bathing the room in bright, pure light.

Miraxis's home was pristine; the walls were unblemished white, the floor tiles polished to a shine, the rug lush and fluffy and spotless. Shadow had the sense that everything here had its place, even more so than in the Hatter's quarters. He'd never been certain if it was a result of Miraxis's tendencies, or because of the praxian's long association with the Hatter.

Alice giggled, and Shadow turned to look at her. She was staring down at her feet, wiggling her toes on the tile. Muddy footprints led from her and Shadow's current positions to the front door.

"I don't think he's going to be happy when he gets back," she said.

Shadow grinned.

Miraxis had been the one to bring Alice to the Hatter, and had led countless others to the Hatter before her, sometimes at the king's command, preying upon the confusion and vulnerability of newcomers. He seemed particularly deserving of the stress this mess would undoubtedly cause him.

"Shall we see where else we can make a mess?" he asked.

She chuckled and nodded eagerly.

Shadow led Alice upstairs, using a finger to tip the precisely spaced pictures hanging on the walls to odd, clashing angles as he passed them. The stairs led directly into Miraxis's bedroom. The bed was neatly made, with tight, squared corners and the throw pillows arranged with perfect symmetry.

"Is that a *shower*?" Alice asked excitedly. She broke away from Shadow's side and hurried over to the open bathroom door. She moved past the threshold and stopped just within the room.

Shadow followed, stopping at the doorway to watch as she looked down at herself.

Alice pinched the sides of her skirt and pulled them outward; the fabric was dirty and stained. "How many days… How long… I *think* it's only been a couple days since I came here, but it feels like forever."

"Days don't mean much here," Shadow said. "Time doesn't mean much."

She turned toward him with a thoughtful look on her face. "Sometimes you say things, like that, that make it sound like you know there *is* another place outside this one."

End him beyond, only beyond!

Shadow squeezed his eyes closed as an unfamiliar, blurred image danced in his mind's eye; it was too hazy for him to identify, but it seemed like a place—a place he couldn't possibly have been to, a place that couldn't have been real. During that moment, it felt as though his head would split in two, as though his skull was being wrenched in opposing directions.

His jaw muscles ticked, but he managed a normal tone when he said, "If I know there's another place beyond, I'm not aware of that knowledge."

When he opened his eyes again, Alice was staring at him, her head tilted at an endearing angle that left some of her golden hair hanging across her cheek. Rather than push the subject, she smiled, turned her back to him, and stepped farther into the bathroom. She shrugged off his jacket and hung it on the clothes rack beside the counter.

"Oh, I can't wait to get all this mud off me." Alice glanced at him over her shoulder, and her smile grew. "Could you help me unlace this dress, Shadow?"

Whatever doubts Shadow might've had about his reality were suddenly forgotten; they were wholly unimportant compared to the opportunity currently presented to him. With a few long strides, he entered the bathroom and eliminated the distance separating him from Alice. "I would be delighted to assist."

Gathering her hair, she pulled it in front of her shoulder and faced forward.

Shadow ran his tongue over his lips as he stared at the back of her elegant neck. His gaze dipped along her spine, which was visible through the ribbon lacings securing her dress. The kisses they'd shared had not been taste enough, not by any means. He wanted to explore every inch of her skin with his mouth. He forced his hands into motion, taking the ends of the silk ribbon bow positioned just above the flare of her hips and the tantalizing curve of her ass, and untied it with oddly clumsy fingers.

Once the bow was undone, he hooked his fingers beneath the lacings. Their backs brushed over her soft skin as he worked his hands up, loosening the laces a little at a time.

Alice shivered, and her breath quickened.

The dress parted, and the top sagged when he pulled the ribbon free of the uppermost loops, giving him a clear view of her bare back. He couldn't stop himself from lightly trailing a finger down her spine.

Her breath hitched, and she tensed. "Shadow…"

He caught a hint of her arousal on the air as he slid his finger beneath the lowest open portion of the dress to brush his claw along the cleft of her ass. "Alice…"

A tremor ran through her. Suddenly, she stepped away, turned, and pressed a hand against his chest. Without a word— without even making eye contact—she pushed him out of the room and closed the door in his face.

Shadow's tail twitched, and he blinked. He'd been too caught up in his own excitement to realize what she was doing before it was too late. Curling one hand into a fist, he settled it lightly on the door and leaned his forehead against it while dropping his other hand to his groin. His cock ached; he couldn't recall ever reacting this way to a female. He couldn't recall ever being in discomfort—especially *this* much discomfort—for wanting something so badly.

Against his will, his fist opened, and his claws scratched the wood. "Alice? Did I do something wrong?"

"No," she said, her voice slightly muffled by the door. "I'll be out soon. Promise."

Suppressing a groan, Shadow squeezed his throbbing cock. Her scent lingered on the air and in his nostrils; how easy it would be to open the door, to go through it, and have her. She was on the cusp of giving in to her desire. She was so *close*. It would only take a little push for her to cross that line and fall into his arms.

Shadow glanced down at himself, noting the dried mud, muck, and grass clinging to his clothing. He had some cleaning up of his own to do. She could have this bit of time to herself; when he returned, she would be his.

He grinned. "Take your time, sweet Alice. When you get out, I'll be waiting."

CHAPTER 12

ALICE STARED across the bathroom with wide eyes. Her back was pressed against the door, and her chest rose and fell with quick, shallow breaths. She could almost *feel* Shadow on the other side of the door. The warmth left by his fingers brushing over her back lingered, and, for a moment, she wished he'd come through that door to pursue her, to touch her again, to follow his hands with his lips and tongue...

So why had she just run from him?

Because I'm confused and scared.

She was scared of his intensity, scared of what he made her feel, scared of what would become of them, just...*scared.*

But God, I want him.

It would have been so easy to have just turned around and embraced him, kissed him, welcomed him into her body.

He's an alien! He has cat ears, claws, a tail, and—

Oh, who was she kidding? She didn't care about any of that. Interspecies relationships were common all over the place, and though she'd never been in one, she found his differences even more intriguing.

He's utterly insane!

Even that didn't matter. She knew that, beneath the surface, he was a broken man.

He's dangerous, unpredictable.

She still wanted him. Her body trembled with need, and her thighs were slick with desire. His slightest touch had aroused her so swiftly.

He'd never hurt me.

Why was she fighting this? *Why* was she resisting? What did it matter that she didn't know him? This place, this simulation, wasn't real. Anything she did in here, with him, wouldn't matter in reality. Why deny herself? No one would know. She could take what she wanted, submit to him, enjoy herself.

Play the game.

Could she?

And even if it was real…

I'd want him anyway.

Taking in a deep breath, she turned and pressed her ear against the door. No sounds came from the other side.

She slowly eased away from the door and approached the counter. She looked in the mirror; the reflection that greeted her made her cringe. There were dark smudges under her eyes, remnants of the makeup Shadow had wiped away, and her skin was too pale. Her hair was a mess, tangled and matted, full of leaves and grass, she was smeared with dirt, and there was dried blue blood on her chin and cheeks.

For a moment, she stared at the blood, tears welling in her eyes. The horror of Jor'calla's death clawed at the edges of her consciousness, but she pushed it away. Her mind couldn't handle that now. Not again, not yet. It had been all too real.

Reaching up, she removed the choker from around her neck —it looked too much like a collar to her, now that she wasn't drug-addled—and tossed it away before plucking bits of debris from her hair. She let pieces of grass and leaves fall to the floor. Once most of the debris had been removed, she picked up a comb from the counter and used it to get rid of the worst of the snarls in her hair.

When she was done, she set the comb down and turned toward the shower. Lowering her arms, she let the unfastened dress fall to the floor, stepped out of it, and nudged it aside. She pulled open the shower's glass door.

The shower, like everything in Miraxis's house, was startlingly clean, but more than that, it was…simple—or maybe *old-fashioned* was the better term. The interior of his home seemed like it would've fit perfectly in the real world—more than a hundred years ago. There were electric lights, but many of the fixtures appeared terribly outdated compared to what Alice was used to, and the single showerhead and its solitary control handle, both made of what appeared to be polished brass, struck her as odd.

There were no control panels, sensors, or additional nozzles on the walls and ceiling like every other shower she'd used.

She turned the handle. Water sprayed from the showerhead in a wide cone. The water was instantly just the right temperature—soothing, but not painfully, hot—and wisps of steam curled into the air. Alice stepped into the shower and pulled the door closed.

Hot water sluiced over her body, carrying away the dirt from her travels. She moaned and closed her eyes, holding her face in the water before turning and letting it run through her hair.

Alice took her time, relishing the heat as she scrubbed her hair and body clean using the soaps and shampoos arranged on the little ledge inside the shower. Once she'd rinsed the lather away, she washed again—just because it felt good to be warm and clean.

When she was done, she stepped out onto the mat on the floor, plucked a perfectly folded towel from the shelf, and ran it over her body, soaking up as much water as possible before tipping her head to the side to dry her hair.

She dropped the towel on the floor and grabbed a fresh one, wrapping it around her body. She paused to stare down at her dress. The stains soiling it were only more pronounced against the pristine white floor tiles; she couldn't bring herself to put it back on in its current state. She'd just have to steal some of Miraxis's clothes.

She didn't feel the slightest bit guilty about that.

Facing the mirror, Alice studied her reflection again. Her skin had a healthier flush to it. She felt...normal. She *looked* normal—like she'd just stepped out of the shower, relaxed and refreshed, after a long day. She picked up the comb and ran it through her hair until it was tangle free before setting it back down.

She adjusted the towel around her body—keeping one hand clasped securely at the top—moved to the door, opened it, and stepped into the bedroom.

Alice froze.

Shadow lay atop the bed, leaning on one elbow with his head on his palm. His hair was darker than usual, hanging around his head in damp locks, and he was free of the dirt and muck he had accumulated during their journey. His legs were both bent; one was curled so his foot was behind him, the other so his knee was raised in the air. He wore wicked grin, and his teal eyes burned with lustful heat.

But none of that was what had given her pause.

Shadow was completely *naked* but for a towel—small enough that it might've been a hand towel—draped over his crotch. The cloth did nothing to hide the bulge of his erection.

"Perfect timing, Alice. I was just getting ready to relax."

"Relax?" she asked dumbly, unable to tear her eyes away from him.

Though he was taller and longer of limb than any man she'd

ever met, Shadow was built like a human. His lean muscles were well-toned beneath that velvety gray skin.

"Well, to be honest, I had no intention of relaxing *now*." A low, rumbling purr underscored his words. "That can come *after*."

"After?" She stared at his groin. Had the cloth *twitched*? Was the outline getting...*bigger*? Her sex clenched, and she shifted on her feet, squeezing her thighs together as heat pooled between them.

Shadow's grin widened, and he drew in a slow, deep breath. "Mmm. I don't think I will ever tire of that scent."

Her eyes flew to meet his.

He held her gaze until she blinked. When she opened her eyes again, he was gone. Only the towel remained on the bed.

"There's no need to be so flustered," Shadow said from behind her.

Alice started, but his hands—so soft and yet so strong—settled over her shoulders before she could move away. His hair brushed against her ear as he leaned forward, and when he pressed his body against hers, she felt his hard cock press along her spine. Something lazily stroked her calf; she glanced down to see his tail brushing her pale skin.

"You have no reason to fear me," he whispered in her ear, his hands slowly sliding down toward her elbows. "I would never hurt you. I just want to make you feel good. Don't you want to feel good, sweet Alice?"

Yes.

Desire curled low in her belly. Her nipples hardened against the towel, and her breasts felt heavy and achy—just because of his nearness, his voice. His touch sent ripples of excitement through her. Alice turned her face toward him, lips parting with her gentle pants as her attention fell on his mouth. It was so close, so tempting.

Play the game.

She lifted her eyes to his, which were half-lidded but glowing brighter than she'd ever seen.

Shadow trailed his hands over her elbows and down her sides, brushing them past her hips before settling them on her bare thighs—mere inches from the bottom of the towel. His fingers crept back up slowly, his claws teasing her flesh, and Alice shivered; goosebumps rose on her skin.

For an instant, his fingertips slipped beneath the towel, but they slid back out again as his palms continued up over the fabric. The upward trek of his hands had her suddenly desperate to have the towel torn away, eliminating the barrier between them. She needed to feel his warm palms on her breasts.

"Shadow," she breathed.

"Alice," he replied just as breathlessly. As his hands neared her underarms, he shifted them to her front. They rasped over her breasts; the friction caused by his palms pressing the towel against her nipples almost made her gasp.

He covered her left hand—which was clutching the towel in place—with his, while the fingers of his right hand curled under the towel's upper edge. "You can let go with me, Alice. You don't have to worry. Don't have to hide."

Alice tightened her fingers around the towel. Her heart raced in anticipation and anxiousness.

This isn't real.

So what? Whether it was *physically* real or not, this moment would never happen again. She might never share anything like this with *Shadow* again.

And she wanted *all* these moments with him; they would be the shining light in the darkness, the glimmer of hope that carried her through this ordeal. Something to look back on with fondness when she escaped this place and returned to her comfortable, mundane life.

Even if none of this was real, it was the most excitement she'd ever had.

Alice released the towel.

Shadow drew it aside. The fabric brushed over her sensitive nipples as it moved, and when he let go, it slid down her side, caressing the bare flesh of her hip, thigh, and backside before pooling at her feet. He moved his hands to her waist and pulled her against him. His skin was soft over his lean, solid muscle, and his erection blazed like a brand against her back, throbbing faintly.

He leaned forward and pressed his lips to her neck. Alice shivered. She tilted her head and closed her eyes as tingles spread across her flesh from the spot where his mouth was touching her. Shadow's lips seared a slow path down her neck toward her shoulder, and he ran his hands up over her stomach to the undersides of her breasts. Cupping her breasts in his palms, he kneaded and caressed them, brushing his thumbs over her taut nipples before pinching them.

Explosive currents raced through Alice. She gasped, covering his hands with hers and squeezing them as she pressed her thighs together in the hopes of alleviating the pulsing emptiness at her core.

It didn't help; all it did was make her more aware of the slick evidence of her desire, more aware of that hollow, aching *need*.

"Don't be afraid of what you feel," he whispered, his breath hot against her neck, as his deft fingers teased her nipples. "Don't fight it."

"I'm not." She turned in his embrace. "Not anymore." She met his gaze briefly before she closed her eyes, looped her arms around his neck, and pressed her mouth to his.

She had only ever kissed two other men in her life, neither of whom had been able to steal her breath with a single touch, neither of whom had set her body aflame merely by looking at her.

Shadow returned the kiss. His tongue slipped across the seam of her lips, demanding entry, as his hands dropped to cup her backside and draw her pelvis against him. He made a low, satisfied rumbling sound in his chest. It vibrated like a purr, stimulating her nipples, which were now pressed against him.

Alice made a small sound—something between a moan and a whimper—and parted her lips. His long, rough tongue delved between them. He explored the recesses of her mouth and stroked her tongue, coaxing it to dance with his. She shivered with delight. His mouth was firm, demanding, and divine; she didn't want this to end. Currents of pleasure coursed through her, heightening her need.

Without breaking the kiss, he lowered his hands to her thighs and lifted her, palms sliding to her knees as he did so. She instinctively wrapped her legs around his waist. The new position pressed her open sex to his cock; it glided along her folds and stroked her clit, and she gasped against his mouth, moving her hands up to grasp his hair. When he walked forward, his stride intensified the sweet friction at her core.

A shudder wracked him, and he squeezed her legs with his strong fingers. The points of his claws pressed against her flesh, but she wasn't afraid; she was eager to feel more. Those tiny pricks of pain only stoked the flames of her desire.

He finally broke the kiss as he laid her on the bed. Alice's lashes fluttered, and she opened her eyes, looking up to meet his half-lidded gaze. For a moment, he lingered over Alice, panting, braced with his arms on either side of her.

Lips parted with her ragged breaths, she loosened her grip on him and smoothed her palms over his shoulders and arms, memorizing the feel and texture of the muscles beneath.

In this quiet moment, everything felt *right*—like this was meant to be, like they'd been destined to meet and come together here. There was no reality, no simulation, no other places or people, only Alice and Shadow, drawn together by their attraction and something more, something indefinable.

When he lowered his head, he pressed slow kisses along her jaw and down her neck, pausing at her chest to suck her nipple between his lips and flick it with his tongue. The roughness of his tongue rasping over the taut bud sent a pleasurable shock through her. Alice grasped his upper arms and tilted her head back with a moan. He lavished her other nipple before continuing down her body, trailing kisses as he moved. He crawled backward as his lips caressed lower, sliding his arms out of her hold, until he was kneeling on the floor at the foot of the bed.

She sat up on her elbows and looked down at Shadow, her stomach quivering as his tongue flicked her belly button. Hunger burned in his eyes. He held her gaze, lips curving upward in a wicked grin as he settled his hands on the tops of her knees and spread her legs wide.

Alice's heart leapt, and she grabbed fistfuls of the bedding. She couldn't deny her excitement despite how exposed and vulnerable she felt.

Shadow slid his tongue down her lower belly and over the short hair on her pelvis, stopping just before he reached her sex. "It feels like I've waited an eternity for this taste. Are you as hungry for this as I am?"

Alice's core clenched at his words, and his warm breath against her slick flesh flooded her with a fresh wave of heat.

"Yes," she rasped.

His grin widened. "Good, because I'm cashing in my token either way."

Lowering his head, he extended his long tongue, pressing its tip to the entrance of her sex, and ran it upward until it flicked her clit. Alice's breath hitched, and her pelvis rocked as she was jolted by pleasure. Her arms nearly gave out beneath her. It was unlike *anything* she'd ever felt before.

Shadow's satisfied purr vibrated into her. "Oh, sweet, *sweet* Alice, I am *never* letting you go."

He curled his fingers around her upper thighs, pinned her to the bed, and pressed his mouth fully against her sex. She wasn't prepared for what followed—he *devoured* her with his lips and tongue, stroking, sucking, and lapping ravenously, and she yielded to her searing need.

She fell upon the bed, desperately clutching the blanket. Waves of powerful sensation blasted through her, but she needed *more*; he seemed to dance around her clit, teasing it, bringing her close to the point of no return only to back away and leave her desperate for release over and over again. Perspiration beaded on her skin.

"Shadow, please," she begged, attempting to undulate her hips, to grind herself against his mouth. Her entire body trembled with the need for release.

He made a sound that was half purr, half growl. "But I love the way you writhe. The way you *taste*."

Shadow speared her sex with his tongue. Alice moaned and bore down, needing him deeper, but his grip on her thighs tightened, holding her still. The tip of his tongue curled against her G-spot, its rough surface rubbing her sensitive inner flesh relentlessly. A rush of pleasure flooded her, prickling along her limbs and making her toes curl.

But it wasn't enough.

Alice reached down to touch her clit.

He caught her wrist in one of his long-fingered hands and lifted his head, withdrawing his tongue from her channel. Alice nearly cried at the sudden sense of loss.

"Mine," he snapped, eyes blazing. Tossing her wrist away, he returned his hand to her hip, dropped his head between her legs, clamped his lips around her clit, and sucked hard.

White-hot pleasure burst through her. She came with a series of cries, and he didn't stop her from thrashing and bucking her hips now—though he didn't let her get away, either. Alice moved one of her hands to his head, curled her fingers into his hair, and pulled him closer to grind against his mouth as he ruthlessly licked, sucked, and nipped.

Her cries descended into a moan of ecstasy as liquid heat flowed from her core. Shadow groaned as he greedily licked up every drop.

As she came down from the peak of her bliss, Alice lay limp with eyes closed and breath ragged. She should've felt sated, should've felt satisfied after the orgasm that had ripped through her, but instead, she needed more—she needed to fill the emptiness inside her.

Shadow's tongue shifted to her inner thighs, licking them clean before he placed a kiss upon the center of her sex. She twitched and forced her eyes open, looking at him down the length of her body.

Shadow lifted his face to meet her gaze, and his tongue trailed over his lips, licking away the glistening evidence of her slick and granting her a glimpse of his fangs. Her sex clenched at the sight. He released his hold on her, pressed his hands atop the bed, and curled his claws into the bedding as he pushed himself to his feet; his abdomen slid over her sex as he moved, followed swiftly by the slow, hot brush of his cock. Alice jumped.

She pushed herself up into a sitting position and ran her hand through her damp hair as her eyes skimmed down his torso, ultimately settling on his shaft. The outline she'd seen through his towel had only hinted at his size, offering no clue as to his appearance. His cock was long, thick, and *ribbed*, with ridges ringing it from its head all the way down to its base.

His erection twitched as she stared.

Alice's gaze snapped back to his. Before she could speak, before she could react, he dove upon her, his arms slipping around her as his mouth captured hers in a heady, consuming kiss. She returned the kiss without hesitation. She tasted herself upon his lips, tasted *him*. She kissed him deeper as the flames within her blazed into an inferno.

He rolled onto his back, taking her along with him; before Alice knew it, Shadow was sitting up with her on his lap, her knees on either side of his legs and his shaft pressed along the cleft of her ass. His hands roamed over her back, and the light scrape of his claws left a thrilling sensation in their wake.

"I want you," she rasped against his mouth.

"I *need* you," he rasped against hers.

Alice broke the kiss. She wrapped her arms around his neck, pulled herself up, and looked down. Shadow slipped a hand between their bodies, grasped his cock, and positioned it beneath her. She lowered herself until she felt its blunt head against her entrance. His other hand settled on her hip, his grip firm but inflicting no pain.

Shadow leaned his head forward, capturing her lips with his again, and pulled her down onto him. The head of his cock entered her smoothly, eased by her slick, but it quickly became a tight fit as more of his shaft slid in.

Alice squeezed her eyes shut, her brow furrowing in concentration as she panted against his mouth. Shadow groaned, settled both hands on her hips, and lifted her only to pull her down again, flexing his pelvis to press deeper. He repeated the action again and again, stretching her a little more—and forcing her to take in more of him—with each pump. She felt *every* ridge on his shaft as it stroked the inside of her channel.

When she'd taken nearly all of him into her body, Shadow tightened his grip on her hips and yanked her down the rest of the way, burying himself in her to the hilt.

Alice gasped and clung to him, pressing her face against his neck as she breathed raggedly. His scent—oakmoss and amber —filled her senses. Shadow's palms smoothed over her sides and back, soothing her, as he brushed his nose in her hair. He didn't move otherwise. She felt him, *all* of him, inside her, felt every pulse, every twitch. Her core tightened in response. The faint sting of her being stretched faded, and was replaced by that urgent need for more, by the need to *move*.

She rose on her knees, causing her sex to slide up along his shaft, and lowered herself again. A shiver ran through her.

"Alice," Shadow hissed, his hands swiftly returning to her hips.

She moved again, lifting herself higher. This time they both moaned when she eased back down.

Tilting her head back, Alice met Shadow's eyes. Desire burned in their depths, but it was paired with a lucidity that she hadn't quite seen before. It was as though Shadow—*all* of Shadow—was there with her, like in these precious moments he was both the unstable, unpredictable being he showed this world *and* the broken man she'd glimpsed beneath the surface.

Like he was *whole*.

That was the Shadow who took control.

And she surrendered to him.

THE FEEL of Alice's tight, desire-slickened heat around Shadow's cock was euphoric, divine, and intense—it was almost too much for him to bear. Yet despite the overwhelming pleasure, he craved more, *needed* more.

Alice offered it freely.

Keeping firm hold of her hips, he set a quick pace, lifting her up and slamming her down again, bucking his hips to meet her with increasing strength and speed. She moved sensually upon him, her body flowing easily, her skin radiant with passion. He held her gaze as he moved, fighting the building sensations threatening to force his eyes shut. He needed to stare into her eyes, to see his pleasure mirrored in her expression. He needed to know, without a doubt, that they were linked to one another in these moments.

Her blunt little nails dug into the backs of his shoulders. She further quickened their pace as soft pants and moans escaped her parted lips. A crease appeared between her brows, and her eyelids fluttered as though they would close.

His chest vibrated with his deep purring, which gave his voice a gravely undertone when he said, "Keep your eyes open, Alice. Look at me. *See* me."

She brought a hand to his face and cupped his jaw. "I see you. I—*ah!*" Her chin tilted up and she shuddered as her sex clenched around his shaft.

She was so beautiful—more so than ever before, with passion burning in her eyes and her cheeks flushed with pleasure.

Shadow raised a hand to cradle the back of her head, tangling his claws in her golden locks. "See and know that you are *mine*."

The convulsions of her inner walls intensified, and whatever control Shadow had maintained up until that point shattered. He pounded into her frantically, using the springiness of the bed beneath him to increase the force of his thrusts. His conscious thoughts were swept away by a gale of pleasure that blasted outward from his center.

Alice pressed her forehead to his as she cried out, her breathy moans escalating in volume with every thrust. Her body went rigid, and she trembled, but her eyes remained locked with his.

His fingers flexed as the pressure within him reached a breaking point. He forced his hips and hands to keep moving as he exploded inside her; his movements were made stiff and erratic by the tension his climax produced in his muscles. Though his eyes strained, he would not allow them to close, would not allow himself to look away from her—not while the same intensity, the same intimacy, he felt in himself was blazing in Alice's gaze.

His cock pulsed in his release, and her sex coaxed more and more out of him until there was nothing left to give. Shadow threw his head back, his body shuddering in the aftermath of his climax. Alice sagged forward, leaning against him, and he eased his back onto the bed, wrapping his arms around her.

They lay like that for a long while, their breath ragged, their skin slick with sweat, as they slowly descended from the heights to which they'd climbed.

Alice drew in a deep breath and released it in a contented sigh as she snuggled against him, rubbing her cheek on his chest. It was followed by a yawn. "I don't think I've ever felt so… sleepy before."

"I don't believe that's quite the feeling I was aiming for," he said, smiling softly as he idly traced the pads of his fingers up and down her back, "but I suppose it will do."

She chuckled; it made her body shake gently, but that was enough to send another flare of pleasure through him. There was a soft moan—Shadow wasn't sure if it had come from him, from Alice, or from both of them at once.

"Whether this world is real or not, dear Alice, I will *never* forget this."

"I won't either," she murmured. Her body went slack a few seconds later, and her slow, even breathing suggested she was asleep.

He remained in place for some time, continuing the slow slide of his fingers from her shoulders down to her hips and back again. He couldn't deny his reluctance to withdraw from her body—she was warm and soft, and even as she slept, the faint movements of her inner walls sent tingles of pleasure through his cock. There was nowhere else he would rather have been.

Part of him also recognized that, somehow, she was the only

thing keeping his mind from being consumed with worry. To withdraw from her would mean an end to the sensations currently distracting him. It would mean facing their current situation head-on.

Shadow sighed softly, lifted his head, and placed a kiss atop Alice's hair. "Nothing is the same since you came."

Moving as carefully as he could, he slowly rolled Alice off him, withdrawing his still erect cock from her heat with a pang of regret. She stirred as he settled her onto her back but did not wake. His heart thumped when he caught sight of the faint smile on her lips. He reached forward and delicately brushed away a strand of hair from her face with the back of a claw.

Propped up on an elbow and with his tail lazily flicking beside him, Shadow happily took time to admire her body— their joining had offered unfortunately little opportunity to do so.

Her skin was as fair on the rest of her body as it was on her face, its pure white broken only by a pair of moles on her inner right thigh and a light pink birthmark on her hip. Even now, he couldn't keep his hands off her. She was so soft, so smooth, so warm. He traced her collarbone with the pad of a finger before running that finger between her breasts, which were round and pert, each a perfect fit for his palm. He followed the progress of his hand with his eyes as it trekked steadily lower.

Alice's flaring hips curved in such a way that they also seemed designed to fit precisely in his hands. He ran his finger around her belly button before continuing down. His hand halted at the uppermost edge of the little patch of hair on her pelvis. The hair was neat and short—though he could tell, despite its length, that it tended to curl—and was a shade darker than the blond hair on her head.

He dipped his eyes lower still, and barely contained a lustful groan. Alice's legs were parted, granting him full view of the drying nectar on her thighs and the pink petals of her glistening sex. The air was perfumed with the lingering scent of her arousal.

His cock throbbed, and he wrapped his fingers around it, squeezing it with the hope of alleviating some of the sudden ache.

Despite what they'd just shared, Shadow yearned for more. Had she not looked so exhausted when they'd come down from their climaxes, he would've woken her now—perhaps with the tip of his tail brushing over her folds, or by spearing her with his tongue again. But his Alice needed rest. Even if he could not understand the stresses and fears she'd endured in Wonderland —because this place had never affected him like it affected her— he *did* understand that it was all taking a toll on her.

Yet his gaze lingered on her sex a little longer. Something seemed wrong, seemed *off*, but he couldn't immediately place it. It wasn't Alice or her body, wasn't her sex...but *something* was missing.

His mind stilled when he realized what it was—none of his seed had seeped out of her.

With brow furrowed, Shadow sat up. He raised his hand from his shaft and sniffed his fingers. All he could smell was Alice's scent, as thrilling and intoxicating as ever but not enough to pierce his sudden unease.

He'd felt himself come, had felt heat pouring out of him, and her body had demanded more.

So where was the evidence of it? Where was his seed, which should've been trickling down her pale skin or seeping from the slit at the end of his cock? Where was its scent?

Shadow lifted his gaze to her face. Her features were serene in her slumber, unburdened by worry—for now, her quest to escape Wonderland was forgotten. For now, she'd accepted him, had accepted this place, and had found some peace in that acceptance.

But what if...

What if she'd been right all along? What if Wonderland wasn't real?

What if I'm not real?

He leapt off the bed and paced at its foot, the fur of his tail standing on end as it lashed restlessly behind him. He shoved the fingers of one hand into his hair, tugging the strands back, glancing at Alice's peaceful form each time he passed her. His chest felt tight, like his organs were constricting.

Everything she'd said flitted through his head, colliding with Jor'calla's nonsense—much of which didn't seem quite so nonsensical right now. Even the Red King's words supported Alice's claims, if only from a certain perspective.

"No, no," he muttered under his breath, "the rules can't just *change*. This is all...all..."

Not real? I don't seem to follow any of the rules, myself. That can't be how reality works, can it?

Shadow lifted his other arm to clench two fistfuls of his hair —as though the sting on his scalp could somehow end this bout of madness.

It's true *death, Shadow!*

No. The only true death in Wonderland was the kind where people came back a little while later.

He halted abruptly and fixed his gaze on Alice. Sweet, sweet Alice—so beautiful, so small, so vulnerable. Could he risk disbelieving all this talk about true death? Could he risk the chance of losing her forever?

He hurried to the bed and knelt beside it, sliding his arms beneath her. With all possible gentleness—and while holding his breath—he lifted her off the bed and cradled her against his chest. Her only reaction was to curl trustingly against him.

"I'll keep you safe, Alice," he whispered. "No one will harm you. You're mine."

Using a combination of one foot and his tail, he peeled the bedding back. He settled her on the mattress. Lying on her side, she nuzzled her cheek into the pillow and let out a contented sigh.

Shadow wanted nothing more than to lie down beside her and hold her in his arms through the night, but he covered her up without joining her. These questions of reality were too loud inside his head; he needed a distraction until he calmed down, until he came to his senses and could see past all this madness.

He turned away from the bed. He would occupy himself by washing their soiled clothes—the mess he'd undoubtedly make of Miraxis's home in the process would be satisfying, and Shadow and Alice would appreciate clean clothes to put on in the morning.

Why speculate about reality? Wonderland *was* reality. There was nothing else.

The visions struck him so quickly, so powerfully, that his stride faltered, assailing his senses in an onslaught against which he could not defend. Sight, hearing, smell, feel, and taste were hijacked; all that remained of reality was his own thundering heart.

He was at the controls of a strange vehicle, struggling with the sticks that operated it. The wide window in front of him was dominated by orange fire, and the tang of burning metal stung his nostrils. Everything around him was rattling so hard and fast that it all seemed on the verge of breaking apart. Countless voices chattered in his ear, and people nearby where shouting in panicked tones.

Shadow shook himself out of the jarring vision, but another swept in on its heels.

He lay on his back atop some sort of bed in a dimly lit corridor. Strong, cruel hands were clamped on his arms and legs as the bed was wheeled into a room, and Shadow couldn't move, couldn't shake the nauseating odor of chemicals.

"Welcome," someone said as Shadow was lifted and lowered into another, narrower bed with high walls. They said more, but he couldn't

hear the words because sharp objects were piercing his skin, and he still couldn't move, still couldn't get away.

Then the lid closed, because he wasn't in a bed—he was in a box, in a tomb. In his coffin.

When he snapped back to reality, Shadow was on one knee, leaning against one of the corners of the foot of the bed. His heart was pounding, his breath ragged, his limbs trembling. He was in Miraxis's bedroom, not in a strange, fiery vehicle or a cramped coffin.

He glanced over his shoulder. Fortunately, Alice was sleeping soundly, undisturbed by his...*episode.*

What was that?

He'd never experienced those things, had never seen those places. Just like everyone else, he'd come into being in Wonderland, and he remembered everything from his awakening.

Those weren't memories. Couldn't be.

It was my imagination. A...temporary lapse of sanity.

Shadow pushed up to his feet and, on shaky legs, made his way to the bathroom to collect Alice's clothing, pausing only to gather his own along the way.

"Not real," he whispered to himself. The words echoed in his head.

Not real.

CHAPTER 13

ALICE WOKE from another dreamless sleep; were dreams unnecessary in Wonderland because she was already dreaming? She was lying on her side, and Shadow's body was tucked against her back. Her head was resting on one of his arms, and his other arm was curled around her, holding her securely in his embrace, wrapping her in warmth. His breath stirred her hair and tickled her scalp.

Waking up with someone holding her was strange, but it was a good feeling. She'd had sex once, after her so-called friends had plied her with alcohol and loosened her up enough to convince her to try it, but the act had been followed swiftly by regret—especially when the guy had tossed her wadded-up clothes to her and pointed at the door.

She couldn't have left fast enough.

At that moment, it hadn't been fear of what her father would think—or fear of what would happen if her indiscretion were discovered and made public—that had driven her away. She'd felt so unsatisfied, so dirty, so *used* that she'd been overwhelmed by shame and regret. That man had wanted nothing but a place to put his cock. That's all she'd been to him. After that, she'd

concluded that one-night stands weren't for her. Alice needed an emotional connection, she needed something meaningful. There were so many other ways to find pleasure without the needless complications of sex that it just wasn't worth it without something deeper.

But lying here with Shadow, she didn't feel even a sliver of regret. She felt...cherished.

A slow smile spread across her lips as she took a deep breath and turned in Shadow's arms to face him. She found his eyes open and alert, and his smile—so soft and tender compared to his usual grin—made her chest ache.

"Good morning, sweet Alice," he purred.

A blush warmed her cheeks. His deep, rumbling voice went straight to her core. How could someone's voice sound so sexy upon waking?

Alice brushed her fingers over his chest, tracing the toned muscles beneath. "Good morning."

"I don't think I could possibly have woken to a more beautiful sight." He settled the pad of a finger on her cheek and slid it down along her jaw, stopping it on her chin.

She trailed her own finger down the center of his abdomen —toward his pelvis. "Are you sure of that?"

His smile widened slightly, enhancing the glow of his vibrant eyes. "I *was*, a moment ago..."

Emboldened, she moved her hand lower and wrapped it around his already erect cock, which twitched in her grasp. Shadow groaned, eyelids fluttering shut.

"You seem to be a new woman today, Alice."

She stroked her hand up and down, relishing his response and the feel of him—warm velvet over steel—against her palm. An empty, needy ache, a *craving* for what was in her hand, grew between her legs.

And the look on Shadow's face said he'd give her exactly

what she wanted without resistance. That made her feel... powerful. Confident. Desired.

"What do you mean?" she asked, tightening her fingers infinitesimally.

Shadow's lips parted with a soft hiss. His eyes opened halfway and met hers. "Until this morning, *I* was the one seducing *you*."

Alice grinned and placed her other hand on his shoulder, pushing gently until he rolled onto his back. Without ceasing the motion of her hand around his cock, she swung her leg over him and straddled his thighs. Her hair fell around her shoulders and brushed over her nipples, which were already tight and achy. As Shadow's gaze roamed over her, Alice's desire only increased, flooding her with heat. He settled his warm palms on her hips and curled his fingers around her possessively. The soft fur of his tail ran down her spine, toward the cleft of her ass.

Lifting herself up on her knees, she shifted forward and positioned the head of his cock at her entrance. "I decided to let go and take what I wanted. And I want y—"

A door opened and closed downstairs, followed by an agonized cry.

Alice gasped and turned her head toward the bedroom door, which was still open. Her heart now raced for all the wrong reasons.

"Sounds like our host has returned," Shadow said.

Alice looked down at him; his devilish grin was back in place, but there was a decidedly annoyed angle to his brows, and his eyes lacked their usual humor. He gently guided her off him and sat up, leaning toward her to peck a quick kiss on her lips.

The voice from below—Miraxis's—increased in volume as it neared.

Shadow slid toward the edge of the bed. "Cover up."

Eyes wide, Alice grabbed the blankets and pulled them up over her breasts. "What are you going to do?"

"I'm just going to greet our generous host." Shadow stood up; in that same instant, Miraxis entered the bedroom. His already light skin was paled in horror, and his pink eyes were rounded.

"What is this?" Miraxis demanded. "What are you—"

Shadow leapt across the distance separating him from Miraxis, tail trailing behind him. The praxian had time enough only to widen his eyes further—to the point at which they seemed ready to bulge out of their sockets—before Shadow was upon him.

"Stay away!" Miraxis yelped.

Alice couldn't really consider what ensued in those moments a fight—Miraxis wasn't trying to battle Shadow as much as he seemed desperate to avoid *all* contact with him. The praxian squirmed, wiggled, and writhed as Shadow—sometimes phasing into different positions—grabbed his limbs and, eventually, restrained him.

The struggle ended a few seconds later with Miraxis face down on the floor and Shadow—still totally naked—sitting on his back, holding Miraxis's arms together at their wrists.

"Get off, get off! No, let go, go away, *get out*," Miraxis cried.

Clutching the blanket to her chest, Alice eased toward the edge of the bed to look down at them. Sympathy stirred within her, but she quickly dashed it away. She knew what it felt like to be in Miraxis's position, to feel so powerless, weak, and vulnerable, because she'd been put in a similar position at the Hatter's Tea Party—and *Miraxis* had been the one to bring her there, knowing what awaited her. *He* had been the one to restrain Alice and pry her jaw open so Cecilia could drug her.

"Welcome home, Miraxis," Shadow said. "Hope you don't mind that we've made ourselves comfortable."

Miraxis groaned pathetically. "Please, go. Go! You've soiled everything. Ruined everything."

Shadow's tone was almost disturbingly casual when he said,

"Listen, Miraxis, I *know* you're capable of speaking coherently. Take a few breaths and steady yourself."

"You're naked," Miraxis whined. "You were naked in my bed. What did you do?" He turned his face toward Alice, cheek pressed against the carpet. "What have you done? Why did you bring this filthy dolly to my house?"

Alice glared at him. "I'm *not* a dolly."

"Just a plaything no matter what they call you. A dolly. Property."

"She is *not* the Hatter's, and she is *not* the king's," Shadow growled.

"No, no...*no one* is the Hatter's now." Miraxis squirmed again, but Shadow's hold didn't allow him much movement. "Hatter is gone. *You* ended him. *You* ruined it all, ghost."

"I feel like I'm repeating myself, but I only stabbed him a little," Shadow grumbled. "I don't understand why he's taken it so hard. It's not the first time!"

Miraxis shook his head, though his range of motion was limited by the floor. "He's late. Too late. He hasn't come back."

Shadow's brows fell, and his grin faded. He leaned forward. "Elaborate."

Swallowing thickly, Miraxis licked his lips. "Hatter was always punctual. Even when he died, he always came back on time. He was *never* late. That's why he was a great man. But he hasn't come back, and it's been *days*. It's the true death. *She* has brought true death to Wonderland, and now it marches with the Red King."

Shadow flicked his gaze toward Alice. His eyes were troubled, but he only allowed her a brief glimpse of them before his attention returned to Miraxis. "That...that doesn't make any sense, and I don't appreciate your insinuation. If true death is in Wonderland, the king won't be doing any marching, regardless of who is responsible for it. I killed him yesterday."

"He is deathless in Wonderland," Alice whispered softly. Ice chilled her blood, and a heavy weight sank in her stomach.

Miraxis nodded and released a panicked chuckle. "He is leading his faceless soldiers to the city, to Rosecourt, to cull the population—and to hunt the Grinning Ghost." His eyes locked on Alice again. "To hunt you. They are marching now, collecting hearts as they go."

SHADOW'S MUSCLES tensed as he pushed up on Miraxis's arms, causing his captive to wail in pain. Thoughts thrashed around his mind in a merciless cyclone, too quick and numerous to acknowledge, too chaotic to decipher. It had taken a while to calm down after his crisis last night, but he'd been in a *much* better place by the time Alice awoke this morning—especially considering the *way* she'd woken.

All that was undone now.

"Lies. Why do you lie, Miraxis?" Shadow didn't even sound convinced to his own ears. "If the king is back, Jor'calla and the Hatter should be back, too. Why him and no one else? It doesn't make any sense. This is all madness!"

"It's the truth, I swear it!" Miraxis's voice wavered. "The dolly is right! The king is deathless."

Growling, Shadow dug his claws into Miraxis's forearms, producing another cry of pain from the restrained praxian. "Do *not* call her that."

Alice muttered something, something too soft for Shadow to hear. When Shadow glanced at her, she was looking down, her brows creased in concentration. He frowned; despite the maelstrom in his head, despite the chaotic jumble in his mind, Alice's troubled expression pierced everything and struck him deep. He didn't like it. He didn't like it *at all.*

Keeping one hand clamped around Miraxis's wrists, Shadow hauled his captive onto his feet. Miraxis's struggles had weakened, as though his distressed sobs had sapped his strength.

Shadow forced Miraxis to the dresser and tugged open the top drawer. An assortment of silk neckties were arranged on one side of it; he used several of them to quickly bind his captive's ankles and wrists. Then he dragged Miraxis into the bathroom—with his legs bound, the pale-skinned praxian couldn't walk on his own—and dumped him on the floor.

Miraxis begged throughout, going on and on about how he didn't want to face true death, how he'd just been doing as he'd been ordered, how he'd never harmed anyone himself. Shadow ignored him; whatever fun he might've had in this encounter had already been leached away, and he saw nothing to gain in killing Miraxis. It simply wouldn't have provided any fulfillment.

Leaving his captive on the floor, Shadow collected the clothing—his own and Alice's—that he'd draped over the shower door to dry. Some of the fabric was still damp, but at least it wasn't dirty anymore.

He stepped over Miraxis without a downward glance and exited the bathroom, closing the door behind him. Miraxis continued his frantic begging; at least it was muffled, now.

Alice was sitting on the edge of the bed, staring at Shadow, still holding the blanket over her chest.

"Jor'calla said the Red King was from beyond," she said. "That he didn't come like us, and that he could only be killed beyond."

Shadow's frown deepened. He didn't want to think about all this, didn't want to stumble along the chain of thoughts that had caused him such distress the night before. Didn't want to acknowledge that there was any chance of losing her.

He stopped in front of her and extended his free hand, brushing her hair back from her face. "Jor'calla said a lot of things that didn't mean much."

Alice raised her hand and gently grasped his wrist. "They mean a lot, Shadow. The king—whoever he really is—could be the key to escaping this place."

The sincerity in her expression made Shadow's chest constrict. It didn't matter how many times he told himself this was madness, that the ideas she—and now seemingly everyone else—was throwing around were ludicrous, that she was simply confused and had a warped perspective; it was all coming together. There were too many things falling into place for him to dismiss them all, and that made him uncomfortable.

Because it challenged *everything* he'd ever known.

He knelt in front of her, keeping his hand on her face, and let the clothing fall to the floor. Miraxis's pleas hadn't ceased, but they were little more than easily forgotten background noise now. Only Alice mattered.

"None of this makes sense to me, Alice. It seems mad." He ran his tongue over his dry lips. "If this isn't real, what is? Where did you come from, where are you trying to go? How did you get here?"

Alice released his wrist and cupped his face, brushing her thumb over his cheek. As she looked down at him, her expression was both tender and sad. "This is a simulation, Shadow. Everything we see here is made up, like a game, and we are the characters. I came from what Jor'calla called beyond. The real world."

"Tell me about your world. About *you*, Alice."

She searched his eyes, leaned forward, and pressed a kiss to his lips. Her mouth was soft and sweet, but, too soon, she pulled away. He was tempted to lay her back upon the bed, to fall into her arms, to pick up where they'd left off before Miraxis arrived. He was tempted to thrust into her hot, tight channel, to become one with her and forget about anything and everything but the woman before him.

But he restrained himself. He'd tried to explain away Alice's claims, had tried to dismiss them as unhinged ravings, and that was in direct opposition to the affection he felt toward her. He needed to know her story. He needed to hear all of it—not just to know why she thought none of this was real, but to learn about her.

He realized now what he should have known all along—their physical connection would never be enough. Not without something deeper, something stronger, something that would link them together whether they were touching each other or not.

"I was born into a wealthy family and grew up with everything I could have ever wanted," Alice said. "I attended a private school and received a stellar education. But my life... It was lonely. I had friends, but I always felt as though I didn't belong, as though I didn't fit in, as though they'd always secretly judged me because of what happened between my parents.

"My mother and father separated when I was little. It was a vicious divorce, and it brought a lot of attention to our family. There were rumors, paparazzi, and so much fighting. My mother reveled in the shame it brought to my father, and fed into the rumors, doing everything she could to squeeze as much money out of him as possible. I didn't like seeing my father so unhappy, so I did my best to be a good, dutiful daughter.

"He remarried a few years later, when I was eight, to a woman named Tabitha Compton. My father said she was a good suit for him, and that I needed a mother figure in my life. A *good* mother figure. She was a pretty lady, younger than him, who'd been widowed a couple years before. She had a son who was five years older than me. But I...didn't like her much. I don't know why. I always just felt uneasy around her, but I never said anything. I didn't want to disappoint my father. He was happy. He *deserved* to be happy."

She went quiet and dropped her gaze to his cheek, which she continued to stroke with her thumb. In her silence, Miraxis's pleas from the bathroom seemed louder and more irksome; were it not for Alice's touch, Shadow would have stood up, walked into the bathroom, and silenced Miraxis without a second thought as to whether death was permanent or not.

Alice slid her hand down to Shadow's chest, settling her palm over his heart. "While I was growing up, every time I thought about doing something bad—even if it really wasn't *that* bad a thing—I always stopped myself by wondering what my father would do if he found out, or asking myself what kind of scandal my actions would bring on our family. I didn't want to make him feel...ashamed or embarrassed of me. I know he loved me more than anything, so I...I couldn't do *anything* that would've hurt him.

"So, I played it safe. I didn't go to parties with my friends, didn't experiment with drugs, didn't drink, didn't have sex..." She looked away from him. "No, that's not true. I *did* do those things—once—and I felt...*awful* afterwards."

Shadow's throat was suddenly tight. He forced his breath through it slowly and, somehow, managed to keep from wrapping her in his arms, clutching her body against his, and taking her right now to prove that she was *only* his, *always* his. It didn't matter how long ago it had been, or if it had only been once—he could not stand the thought of another male having her. He couldn't stand the thought of her carrying another male's scent when he seemed unable to mark her with his own.

"And then, a few months ago"—her eyes welled with tears— "my father died. I don't remember too much after that, just this heavy grief, this pain, this emptiness and loneliness. I had Tabitha and Jonathon, who were basically my family, but there was a chasm between us. Tabitha was always so *cold*, and Jonathon..."

She met Shadow's gaze. "Even though he found success and respect working for my father's company, at heart, he's a coddled boy who does anything his mother tells him. So, I locked myself away as I mourned my father. I barely ate, I didn't answer calls, I just…wanted to be alone. But…but *they* came. I was in…in my father's office, and I was… I…I can't remember what I was doing, but *they* came and took me away."

Alice looked away again, and her eyes gleamed with a hint of fear. She removed her hand from Shadow's chest and slipped her fingers into her hair, clutching a fistful of it. "I'm trying to think, to remember, but it's all getting hazier the longer I'm here…" She squeezed her eyes shut. "Their hands hurt. They were dragging me through a hall. I remember voices, but I can't…I can't remember <u>them</u>. They did something to me, and I was confused, but I remember…the coffin. No, a box, or a *pod*. They put me in a pod and all I remember after that is pain. So, so much *pain*."

Her other hand joined the first in her hair. She squeezed her golden locks as she rocked back and forth on the edge of the bed, her eyes glistening with tears. "I can't remember why I was there, or who they were. *Why* can't I remember?"

Flashes of one of the strange, overwhelming visions Shadow had experienced last night flitted through his mind—dim lights, strong hands, a coffin-like bed. It was eerily similar to what Alice had just described.

She's told me before, she must've. I just…forgot about it until now, and it lingered in my subconscious until last night. That vision was my imagination, sparked by her story.

Clenching his jaw, he drew in a deep breath; his weak attempts at rationalization weren't even convincing to himself anymore. Fear fluttered in his gut, but he refused to let it spread, refused to succumb to it.

He settled his hands over hers and gently pried them out of her hair before guiding them down. Once she'd lowered her arms, he cupped her cheeks in his palms, brushing away her tears with his thumbs. "It's okay, Alice. You're with me now, and everything is okay."

"Why can't I remember, Shadow?" She opened her eyes and met his. "What if I forget my past? What if I forget *everything*, even myself? What if I let myself forget? What if I start believing this place…"

"You won't forget everything. You know in your heart what's true."

She took firm hold of his hands. "*You* forgot, Shadow. You believe this place is real. That all of this is real."

He searched her sorrowful, desperate gaze; it seemed to mirror the ominous feelings brimming in his chest. "I don't know anymore. Don't know what to believe in, apart from you. This is the only reality I know, and if it's fake…what does it matter? You and I are real even if nothing else is, aren't we?"

She nodded, her grip on his hands tightening as though he was all that anchored her. "But we can't stay here."

Shadow glanced around the room. "In this house?"

Alice stared at him for a moment before the corners of her lips twitched and rose into a smile. She laughed, shaking her head, and launched herself against him, wrapping her arms around his neck. Shadow embraced her in turn. Her breasts were soft against his chest, her body warm and supple.

Despite everything—Miraxis tied up and begging in the bathroom, the cracks forming in reality all around him, the emotional weight of Alice's story—Shadow was tempted to make love to her right then. He was tempted to guide her legs around his waist and slide into her welcoming heat.

She turned her face into his hair, nuzzling his neck. "No. We can't stay in this house, but we also can't stay here, in this simulation. In Wonderland. We need to find a way to…wake up."

Shadow rested his chin on her shoulder and squeezed his eyes shut. He didn't want to think about that anymore, didn't want to deal with it. He just wanted to hold her forever. But he knew she was right, even if only a small part of him accepted that knowledge. "How do we do that, Alice? How do we wake up?"

His mind flashed to the swamp of sleepers for an instant—to the tall, gray-skinned sleeper with the tail—before he snapped himself back to the present.

"He travels between worlds," Alice murmured. "The Red King knows the way."

Shadow opened his eyes and drew back to meet her gaze. "What?"

"Jor'calla said that before the king killed him. The king *knew* me. Said he'd been looking for me. And his voice…" She shook her head, brow furrowed as though in pain. "It was so familiar, but I just *can't remember.*"

"Shh," Shadow soothed, lifting a hand to her face to smooth his fingers gently across her brow. "It's okay. It will come back to you, Alice. If anyone can remember despite this place, it's you."

She lowered her head onto his shoulder.

He pressed a kiss atop her hair. "So, we have a direction. If the king knows the way, and he's heading to Rosecourt, that's where we must go, as well. We'll get an answer out of him one way or another."

Placing his hands on her shoulders, Shadow eased Alice back slightly before reaching down to retrieve their clothing from the floor. "Let's get dressed and be on our way. I fear we've worn out our welcome with our poor host."

CHAPTER 14

AFTER DRESSING—WITH Alice donning a pair of Miraxis's pants —they left the praxian's house and resumed their journey through the woods. Alice's dress was clean thanks to Shadow, and she felt much better having her legs covered; she hadn't realized just how uncomfortable it was to walk around in a short dress with no underwear on.

To say Shadow had been disappointed in her putting on the pants would've been an understatement. He'd vehemently objected to her wearing the praxian's pants and had stood with arms folded across his chest and an almost comical scowl as she'd tugged them on. He'd muttered to himself about stabbing their host as they'd exited the building. Fortunately, he'd eased as they put the place and its owner behind them.

Though she had no idea how long she'd been in Wonderland —she had no means of tracking the passage of time in the real world, and time seemed to speed and slow here at random—this strange forest with its oversized vegetation already felt familiar, like she'd spent half her life here. And that made sense, even if part of her whispered that it wasn't right, that it *couldn't be* right.

This place seemed real...wasn't that enough? And it was almost comforting to be out here with Shadow again.

Alice didn't bother asking where they were going or how long it would take to get there. Like Shadow had told her, he always wound up in the places he intended to go; she had confidence in that now.

Shadow maintained an easy stride, setting a pace Alice could keep up with without overexerting herself, and occasionally hummed as he walked. The tunes ranged from joyful and carefree to ominous and gloomy; Shadow himself seemed not to notice the extreme changes in his tone, though Alice sometimes caught glimpses of a worried glint in his eyes that suggested he was not as calm as he otherwise seemed.

She didn't like seeing him so troubled. When she'd first met him, it seemed nothing could've shaken him, and to see him like this now...

She needed to ease his trouble, if only for a little while. Needed to distract him.

Alice edged closer to Shadow and slowed her pace just enough to fall into step behind him. Her eyes fell to his tail, which swayed back and forth restlessly. She grabbed it and gave it a tug.

Shadow jumped and snapped his head to the side to look at her over his shoulder.

Alice grinned and tugged his tail again. "I caught you by your tail."

His ears perked up, and the corner of his mouth twitched in a smile. "That's not fair."

"Why isn't it fair?"

He turned his head away, tilted his chin up, and huffed. "I wasn't told we were playing a game."

Alice chuckled, bringing his tail up to her cheek and nuzzling it. "That doesn't change the fact that *I* caught you."

Shadow pulled on his tail, but not hard enough to free it

from her grasp. "Only because I let you."

"How about we play another game?"

Alice's fingers—which had been firmly around Shadow's tail—suddenly closed on empty air; Shadow was *gone*. An instant later, his hands settled on her hips from behind, and he drew her backside against his thighs.

"What sort of game, sweet Alice?" he asked huskily, his mouth so very close to her ear.

Alice inhaled sharply, both in startlement and pleasure. She grinned, wiggled her backside against him, and twisted her torso to look at him. "Now *that* is unfair."

"Doesn't change the fact that *I* caught *you*."

She pecked a kiss on his lips. His gaze darkened and dropped to her mouth, and she felt the light prick of his claws through her clothes as his fingers flexed on her hips.

Desire flooded Alice; suddenly, she wished she *wasn't* wearing pants. "Let's play hide-and-seek. I'll hide, and you come find me." She trailed a finger along his jaw. "If you find me, we can finish what we started earlier."

Of course, they could've just thrown off their clothes and done it here and now, but where was the thrill in that? She wanted to *play*. The excitement lay in the chase. She wanted him to chase her, wanted to feel her heart racing, to feel excitement and adrenaline pumping through her veins, to feel their mutual passion when their bodies finally came together.

He took her hand and, before she could react, slipped her finger between his lips. His rough tongue swirled around it as he slowly slid it back out again.

Alice stared, panting softly, her sex clenching in need.

Shadow's nostrils flared with a deep inhalation, and his smile widened into a wicked grin. "That was just an appetizer. I'll feast upon the main course soon enough."

A shiver swept through her as she recalled the way his

tongue had felt against her sex. "No cheating, though. You can't phase."

When she pulled her hand away, he released it reluctantly. Alice turned fully toward him.

He took a long step backward and sank into a deep, exaggerated bow, complete with a flourish of his hands. "A true hunter always practices good sportsmanship, dearest."

Alice grinned. "Good. Now close your eyes and count to...fifty."

Shadow rose from his bow and straightened his jacket. His eyes glimmered with an anticipatory light. "For the sake of fairness, I'll make it one hundred—but I doubt I could make myself wait any longer than that."

"One hundred it is, then. Now close them."

He lifted his hands to his face and moved as though to turn, only to stop and peer between his fingers. "One more look, just to hold me over during your brief absence." He raked his gaze over her from head to toe and back again; Alice swore she could feel the heat of his eyes on her skin, and it made her clothing feel irritating and restrictive.

His grin tilted to one side as he closed his fingers, turned away, and leaned against the trunk of a nearby tree. "One...two..."

Alice spun around and raced off. Her grin widened as the distance between them increased; soon, she could no longer hear him counting. Perhaps this game was childish, especially when they should've been focused on finding the king and escaping this simulation, but Alice didn't feel childish. All those worries were far off right now, they were distant while she was in this forest with Shadow. For the first time in as long as she could remember, Alice was truly enjoying herself. She was having fun with the man that she...

The man that she...loved?

No, it can't be that. Can it? This soon?

She barely knew anything about him, and the little she'd seen from Shadow wasn't necessarily *him*—it had been more like…facets of him. Fragments of his broken mind. No one they'd encountered seemed very fond of Shadow. Was that because, as he'd implied, he was simply a misunderstood outcast? Or was it because he *was* the Grinning Ghost, as they'd called him, because he was an agent of chaos?

Keep your eyes open, Alice. Look at me. See me.

Alice shoved aside her doubts. *No.* She'd caught glimpses of Shadow, the *real* Shadow, when his mask fell. She didn't see what everyone else seemed to. She *saw* him. Whatever was between her and Shadow was new, but it was potent, and she would nurture it as it blossomed into something larger, stronger, and deeper rooted. Her feelings for him couldn't be undone—she didn't want them to be undone.

She dashed between huge leaves, giant flowers and mushrooms, and towering trees. Her breath was ragged, and her heart pounded against her ribs. Despite the exertion, she felt *good*; her body seemed lighter than ever, and she bounded through the woods as easily as the wind flowed over a field. The surface of her skin tingled, and heat pulsed in her core, intensified by the knowledge that Shadow would be right behind her, stalking her, eager to catch her and claim his reward—claim *her*.

Over her heavy breaths and drumming heart, Alice heard water running nearby. Darting between two trees, she pushed through the thick foliage only to come to an abrupt stop when she found herself near the bank of a wide stream. She bent over, hands on her knees as she caught her breath, and ran her gaze along the stream.

The water was blue and clear, more like the waters off a tropical beach than any stream or river she'd ever seen. Large, flat, dark stones lined the stream, too neat to be natural. It was exactly what she'd come to expect in Wonderland—a familiar sort of thing that was just a bit *off* from the norm.

She inhaled deeply, straightened, and cocked her head to listen for sounds of Shadow's approach. She heard nothing.

Alice stepped to the edge of the water, knelt, and leaned forward to peer in. The crystal-clear water was deeper than she'd expected; it was always difficult to judge depth, especially through the reflections wavering on the surface, but it had to be at least three feet deep even here along the bank. She reached in to splash handfuls of cool water on her cheeks, distorting her own reflection.

Closing her eyes, she released a soft hum of satisfaction; the water was refreshing against her heated skin.

When she opened her eyes, she started and gasped.

There was a face staring up at her from beneath the surface —a face that wasn't her own.

Alice jumped to her feet and reeled back only to slam into something solid. A pair of powerful arms wrapped around her from behind, banding around her torso and pinning her own arms at her sides. She knew by the feel of the rough skin against hers that her captor wasn't human—and that he wasn't Shadow. Her heart leapt into her throat.

Something moved beneath the stream's surface—a figure, distorted by the rippling water, attached to the face she'd seen. An alien rose out of the water slowly, revealing his hairless head first. His skin—no, not skin, *scales*—were a dull golden brown with olive spots along the sides of his head. He stared at her with two large, yellow eyes with slitted pupils. His face was startlingly humanlike despite his scales, right down to a perfect, aquiline nose, but that nose rested over a too-wide mouth that was curled into a grin from which long, jagged, yellowed fangs jutted like crocodile's teeth.

Where Shadow's grin always held a hint of mischief, a roguish charm, this creature's grin was cruel, sadistic, and smug.

Alice knew what he was, though his species wasn't common on her home planet—a boruk. The images she'd seen had not prepared her for how unsettling they looked in person.

The boruk stood up fully, bringing his torso out of the water. There were more olive spots on his shoulders and upper arms, both of which were powerfully built. The scales of his chest and abdomen were large and segmented, almost like armor plates, and tapered along with his narrow waist.

Whoever was holding Alice tugged her back from the shoreline as the boruk stepped forward. She wiggled, trying to pull her arms free while fighting back a swell of fear.

"King was right," the boruk said, his long, thin tongue flicking out. His voice had a strange, vibrating quality to it that reminded her of a rattlesnake's tail. "What a little pretty we've found."

"Too plain," said the alien behind her—in a voice identical to the boruk's.

"Let *go* of me!" Alice kicked at her captor's legs, took in a deep breath, and screamed, "Shadow!"

The alien restraining her—whose arms were the same as the boruk's, as well—hissed softly and tightened his hold on her, making it difficult for her to draw in another breath after her scream. "Feisty. Maybe I do like it, after all."

Water sloshed around the first boruk as he climbed out of the stream. "Too loud. It should learn when to give in."

As he emerged from the water fully, Alice couldn't help but drop her gaze lower. A thick, powerful tail extended from his lower back, and his legs—as heavily muscled as his arms—were clad in form-fitting black pants, but it was the belt around his waist that held her attention the longest. At least half a dozen sheathed knives hung from that belt, each longer than the last.

"It would be boring if it was submissive," said the boruk holding her. His long, alien tongue flicked over Alice's hair and across the top of her ear.

Alice jerked her head away, then instinctively snapped it

backward, striking the boruk behind her in his mouth. Pain pierced her skull; her captor's teeth were rock solid, and the sting on her scalp suggested they might have broken her skin. And it was that pain that brought clarity to Alice's mind.

This simulation may not be real, but these people were—and they could deliver true death.

The alien holding Alice growled and leaned back, lifting Alice off her feet, before carrying her toward the water.

"See?" the first boruk said. "Too much fight. Pretty but annoying."

"Plain but intriguing," snapped her captor.

Alice's eyes widened as she neared the water. She renewed her fight, kicking and thrashing against the boruk. "No! Stop! *Shadow!*"

Undeterred, Alice's captor stepped off the bank and dropped into the stream. Alice found herself immediately submerged to her chest, and he only moved farther from the shore, into deeper water. Her continued struggles were soon too far below the surface to cause more than some pathetic ripples around her.

He halted when the cold water had reached Alice's chin and twisted around to face the shoreline. He and his companion were both staring at the same place—a mass of leaves between the trunks of two trees. The same spot, she realized, through which she'd arrived.

"He is here," said the alien on land.

"Yes," hissed the alien holding her.

Lifting her chin to keep her mouth above the stream's surface, Alice stared at the foliage. Her heart pounded, and her body trembled with fear and cold. Were they talking about Shadow? How could they be? There was no sign of him, no way they could've known where he was, especially if he didn't want them to know.

He's already taken out two very dangerous men like it was nothing. He'll do the same with these two.

For several seconds, both boruks were still, and everything seemed unnaturally quiet. Even the rustling of the leaves overhead and the stream's burbling around Alice were muted.

Then everything moved faster than her fear-addled mind could keep up with.

The boruk holding Alice spun around suddenly, swinging her to face the opposite bank. Shadow was standing in the stream no more than five feet away. The water was barely up to his chest, even though she had to stretch her neck to keep her chin above the surface. But the relief she should've felt at his presence, at his nearness, was cancelled out by the look on his face.

There was a crease between his eyebrows, which were drawn tight over rounded eyes, and his mouth was agape. No grin, no playful sparkle in his gaze, no hint of his normal carefree demeanor. He wore only concern and shock on his face. Both his arms were raised, claws poised as though to strike, but he was unmoving.

That was the last thing Alice saw before she was pulled under water—Shadow frozen in an unending moment of time, stunned and helpless.

CHAPTER 15

FOR SHADOW, the space between those heartbeats stretched into eternity.

Thump-thump.

He'd phased behind the boruk holding Alice—that one posed the most immediate threat, directly endangering her life, and therefore needed to die first. It should've been quick and simple.

But the alien spun around before Shadow could strike—as though he'd somehow known the very instant Shadow had meant to attack. Shadow only had time enough to meet Alice's terrified gaze before her captor dragged her below the stream's surface.

That instant—it couldn't have been longer than a fraction of a second—was more than adequate to flood Shadow with horror and despair. He was losing her. Right before his eyes, Alice was being taken.

Thump-thump.

The blurred figures of Alice and her captor sped away along the bed of the stream, propelled by the alien's thick tail and the water's swift current.

As Shadow spun to follow them, movement flickered at the

edge of his vision. He turned his head to see the other alien—who looked identical to the first—in the air, hurtling toward Shadow with a knife in each hand.

Shadow swayed to the side, but the deep water made his movements jarringly sluggish. He narrowly avoided a full-on collision with his attacker, who landed with a huge splash, but a heavy, piercing impact on Shadow's shoulder made it clear he hadn't avoided harm.

The pain was as distant and diminished as usual, like his body was a thousand miles away from his mind. He kicked off the bottom of the stream, launching himself away from the boruk and into the water current; his attacker's knife remained embedded in his shoulder. The stream swept Shadow along swiftly as he wrenched the knife out of his shoulder, plunged under the surface, and swam.

Alice's blond hair, pale skin, and blue dress stood out starkly against the rocky bed of the stream forty or fifty feet ahead. She was still underwater—and still in the clutches of the other boruk, who was carrying her steadily farther ahead of Shadow.

Something else caught Shadow's eye, glittering in the sunlight that filtered through the surface—a thin, barely perceptible silver thread trailed in his target's wake.

Shadow sensed movement behind him and spun toward it just as the knife-wielding boruk charged forward, churning water with the swinging of his powerful tail.

The alien moved as quickly and easily in the water as Shadow could move on land and was upon him within a second.

Shadow twisted to avoid the boruk's first thrusting blade, but a second knife in the alien's other hand sliced across Shadow's abdomen.

The attack had brought the alien in close. Shadow retaliated by burying his knife in his foe's back, punching the point through thick, tough scales.

The alien seemed unfazed. He whipped his tail around,

striking with enough force to flip Shadow end-over-end, making him lose his grip on the knife.

Water filled Shadow's nostrils and mouth as he flipped and tumbled. The sky above and the smooth rocks below reversed their positions at least twice before he recovered.

Alice needs me. Can't waste time.

Before Alice, Shadow would've thought this an exciting game with two Wonderlanders he'd never encountered, made particularly thrilling due to the unique and unexpected challenge he'd been presented. Now, it was simply another threat to her safety—possibly more serious than even the threat posed by the Red King himself.

Stop thinking and act!

He wrenched himself through reality. The phasing felt slow, *heavy*, as though he were weighed down by his water-logged clothing, but it worked. He stumbled as his feet came down on the stones that ran along the stream's bank, but he remained upright.

As grateful as he was to have solid ground beneath his feet—and for up and down having been restored to their proper positions—Shadow wasted no time in racing along the stream in the direction Alice had been carried.

His injuries were nearly forgotten, just like every nonlethal wound he'd suffered, regardless of its severity. The boruk who'd stabbed Shadow was a blurred form speeding through the water; despite the damage Shadow had inflicted upon him, there was no trace of blood in the water. It was almost as though the boruk hadn't been wounded at all.

Shadow glanced downstream to see the other boruk emerge from the water with Alice still caged in his arms. The instant her head broke the surface—the only part of her body to do so—she sputtered, coughed, and sucked in a deep, ragged breath. Her golden hair hung in wet, clumped strands that concealed most of her face.

Fear clawed at the edges of Shadow's mind; how long had she been under? How close had it been to *too long*?

The knife-wielding alien surfaced beside his companion, and the two stared at Shadow with calculating, *identical* yellow eyes.

Shadow halted once he was perpendicular to their position along the bank.

Something shimmered in the water—the silver thread he'd glimpsed before, thicker and more substantial now. It seemed to be connected to both boruks.

"As dangerous as the king said," the knife wielder said.

"Not as dangerous as the stories," the other replied.

"But he *is* a ghost."

"As much as you are a ghost."

The boruks' jagged-toothed grins spread as the knife wielder said, "Your tether is long, Grinning Ghost, but I will follow it."

"I will find you," the one holding Alice added.

Alice's hair wavered as she panted. She flicked her chin up and aside to flip some of the strands away, uncovering one piercing blue eye. It was bright with panic and worry, but there was something more in it, something Shadow couldn't fully identify—as though it brimmed with a thousand words left unsaid.

As though were overflowing with *caring* she longed to express.

Shadow's aching heart swelled until it seemed likely to burst from his ribcage. He'd promised her she was safe with him. This was his failure, staring him in the face.

This was no game. There was no fun to be had here. Shadow had to assume death had become a permanent state now, that there'd be no coming back. Not for Alice.

That made her the most precious, invaluable thing in all Wonderland—the one thing for which he'd gladly give *everything* up. The only thing he needed to be real.

The only thing he *knew* to be real.

She's been that to me all along.

Shadow clenched his fists at his sides, digging his claws into his palms.

Save her, protect *her.*

"Who are you?" Shadow asked through gritted teeth.

"I am Sithix," both boruks replied in unison. They glanced at one another and said, "*I* am Sithix."

"You seem confused, Sithixes." Shadow raised a hand, holding up his pointer finger. "You get *one* chance. Release her and walk away."

"Voices whisper and claim the ghost enjoys games." Knife-Sithix inched closer to Alice and his companion. "Play."

"What color is her blood?" other-Sithix asked.

Knife-Sithix settled his blade on Alice's cheek. "Does her flesh taste foul or sweet?"

Alice squeezed her lips together in a tight line; the already pale flesh around them somehow paled further. Her nostrils flared as the blade pressed into her skin, producing a crimson line on her cheek. Blood trickled from the small wound. A high-pitched whimper escaped her.

Shadow's lips peeled back, baring his teeth, and his fingers curled to ready his claws.

"King won't mind if I take a small taste," knife-Sithix said, staring at the blood.

Other-Sithix leaned close to Alice's ear and ran his long, thin tongue along its outer edge. "I want *more* than a taste." He dipped his face lower and dragged the point of a tooth just below her jaw. She flinched with a cry. Blood dripped from the cut opened by his tooth, falling into the water to vanish in the current.

Their brief exchange saw Shadow frozen in place; even had he been able to think, his legs wouldn't have moved. For those few seconds, he was an immovable mountain with roots that ran unfathomably deep—but even though his body was still, there was no peace within him.

Alice, my Alice, mine, sweet, sweet Alice...

Heat roiled in his gut like a churning mass of molten stone and fire, and as it built, so did the pressure accompanying it. The heat flowed through his veins and made his scalp, fingertips, and toes tingle; it flared in his eyes, tinting everything crimson, and when it coalesced in his chest, it met the jumble of powerful emotions he felt toward Alice.

That combination of fire and emotion triggered an explosion.

Rage like Shadow had never experienced, like should never have been possible, enveloped his mind and body, and it wouldn't allow a single moment of inaction.

Shadow charged. He leapt over the stream, perceiving the Sithixes only as threats, only as vessels for blood that needed to be spilled.

Their already wide, reptilian eyes somehow rounded further, but their grins did not falter. They were confident, especially in the water.

Confidence didn't frighten Shadow.

Knife-Sithix raised his blades, which gleamed with droplets of water—and one of them with a hint of Alice's blood. Those droplets fell away and were swallowed by the stream like tears lost to the flow of time.

Halfway through the arc of his leap, Shadow phased, driven by instincts that had been honed by the intensity of his fury and hatred. He rematerialized in the place his jump would have taken him naturally—in front of knife-Sithix's position—but his foe was already in the process of turning around, having likely anticipated another attack from behind.

Shadow came down with a huge splash and grabbed the knife handle still jutting from knife-Sithix's back. The alien reversed his turn but wasn't fast enough—Shadow pulled up hard on the knife, tearing through thick scales and powerful muscle. The blade only stopped when it hit bone.

With a sharp, hissing roar, knife-Sithix whipped around, swinging one of his knives at Shadow.

Shadow ducked under the swing and slashed his claws across knife-Sithix's exposed ribs. None of the boruk's wounds bled, despite their severity, but knife-Sithix seemed to *feel* them, at the very least.

Other-Sithix, maintaining his hold on Alice, was backing away. He remained the true threat.

Shadow phased to knife-Sithix's opposite side, caught the jutting knife handle again, and twisted it. Howling, the boruk took another swing.

Shadow swayed away from knife-Sithix's attack, slammed a foot against the boruk's hip, and straightened his leg. He held tight to the knife grip as knife-Sithix stumbled away, wrenching the weapon free of the boruk's body. Shadow phased again before his foe could recover, appearing behind other-Sithix.

When other-Sithix spun to face Shadow, creating a small wave on the water's surface, Shadow plunged into the stream fully and phased again. He rematerialized near the bed of the stream, lying on his back, with other-Sithix's legs directly in front of him. He thrust the knife into the back of his enemy's knee and dragged the blade down. It tore open a long, wide gash along the boruk's calf.

Dark blood clouded the water.

Shadow grinned. A metallic tang flowed into his mouth; that hint of flavor was oddly satisfying.

The ambient sounds of running water were overpowered by a rush of movement. Shadow twisted to see knife-Sithix speeding toward him along the stream bed, tail lashing side-to-side to propel him forward. The charging boruk struck with jolting impact, throwing his arms around Shadow's torso as they collided. Knife-Sithix's momentum carried him and Shadow away from Alice and *real*-Sithix.

Shadow slammed his hands down on knife-Sithix's back, sank his claws deep, and kicked off the stream bed. He glanced toward Alice as he broke the surface; her captor, bleeding profusely, had released his hold on her, and she used that freedom to push to the surface and snatch a knife from his belt even as she was drawing in a ragged breath. Before real-Sithix—who was struggling to staunch the flow of blood from his leg—could react, Alice plunged the blade into his left eye. The first inch of the blade pierced the large yellow orb before the metal was stopped by scale and bone.

Real-Sithix roared as Alice frantically swam toward the shore.

Maintaining his hold on knife-Sithix, Shadow forced another phase.

Suddenly, he and knife-Sithix were high in the air, level with the uppermost branches of the trees around the stream. Shadow was weightless for a moment; hundreds of water droplets hung in the air around him, sparkling in the sunlight like a cache of diamonds tossed into a summer sky. Even through the haze of his rage, the sight was beautiful—but its beauty was *nothing* compared to Alice's.

Gravity reasserted itself.

Shadow's stomach lurched, and his insides seemed about to force their way up and out of his skull. Knife-Sithix's weight tugged on his claws, but the boruk's arms had released their hold on Shadow's middle to instead flail wildly—as though they would somehow sprout feathers and keep their owner aloft.

Shadow tore his claws free, ripping off chunks of meat and clumps of scale, and glanced down. Alice was on her hands and knees at the shoreline, head down and shoulders heaving. Real-Sithix was nearby, having hauled himself partially out of the water—which was murky with blood around his legs. He reached up to tug the knife from his eye. Blood spurted from the wound. The ground was at least a hundred feet below Shadow, though that distance was fast shrinking.

He knew what Sithix was now—even if he didn't understand how it worked, even if he didn't have a name for it—because it was *very* close to what Shadow was.

Ghost wasn't quite the right word for Sithix, however.

Regardless, Shadow's work wasn't done. Alice wasn't safe.

Shadow drove his foot into knife-Sithix's gut. The blow shoved their free-falling bodies away from each other—and away from what might've been relatively safe landings in the stream. Knife-Sithix tumbled, head over feet, toward the vegetation crowding the edge of the forest below.

Shadow didn't have time to wait until he hit the ground; Alice was only a few feet away from her former captor, and real-Sithix was wounded but not incapacitated.

The world blurred for an instant as Shadow phased. Hard stone materialized beneath his boots, and his insides settled into their normal positions. He raised his head to find himself crouched on the bank of the stream between Alice and real-Sithix.

Alice's fingers were clutching one of the stones beside the stream, and her wet, tangled hair hung around her face in thin strands. Her breathing was quick and ragged, but she *was* breathing—that was what mattered.

Shadow turned his head toward real-Sithix just as something heavy crashed through the nearby vegetation, creating a chorus of shaking leaves and snapping branches that ended with an abrupt, bone-crunching *thud*. Real-Sithix's attention was fixed on that spot for a few seconds before he looked at Shadow. One of his eye sockets oozed blood, while a glint of fear shown in his remaining eye.

Shadow rose and stepped toward real-Sithix.

"Stop him," real-Sithix hissed through his jagged teeth. He dragged himself along the bank, away from Shadow. "End him!"

The foliage beside the bank rustled. Shadow glanced toward the movement.

Knife-Sithix—limbs sporting new bends and angles that were wholly unnatural—crawled out of the vegetation, dragging himself by two fingers. Despite the extent of the damage, there was still no blood. The mangled, broken creature curled his fingers and pulled himself forward a few inches before extending them again.

"Oh, my God," Alice rasped.

Shadow returned his attention to real-Sithix and took another step toward him. "No more help. No running."

Real-Sithix's eye flared, the fear in them becoming dominant. He shoved off the shore as though to swim away. Shadow darted forward and dropped to one knee, plunging a hand into the water. His fingers closed around Sithix's tail, and he squeezed to bury his claws deep.

Part of Shadow wanted to toy with Sithix—but it wasn't the playful part of him, wasn't the part of him that delighted in the games he played with the other denizens of Wonderland. This was something deeper, something primal; not the trickster but the beast that dwelled in the darkness buried in his heart.

He wanted to make Sithix suffer. He wanted to prolong this being's death because *no one* was allowed to touch Alice but Shadow, because *no one* was allowed to harm her, *no one* was allowed to threaten her.

Sithix thrashed, churning the water. Shadow's arm jerked, but he held fast, and—with a deep, rumbling growl—dragged Sithix toward land. Despite his struggles, Sithix couldn't escape.

Shadow stood up, braced his feet on the stone, and stepped back, giving his foe's tail a sharp tug. Sithix's legs emerged from the water first. His right calf bled profusely as he scrabbled for purchase. Shadow took another step away from the stream, leaning backward with all his weight. Sithix's torso slid onto land. He clawed at the stone slabs, breaking several of his claws in his desperation but failing to latch on.

With another great heave, Shadow dragged his foe farther back, leaving the water several feet outside Sithix's reach. He snarled, "No running."

Sithix twisted onto his back and kicked at Shadow with his left leg. His intact eye was bulging, his slitted pupil blown wide.

Shadow released Sithix's tail and batted aside the boruk's flailing legs. He dropped down atop Sithix, driving his knee— with most of his weight behind it—into Sithix's gut, and drew one of the knives from the terrified alien's belt.

The broken creature—formerly knife-Sithix—hissed from somewhere behind Shadow, who didn't bother to look back. It was too late for Sithix to save himself. It was too late for Shadow to reject the crimson miasma that had consumed him.

Sithix threw up his arms, swinging, grasping, and scratching in a wild struggle.

This is real, Shadow thought. *His terror is real.*

Tightening his grip on the knife's handle, Shadow swung it downward. He felt it bite flesh; that was enough to urge him on. He lifted his arm and brought it down again and again, and when warm, sticky blood splattered on his arms and face, he was driven even faster, even harder. Shadow roared his fury, his bloodlust, his sense of helplessness; he roared with all his caring for Alice. And he kept the blade moving up and down as that roar ripped out of his throat, burying metal deep in flesh only to tear it out again. The squelching sounds of the knife's impact were wholly gratifying.

"Shadow?"

The voice was familiar, but it was so soft, so far away…

And Shadow *had* to keep attacking. He had to make Sithix pay, had to make sure he was *gone* forever.

"*Shadow!*"

His arm came down again; a jolt ran through the blade and up his forearm as the metal lodged in bone. Shadow stilled his arm. For what felt like a long while, he remained in place, shoulders heaving with his panting breaths, eyes fixed on his enemy without actually seeing. The red haze didn't fade; it took some time for him to realize why.

He was staring down at a bloody, mangled, crimson mess—at meat so torn and tattered that it would've looked less damaged had it been put through a grinder. Shadow's hands and arms were bathed in glistening crimson, and he could feel droplets of blood clinging to his face.

He could even *taste* the blood—some of it must've splashed into his mouth through his painfully wide grin. That taste…it wasn't unpleasant.

Shadow released the knife abruptly. His palm was slick with blood.

What is this? What…what am I?

He shoved himself back and landed on his backside in the grass beside the stone slabs, hands planted to either side of his hips. Rivulets of blood flowed from around Sithix, running over the flat stones to drain into the stream and drift away.

A gentle hand settled on Shadow's shoulder, and he turned his head to see Alice kneeling beside him. Water-thinned blood trickled from the shallow cuts on her cheek and arm.

She's mine. Mine! *My Alice, my sweet.*

Alice raised her other hand and cupped the side of his face. Her eyes were steady upon his.

"It's done," she said softly. "It's over. He's gone now."

Shadow held her gaze, searching her eyes. She wasn't lying, but her words still didn't ring true to him; this felt somehow like a beginning, like everything had just started—and, ominously, like the worst was yet to come.

CHAPTER 16

SHADOW DIDN'T KNOW how to articulate any of his feelings, but that didn't matter at that moment. Only *Alice* mattered.

He wrapped her in his arms and drew her against his chest, lowering his face to her hair. She embraced him, holding him tight as she ran a hand down the back of his head. Despite the stench of blood, despite the chill of their soaked clothing and the thundering of Shadow's heart, her presence soothed him. Her scent, her warmth, and her touch enveloped him, carrying his mind far away from all that had just happened.

But one thought refused to be silenced, one voice continued to whisper in the back of his mind—*I almost lost her.*

The truth of it was undeniable, and its implications staggering, terrifying, *soul-crushing*. He could not shake it. His nascent calm was swallowed up in a flare of desperation—but that desperation was not purely driven by despair. A familiar fire rekindled low in his belly.

He needed Alice. Needed to be as close to her as possible, needed to feel her body, warm and *alive*, against his. He needed to feel as though he were one with her.

Shadow drew his head back, buried the fingers of one hand

in her hair, and slammed his mouth down on hers. After her initial shock, she returned his kiss, matching his fire and desperation. Her fingers curled over his shoulders, and the press of her little nails, even through his clothing, was divine in the wake of all they'd just experienced.

Holding her tightly against him, Shadow shifted to get his feet beneath him. Once he was standing, he guided her legs up and around his waist, supporting her weight with one hand on her ass. He didn't want to pull his lips away, didn't want to break this physical contact with her, but he also couldn't have her *here*, like this, amidst the aftermath of the attack.

He forced his eyes open and broke the kiss. Blood—Sithix's blood, primarily—was smeared on her face, dress, and arms. He wouldn't have that. Wouldn't have her tainted by this. Wouldn't have Alice, his sweet, determined female, mired in the trappings of death.

She opened her eyes, brow creased in concern and confusion. "Shadow?"

And still, he couldn't help but look at her lips and long to kiss her again, right now. "Hold your breath, dear Alice."

She searched his face for a moment before offering him a small nod. She drew in a deep breath and pressed her lips together tightly.

Shadow phased into the middle of the stream. The cold water was a jolt, but the discomfort was worth it for the way Alice clung to him. The rushing water washed away the blood that had clung to their clothing and skin within a few seconds. He phased again, much farther this time; they rematerialized hundreds of feet upstream, on an embankment overlooking the water.

Alice's lips parted as she gasped for air. Within the next instant, Shadow reclaimed her mouth in a hungry, desperate kiss. Her hands clutched at him, and her thighs tightened around his waist. Though he could still smell a hint of blood, it was Alice's scent—warm honey and creamy vanilla—that engulfed him.

He moved forward blindly. Water weighed them both down, pouring from their bodies and clothes, but he clasped Alice to him, refusing to let go, and stopped only when her back was against the trunk of a tree. He kissed her in reckless abandon, making full use of lips, tongue, and teeth, and she returned the kiss just as eagerly, her breath raw and ragged. Fire blazed through his veins.

"Now," Alice rasped against his mouth, dropping her legs from around his waist. "I need you now, Shadow."

Whatever conscious thoughts remained in Shadow's mind were swept away, replaced by a driving, consuming need. In a flurry of motion, he moved his hands under her skirt, hooked his fingers under the waistband of her pants, and shoved them down. The scent of her arousal struck him immediately, and he groaned. His palms brushed over the smooth skin of her legs until her pants were at her ankles. She kicked the garment aside while he removed his own pants, nearly tearing the fabric in his rush to have them off, in his desperation to feel her bare skin against his.

His erect cock sprang free, throbbing and hungry. He looped his arms behind her knees, lifted her high, pinning her against the tree, and thrust into her eager sex with a guttural growl. Alice gasped, head thrown back, and grasped his shoulders. A powerful shudder coursed through his body as her tight, hot, slick walls clamped around his shaft. He released a shaky breath.

This was what he'd needed. *This* was where he wanted to be. Where he *belonged*.

In her arms.

· · ·

THE PAIN of Shadow's entrance into Alice's body was a flicker compared to the all-consuming need raging within her. Her mind and body were swept up in a maelstrom of desire that left room only for *him*. His cock, thick and hard, throbbed inside her, spearing her with its heat, and his body caged her against the tree, leaving no room for escape.

But she didn't want to escape. She was exactly where she wanted to be. With Shadow.

Limbs trembling, Alice lowered her face, opened her eyes, and met his gaze. His eyes blazed with unspoken words—they were filled with so much passion that there couldn't possibly *be* the right words, in this world or any other, to adequately convey it.

Shadow rolled his hips back, sliding his shaft almost entirely out of her, and slammed forward again. Alice's breath hitched as pleasure unfurled inside her. He did it again, and again, each of his movements measured and deliberate but at once savage in their intensity. Breathy moans escaped her lips, and her fingers tightened on his shoulders. Her breasts bounced with his every powerful pump.

His rhythm faltered as he released another low, rumbling growl. He shifted a hand to her ass, squeezing her flesh, and slapped the other against the tree trunk. She heard wood splintering near her head and glanced toward his hand to see his claws buried deep in the bark.

Alice brushed her forehead against his arm, eyelids fluttering as the sensation within her continued to build, coalescing within her core. Every stroke of his ribbed cock sent an electric shock through her body.

Lifting her legs, she wrapped them around his waist and turned her face back toward him. His eyes—burning with teal fire—fixated upon hers; she felt like he was looking straight into her, like he'd opened something within himself so she could look back into him.

No one had ever looked at her that way. She'd never thought it possible to see so deeply into a person, had never imagined that simple eye contact could carry so much weight.

But she knew he was holding back—and she knew it was because he feared doing her harm.

Alice trusted Shadow. His dangerous hands, with those lethal claws that could tear flesh to shreds, had always touched her only with gentleness, reverence, and care.

Sliding her hands over his shoulders and up his neck, Alice slipped her fingers into his hair and rasped, "Let go, Shadow. Give me everything. All of you."

His eyes flared, and the heat in them intensified. He slipped his tongue out and ran it over his upper lip, which peeled back to reveal his fangs. This wasn't his mischievous grin—this was a ravenous expression, and it ignited an inferno in her core.

Shadow sped his pace, grunting between his thrusts and his ragged breaths. Each time he pounded into her it was with more force than the last. Soon, his hands dropped to her hips, anchoring her in place and leaving her no choice but to take *all* of him. He dipped his head and ran his lips roughly over her cheek, jaw, and neck. His breath was hot, and the light graze of his fangs against her sensitive, flushed skin was thrilling.

Alice wrapped her arms around his neck and did all she could—she held on. She was his, wholly and completely *his*.

Her back scraped against the bark, and she could feel the bite of his claws as they curled into her skin, but she didn't care. All she could focus on was his body and the way it moved, on the way he moved *inside* her. She was mindless with growing pleasure, which spiked higher and higher with every brutal thrust of his cock; the tiny twinges of pain on her flesh only enhanced that pleasure.

Shadow snarled against her neck, thrusting into her once

more, and Alice shattered. She cried out as waves of ecstasy swept through her. It was unbearable, it was rapturous, it was *glorious*. She clung to him as her body shuddered and tightened around him. Her sex gripped his cock, seeking to pull him in deeper and hold him captive, but Shadow pounded in and out of her in a frenzy. She buried her face against his neck. The pleasure was staggering, almost too much to endure.

"Everything, Shadow. Everything," she moaned. The sensations roiling through her were so powerful that she couldn't hold back the words burning in the back of her mind; they came out in a muffled rasp against his throat. "*I love you.*"

Shadow's motions faltered. He tensed, and spasms wracked his body. The sound he released rumbled up from deep in his chest, emerging as something half-growl, half-roar—but it was, unmistakably, her name. He pounded into her with one final, forceful thrust, and then sagged forward, pinning her against the tree with his body as he buried the claws of both hands in the bark.

Alice held onto him, her limbs trembling and weak, and tried to catch her breath. Her sex continued to contract around his cock as aftershocks of pleasure swept through her. She loosened her grip on his hair, released a contented sigh, and stroked her hand down his back, wishing it was his bare body against her palm and not his jacket.

Sweat coated her skin, her damp clothing clung to her uncomfortably, chafing her, and the bark dug into her back, but for all that, Alice was perfectly happy where she was.

They stayed like that for a time—not that time held much meaning to Alice in those moments—their bodies connected as they slowly eased from the heights of their passion. When his breathing was finally steady, Shadow leaned back and looked down at her. He searched her gaze before he spoke.

"What was it you said to me, Alice?"

It took Alice a moment to understand what he was asking, and once realization struck, her eyes rounded.

I love you.

She hadn't meant to say those words out loud. They'd been lurking in the back of her mind, whispering to her, but she hadn't yet acknowledged them, didn't even know if they were true.

They felt *true when I said them.*

Even spoken in the heat of the moment, they hadn't felt any less true.

"Am I crazy, Shadow?" she asked.

His brow furrowed as he tugged a hand away from the tree and brushed the backs of his fingers down her cheek, his current tenderness wholly at odds with his wildness from only minutes before. "Why would you be crazy, my sweet?"

"Because of this place. And you've called me crazy more than once before. So…I must be losing my mind."

"Firstly," he said, his lips tilting into a strange combination of skeptical frown and amused smirk, "I ought not to be looked at as a good judge of anything like that. You may be surprised to know that I've had a brush or two with madness in the past, myself. And this place…" He raised his eyes, looking straight up, and then looped them around in a circle—without moving his head at all—until he met her gaze again. "Well, it's not real, so there's no need to let it affect you."

"But this is real," she said, tightening her arms and legs around him, pulling him closer. "*We* are real."

He groaned, and his eyelids fluttered for a moment. "Yes, we are. And the things you do to me, Alice…" Shadow grinned and purred appreciatively.

Alice's sex contracted around his cock as his purr rattled through her.

He shuddered, his shaft twitching, and leaned his forehead against hers. "Now, what was it you said to me?"

Alice closed her eyes. "I *must* be mad. We only met a few days ago, but I already feel like I know you better than anyone, like I...*need* you. But I don't *really* know anything about you."

"I wouldn't worry yourself too much on that last point," he said, with oddly morbid humor in his voice. "I don't know much of anything about me, either."

Alice smiled, and tilted her face up just enough to rub her nose against his cheek. She opened her eyes and met his. "And despite all that...I love you."

His grin vanished, and his face became suddenly solemn— more so than she'd seen since she met him. He searched her face, nostrils flaring with his slow, steady breaths, and swallowed audibly. A troubled crease appeared between his brows, and the muscles of his jaw ticked.

Doubt and embarrassment washed through Alice, chasing away the pleasure she'd felt only moments prior. She drew her head back and looked away. It'd been foolish of her to let the words slip, to have admitted to saying them. She and Shadow had only just met. They were still strangers. Circumstance had brought them together in this virtual world, and though they were attracted to each other, though they desired one another, that didn't necessarily equal love.

Maybe...maybe what she felt *wasn't* love. Maybe...

No. It *was* love. And the knowledge that he didn't feel the same for her, the chance that he would laugh in her face or reject her, was too painful to bear.

"I-I'm sorry. I shouldn't have..." She pulled her arms away and allowed her legs to drop from his waist. "You can set me down now."

But his hands caught the backs of her thighs well before her feet touched the ground, forcing her legs back up. He released one only to cup the side of her face, press his thumb under her chin, and turn her face up.

The seriousness hadn't left his face, but something burned in his eyes—something subtle but intense.

"You have changed everything for me, Alice. Turned my world upside down. I can't even tell what's real anymore, can't tell if everything I've ever known is true or an elaborate lie...but like you said, *this* is real. *We* are real. And even if I don't fully understand it, I know my love for you is real, too."

Her heart thumped as warmth blossomed within her chest. "You do?"

He answered her with a kiss, wholly unlike the one he'd given her before their joining. His lips were tender, sensual, and caressing, and his tongue worshipped her mouth once she granted it entry.

Alice wrapped her arms around him and moaned as he slowly pumped his hips. There was no desperation in their lovemaking now, just a gradually building pleasure, just the joy of sharing in each other's warmth, the contentment of their bodies and hearts coming together as intimately as two people could. Despite the slower pace, they were soon carried away on a swelling tide of pleasure that left them trembling against each other.

CHAPTER 17

ALICE AND SHADOW spent the night in the woods, with the stream's burbling long forgotten behind them. When darkness came—*true* darkness, during which not even stars or moon gave off any light—she curled up in Shadow's arms, unburdened by fear. He would keep her safe.

She knew what they had to do, but Alice was reluctant to proceed with their plan. What if, once they left this simulation, once they left Wonderland, nothing was the same? What if she never saw Shadow again? What if he wasn't even in the same facility as her? It wasn't impossible that Wonderland was a network connecting numerous facilities, each containing hundreds or *thousands* of patients. And Shadow didn't even know who he really was, didn't even know his real name. How would she find him once they got out?

Alice snuggled closer to him, and Shadow released a contented purr and tightened his arms around her. Her connection with him was stronger than any relationship she'd had in her life.

I don't want to lose this. I don't want to lose him.

227

And it was with those thoughts that she'd succumbed to sleep.

They resumed their trek shortly after waking in the morning light, with only a brief side excursion—Shadow vanished for nearly a minute, and when he returned, Sithix's knife-laden belt was buckled around his narrow waist.

Though his nearness urged her onward, Alice's reluctance to go to Rosecourt, toward what was meant to be their escape from Wonderland, hadn't diminished. They held hands through most of the journey, and even when their hands weren't touching, they remained in contact—with his tail brushing softly against her leg, or Alice holding onto it while he walked slightly ahead. He seemed unwilling to let her out of his sight, unwilling to let her out of reach. And she understood; she felt the same way about him.

Even in this world, there were too many things that could tear them apart. There was too much threatening their togetherness.

Night did not fall again, but it felt like they walked for days, like they crossed hundreds of miles. Despite that sense, Alice was never once bored or tired. Shadow's presence soothed her, and his conversation—sometimes rambling, sometimes more lucid than she'd ever heard him, but always entertaining—filled the time perfectly.

At some point during their travels, she realized that she hadn't eaten anything since arriving in Wonderland. Even that realization didn't awaken her appetite. Thirst and hunger didn't seem to apply here—she'd only had some water at the stream in all her time in the simulation, not counting the drug-laced drink that had been forced upon her by Madame Cecilia. By now, she could simply accept that food and drink were for enjoyment rather than necessity in this simulation; it made as much sense as anything else. She still found it odd that she needed to sleep—

it was as though her mind needed a break from Wonderland every now and then.

Alice's favorite times were the handful of stops they made—not because they delayed their arrival in Rosecourt, but because those were the times during which she and Shadow made love.

The forest was, maddeningly, both incredibly consistent and impossibly varied. Though their appearances remained the same, the plants seemed, at random intervals, to change sizes, and at a few points all the colors were completely different—blue leaves, purple trunks, flowers that were the inverse of their usual colors. Alice and Shadow occasionally traveled through areas that were decidedly not part of the forest, the most memorable of which was a neatly tended garden that seemed to be made in the proportion of the trees and plants surrounding it. The barriers between flower beds—barriers that would've been perhaps six inches tall back home—stood almost as tall as Alice, and the stone benches set throughout the garden were high enough that neither she nor Shadow could even see onto their seats. The weatherworn statues, many of which depicted cherubic figures in various carefree poses amidst the flowers, were titanic.

The strangest part of it all was how normal it seemed now. Only a few days ago—a few days ago according to the slowly suffocating rational part of Alice's mind—such sights would've been mind-boggling. Now they just seemed mundane. However…

"Are there giants here?" she asked.

"If there are, I've never seen one," Shadow replied. "Though…I'm sure it's all just a matter of perspective, isn't it?"

Alice looked at him, cocking her head. "What do you mean?"

Shadow shrugged nonchalantly. "Perhaps we are just very small—or otherwise very big. Who's to say our normal is normal at all?"

She chuckled. "Here in Wonderland? I guess no one."

Of course there was a giant garden. Just like there was a place where one of the purple cobblestone paths wound in a huge spiral, its loops growing smaller and smaller as it curled in on itself. Shadow and Alice followed that path, and when they reached the center, they were simply...somewhere else in the woods. She shrugged it off without a second thought and continued onward.

As Shadow had said—they would get to wherever they were going. Direction made little difference.

Despite having never been to Rosecourt, Alice knew when they were close—the atmosphere shifted. They emerged from the trees and stepped onto another cobblestone path, but this one was at least thirty feet wide—a cobblestone *road*. The trees along its edges were bent inward, creating a tall natural tunnel that ran as far as she could see. The air here was thicker, charged with a strange mixture of frantic energy and heavy foreboding. Posts set at irregular intervals along the road were topped with flickering electric lanterns that filled the tunnel with uneven, dancing light. The sunshine did not penetrate the leaves overhead.

"Almost there," Shadow said, his voice lower and quieter than normal as he stared down the road, the end of which was lost in a distant mist.

A chill skittered down Alice's spine, and she looked at Shadow. "What's wrong?"

"The air feels...*bad*." He looped his arm around her waist and drew her against his side. "We know why the king was coming here. We just..." Shadow turned his head to look down at her, his eyes solemn. "We just need to be careful and keep alert."

It was at moments like this that Alice *knew* Shadow had changed; he was different from when they'd first met. He was more lucid, more himself. Something drastic had shifted within him, and it had started during their visit to Miraxis's house.

"What are we going to do?" she asked. "We can't just...go in there and confront him."

Shadow walked forward slowly, and she matched his pace, though part of her didn't want to take even a single step more toward Rosecourt. The urge to turn back, to find a quiet place to hide with him, to *live* with him, swelled in her chest and made her throat tight.

But it wouldn't really be *living*. This place wasn't real, and they would never be able to live here peacefully. Their lives would always be in danger so long as they were in Wonderland, so long as their bodies—their real bodies—were left to waste away in the real world.

"That absolutely was *not* my plan," he said unconvincingly.

Despite the situation, Alice couldn't help but smile. "I don't believe you ever really have a plan for anything."

"I have all sorts of plans all the time! Like goad the Hatter into anger, or irritate Jor'calla, or toy with Miraxis, or... You know, the specifics don't matter. I'm an *excellent* planner."

"I believe specifics are usually required when you're planning something. That's why it's called a plan, Shadow."

He threw up his free hand, palm turned skyward. "The best plans are adaptable, which means fewer specifics. You really just need the general gist of the plan. Any more is a waste of time."

Alice nodded once. "Okay. We can do this."

I hope.

She faced forward, and they continued to walk along the tunnel. The mist only seemed to thicken as they moved. It was reminiscent of the swamp of sleepers; Alice cast those unsettling memories aside.

"So...we're going to confront the king and his army with your beltful of knives, overcome them, and force him to tell us how to get out of Wonderland," she said.

"That is the essence of the plan, yes."

"That sounds like a terrible plan. Shouldn't we worry about their guns, or that he has at least twenty or thirty robotic soldiers?"

"I've never much worried about any of that before." His hold on her tightened. "Though the stakes are much higher now."

Alice curled her fingers into his jacket and tilted her head, resting it against him as they walked. "You can disappear."

His voice was uncharacteristically thick when he said, "But you can't."

Those words bolstered her—because his caring was evident in them—while also reminding her of the immense risk they were taking. Shadow was different from everyone else Alice had encountered in Wonderland so far; he was unique. But there was something different about the Red King, too, something inherently more dangerous—and it all had to do with Jor'calla's cryptic words about *beyond*.

Alice had no doubt that the king knew this was a simulation. She just couldn't figure out how he knew, or why he was able to come and go as he pleased.

The road continued straight—*too* straight, if that was possible. After experiencing all the nonsensical winding pathways and unnatural angles in the rest of Wonderland, this road, a seemingly normal road, was totally out of place. That only enhanced the unsettling air around it.

Alice's unease increased with every step. She couldn't ignore the possibility that they'd find a dead city, its streets piled with corpses and its gutters flooded with crimson streams. The king meant to cull Wonderland, after all. He was marching on Rosecourt to *kill* people.

A wall materialized from the mist. It was at least fifteen feet high, and as Alice neared it, she realized that it looked to be made of concrete—though the concrete was covered in layer upon layer of colorful graffiti, much of it faded by age and weather. The road ran through a wide gap in the wall, to either side of which lay two massive, rusted metal doors, neither of them attached to the concrete any longer.

Shadow guided her through the gap.

The mist cleared instantly, and Alice halted in shock. There'd been no sign of the tall, vibrantly colored buildings lining the road beyond the wall a moment ago, no sign that there was *anything* on the other side of the wall but more fog, and yet she now stood on a bustling city street.

The buildings were painted in colors that were sometimes complementary but were just as often clashing, and their architectures presented some of the same odd, impossible angles and shapes that had been so prevalent at the Hatter's. Alice could only liken it to a child's crayon drawing made real—none of it seemed right, but everything was clearly what it was, regardless.

Ten-foot-tall flowers and oversized plants were visible in great concentration all over, many of which were in crooked planters along the sidewalks or comically cramped balcony gardens on the buildings. Most prominent of the vegetation by far were the roses. They grew in vine-like tangles that clung to the sides of buildings and in bushes around the few open common areas in addition to within the planters, the blooms varying in size—the smallest were the size of golf balls, while the largest were likely wider than Alice was tall. Regardless of their size, their petals were all the same shade—deep crimson.

Dozens, perhaps hundreds of people milled about in the streets. Most were human, but many were aliens of countless species. Their clothing was so varied it defied categorization— fashions from numerous historical Earth eras clashed with more modern attire and an eclectic array of alien clothing.

A few of the people weren't wearing anything at all.

There were interactions and conversations happening all over. A few of the people were talking to themselves, while others danced wistfully to inaudible music. One man was even smacking his head against a wall, over and over, his lips moving as though he were muttering. If the king had arrived in Rosecourt, he clearly hadn't been here yet.

This was closer to what Alice might've expected to see in an asylum. Not what she'd witnessed at Hatter's Tea Party.

"Why is everyone so different here?" Alice asked.

"Different how?" Shadow asked. He maintained his easy pace, leading her along as he gracefully wove between the people crowding the street.

"They're...troubled."

A dancing woman spun, eyes closed and a joyful smile on her lips, as Alice passed her.

"Well, not troubled," Alice continued, "but...some of them seem closer to the sleepers than they do to the people that were at the Hatter's. Like they're not entirely *here*."

Shadow hummed thoughtfully. "Perhaps. But there are many more people here than at the Hatter's; it's only natural that you'd see more of the crazy ones. Just a matter of population density, I imagine."

"How many people *are* here?"

He shrugged. "I don't know. I'm not sure anyone does, really. Thousands, tens of thousands. Maybe hundreds of thousands? It's difficult to say. I don't believe anyone even really knows how big Rosecourt is."

Alice hadn't seen the asylum from outside, though she supposed even if she had, it wouldn't have helped her guess how many of those pods were inside. If there really were hundreds of thousands of people in this simulation—and she couldn't bring herself to believe that was true—it was highly unlikely that they were all linked in from a single facility, but she simply didn't know either way.

"So, what do we do now?" she asked. "We came here to find the king, but if he's not here..."

"We go to the likeliest place for information. The Stark Rave."

Shadow's words from Jor'calla's—it seemed like that had been a lifetime ago—drifted back to her.

See? Stark raving mad.

"The Stark Rave? That...doesn't sound very appealing, does it?"

Shadow shrugged. "I think people are more interested in what they can *do* there. What it's called isn't very important."

They came to an intersection, and Shadow turned left. The next street was just like the last—not that anything was actually the same, but it was equally colorful, disjointed, and crowded.

"The Stark Rave is just like Hatter's Tea Party," Shadow said. "Just no dollies and infinitely more drugs. It's run by Bokki and Grithis; they're friends of the Hatter's. But we don't need to worry —that mean woman with the bird mask, Cecilia, is never there."

"And you think they'll know something?"

"People are in and out of the Rave constantly, and they're always high while they're inside, so they talk. Bokki and Grithis make a point of keeping abreast of all that talk. Jor'calla *knew* things, but those two *hear* things. Everything."

Alice's brows lowered. "That doesn't mean they'll just tell us."

Shadow's lips stretched into a slow, wide grin.

"Okay, so maybe they will," said Alice. "You seem to put fear into everyone here, and I'm sure they'll only be more scared with the threat of true death."

"I'm not frightening, just *persuasive*. But I probably ought to inform you that I'm not actually welcome in their establishment, so we'll have to avoid entering through the front door."

"I'm sure that has nothing to do with you being scary, right?"

Shadow shook his head. "Not at all. They were just upset that I continuously came out on top in our games."

Alice stared at him. "You killed them, didn't you?"

"Yes, but they always came back!"

"They won't anymore."

"That means they should be *especially* friendly and talkative today."

He increased their pace. Despite everything, Alice's heart beat with a touch of excitement; hurrying through the streets with Shadow was, in its own way, thrilling, and that thrill was certainly more pleasant than dwelling upon the uncertainty and danger they were rushing toward.

After more turns than she could count—including several through alleyways of varying sizes and degrees of filth—they turned onto a street wider than the rest. The electric lampposts, which lined the streets all over Rosecourt, were positioned at more regular intervals here, and the open space seemed designed specifically with pedestrians in mind. More oversized vegetation was on display in sculpted planters along the street, but they weren't what caught Alice's attention now—her eyes were drawn to the building directly ahead, at the end of the street.

At least one or two hundred people were gathered outside of it, their degrees of intoxication implied by their levels of unsteadiness. There was plenty of space for them—the Stark Rave itself appeared to be comprised of more than a dozen smaller buildings mashed together, all perched upon a single column that ran to the ground. It reminded Alice of a bird house. Every one of the clashing planes on the structure was a different color and pattern. Vibrant reds, oranges, yellows and pinks hit cool splashes of green, blue, teal and purple, some-times in stripes, checkers, or spots, none of it matching and yet somehow comprising a greater, oddly coherent whole. Some of the smaller buildings had balconies upon which more revelers were dancing and talking—the highest of which had to be at least a hundred and fifty feet off the ground.

As far as Alice could see, there was only one entrance—a

pair of large doors at the base of the column, which itself seemed far too thin to support the structure above it. A pair of burly guards in dark suits flanked the doors, occasionally stepping forward to block people's entry.

The guards would've looked right at home at the Hatter's Tea Party.

Alice's eyes widened as they neared the Rave's grounds. There were several people having sex outside—on the ground, amidst the large-leafed bushes, on the benches and tables scattered all around, even a group of three up against the building's support column. Everyone else was talking, drinking from vials, swallowing pills, or eating little cakes. The drinks and drugs seemed to be provided by masked, tuxedoed waiters wandering throughout the crowd.

Alice eased a bit closer to Shadow. This place reminded her too much of her brief time at the Hatter's. Was this the sort of scene that would've awaited her had she remained there? Would she have wound up as one of these drug-addled revelers, sharing her body with strangers, her inhibitions and free will cast away and forgotten?

Something in her gut told her that it would've been somehow *worse* at the Hatter's.

Shadow led her to the outskirts of the gathering and turned to walk along the edge of the grounds. As Alice swept her gaze around, she noticed several more stoic guards posted at various intervals.

Were all those guards—so big, so intimidating, so calm—patients in the asylum, too?

"How are we going to get inside?" she whispered.

Shadow turned his head to glance up at the building. "I think you already know, dearest."

She followed his gaze with her own. The Stark Rave looked even larger from up close, nearly as tall as the giant trees between which she'd spent so much time walking. At least she had some idea of what to expect inside—the same as out here only more, only louder.

"Hey!" someone shouted.

Alice swung her gaze aside to see one of the guards shoving through the crowd toward her and Shadow, his expression hard. A spike of fear pierced her chest.

"Hold on, my sweet," Shadow said an instant before sweeping Alice into his arms, dipping her back, and covering her mouth with his.

Alice's eyes widened, and she clutched at his arms. Despite her fear, she couldn't deny the heat that sparked within her in response to the feel of his mouth against hers. Her eyelids drifted shut; she was vaguely aware of the air wavering around her, and then music with thumping bass pulsed over her.

Shadow broke the kiss, and Alice opened her eyes. He offered her a grin before raising her from the dip.

Alice glanced around their new surroundings. They were at the edge of the dance floor in a huge, domed room. Countless bodies writhed nearby, their faces obscured by dim, flickering lights and a thin but prevalent cloud of smoke. The air was redolent with a mixture of powerful scents, but alcohol and that sweet smoke were the strongest of them.

Something tickled Alice's scalp, and she turned to see an alien woman beside her with a thick strand of Alice's hair in her fingers. The alien's skin changed wildly from moment to moment under the pulsing lights—vibrant pink when the bright lights touched it, and a deep purplish-blue under the ultraviolet lights.

The female smiled and raised Alice's hair higher, rubbing it against her cheek, before she met Alice's gaze. She extended a webbed hand and ran her fingers along Alice's collarbone and down to her breast, which she cupped in her palm.

Alice's breath hitched.

"Such a pretty thing," the female said, smiling to reveal shark-like teeth.

Shadow spun Alice away from the female, and, with a metallic flash, pressed the blade of a knife to the alien's throat. "Hello. We haven't met, but that won't stop me from slicing you open from top to bottom."

Alice peeked around Shadow's shoulder. He kept an arm around her, his fingers curled possessively on her hip. She could feel the press of his claws despite them being separated from her skin by both her skirt and her pants.

The female alien's glowing yellow eyes flared, and she backed away, raising her hands. "Faceless One, I meant no disrespect. I only sought to taste the pretty."

"She is for *me*," Shadow growled, angling the knife to keep its tip pointed at the female, "and no one else."

The alien recoiled and bowed her head, averting her eyes. "Of course. Of course."

Shadow held his stance until the female had vanished into the crowd before twirling the knife between his fingers—as effortlessly as a person might scratch their cheek—and sheathing it on his belt. "Give people some mind-altering substances and they forget all their manners."

"Did you take them when you came here?" Alice asked, staring at the sheathed knife.

He turned his head to scan their surroundings and shrugged. "They never had an effect on me. Didn't see a point after the first few tries."

Alice glanced up at him. "You tried? You wanted to feel...like *that*? Like you're no longer in control of yourself?"

Shadow sighed and flicked his gaze to hers briefly. In that instant, she saw vulnerability in his eyes, saw the underlying sorrow that he almost never exposed.

"I just wanted to feel...*something*. Something other than empty and alone. Something...*good*. I don't know if I've ever been happy until you came along… But this is hardly the time." He pointed toward a door on the far side of the room—a large, rectangular door that was covered in red, velvety material. The guards posted in front of it were two scaly aliens who looked like hybrids between dragons and bodybuilders. "Bokki and Grithis are through there. I can't allow the guards to see me, or there will be more trouble than we can deal with."

"You want me to go in *alone*?"

"I'll be with you. Just…out of sight."

Of course he'd remain close. Alice should've known that. But the thought of walking into the unknown unsettled her—especially in a place so reminiscent of the Hatter's. If that female alien had wanted a *taste*, what would everyone else want? How was Alice going to get past those guards?

This is our only way forward.

Alice and Shadow needed information, needed answers, so they could escape Wonderland. And once they were out, once they were *safe*, she could let herself forget most of her experiences here—all but those with Shadow—like they'd been nothing more than a particularly vivid nightmare.

"Okay." She took in a deep breath, released it, and stepped away from Shadow. "I'm sure they'll let me in considering I'm a…you know. A *dolly*."

One that's been played with a little too hard, perhaps, considering my appearance.

She slipped her hands under her skirt, hooked the waist of her pants with her thumbs, and shoved them down. She kicked the pants aside; they disappeared under the feet of the nearby dancers.

"Uh…*what* are you doing, Alice?" Shadow asked, ears perking. "I know I wasn't happy when you first put those on, but I've changed my mind. Put them back on, now!"

Reaching up, she ran her fingers through her hair, working out some of the tangles. "I'm a dolly here, Shadow." She tore her eyes away from the door and looked at him. "I need to look the part if I want them to let me through."

Despite the loud music, she clearly heard Shadow's frustrated growl.

His ears fell flat. "If any of them get handsy, I will start cutting their hands off."

Strangely turned on by Shadow's threats of violence in her honor, Alice smiled. She stepped up against him, slipped her arms around his neck, and drew his face down close to hers.

"I trust that you will," she said before kissing him deeply.

Shadow groaned against her mouth and gave in to her kiss; within a moment, his hands had slipped beneath her skirt to cup her bare ass cheeks, giving them a squeeze. "Remember, sweet Alice—you're *mine*," he said against her lips.

She ground her pelvis against him as a bolt of desire flared in her core, causing her sex to clench in need. She moaned. "*Yours.*"

He purred appreciatively, and his cock hardened as though straining for her through his pants. "I don't want anything more than I want you right now, but we have some people we need to threaten first."

Alice groaned, rested her forehead against his, and closed her eyes. Her body thrummed with the need to be touched, the need to feel his hands sliding over her skin, the need to feel him inside her. But her fear—of something going wrong, of losing him to true death—was stronger than her desire right now. "Be careful, okay?"

He brushed the backs of his fingers down her face, from cheekbone to chin. "Only as careful as I need to be to keep you safe."

She tilted her head back and opened her eyes to meet his. "I love you."

He smiled; the expression was warm, genuine, and charming. "I love you, too, my sweet, sweet Alice."

Her heart leapt with those words. Even though she'd heard them before, they still made her breath quicken.

Alice pulled away from him, and he released her reluctantly. One of his hands lingered on her ass, as hot as a branding iron, but he'd been right—now wasn't the time. Turning toward the large velvet door, Alice stepped out of Shadow's touch and slipped into the crowd.

CHAPTER 18

THOUGH EVERYTHING ALICE had been through since being sent to Wonderland had been bizarre, crossing that dance floor was, perhaps, the most surreal experience of them all.

The press of bodies was thick, and the heat they put off made her skin tingle. She pushed forward regardless. The dancers offered little resistance, parting as easily as stalks of long grass, their arms, legs, hands, and bodies brushing over her as she moved. Many of the touches seemed deliberate—some even seemed intentionally *sensual*—but no one stopped her.

Sweat, alcohol, smoke, and sex scented the air, and though the music was thunderous, it was not loud enough to mask the sounds of the revelers' panting breaths, tittering laughter, and heavy moans. Everyone who met Alice's gaze had the same expression on their faces—lips parted as though in pleasure, brows softened, eyes blank and half-lidded.

She realized after only a few steps that this was more an orgy than a dance.

This would have been me, *had I eaten those cakes...*

Alice broke through the crowd and raised her chin as she walked toward the guards standing at the velvet door. Four wide steps led up to the landing the guards were perched upon; the extra height off the floor made them appear even more massive than they already were. They didn't move except for the slight turns of their heads as they watched her approach.

Once she was in front of them, one of the guards lifted his scaled snout toward the dance floor. "Party's that way, human."

"I would like to speak to Bokki and Grithis," Alice said.

The guards exchanged a glance before the first returned his attention to her. "And who are you?"

Alice ran a finger beneath the cut on her cheek, smiling as though pleased by it. "I was one of the Hatter's favorite dollies, and I heard this is the place to be now that he's gone."

Both guards raked their reptilian gazes over her; the image of Sithix's unsettling eyes flashed through her mind, but she shoved it aside before terror could take hold of her again. These creatures were not boruks; they were not Sithix.

"Looking a little run down, dolly," said the other guard.

She grinned and bent toward them, knees locked, allowing them a glimpse down her cleavage. "I enjoy being played with" —she winked—"*roughly.*"

The guards exchanged another glance, and their lips peeled back in sharp-toothed smirks as they chuckled.

"Bosses might have a place for you here, then," said the second guard. "Go on through. Maybe we'll see you again later."

Though Alice didn't see Shadow, she sensed him close by, and could almost feel rage radiating from him.

Alice climbed the steps onto the landing and smiled at the second guard, trailing the tip of her finger along his thickly muscled forearm. His scales were hard. Her mouth was dry, but she forced the words out smoothly, nonetheless. "Perhaps…both of you at once?"

"Hatter must've been starving you, dolly," he grumbled. "Any time you like, we'll show you what a good time *really* looks like."

Please don't stab them, Shadow. Not yet.

The first guard extended an arm to grasp the door handle; his forearm, as solid and powerful as his companion's, brushed across Alice's stomach as he did so. He turned the knob and pushed the door open. "They breed some of these humans *nasty.*"

What the hell is that supposed to mean?

It took everything inside her to keep smiling, to keep herself from recoiling from his touch and their leering eyes, to keep her disgust hidden.

A long hallway with dark walls and a plush red carpet awaited her beyond the doorway. Alice stepped forward, relief easing her tension. She'd made it.

The other guard's hand was suddenly beneath her skirt. His thick fingers slipped between her legs.

It was only a combination of shock and willpower that kept Alice from jerking away from the repulsive touch and showing just how horrified and revolted she was in that moment, preventing her from hitting the guard as hard as she could; she needed to keep up the act a little longer, needed to be a dolly just until the door was closed behind her…

The guard rubbed his finger along Alice's sex—which was still slick after the desire Shadow had stoked in her on a few minutes before. He withdrew his hand and raised it, slipping his finger into his mouth. He groaned. "Not nasty. *Sweet.*"

Oh, no.

Alice spun around just in time to see Shadow appear on the lowest step. His features were swallowed in darkness but for his gleaming eyes and enraged grin. *This* was why he was called the Grinning Ghost. *This* was what everyone else saw when they looked at him.

Before the guards could react, Shadow darted forward. Metal glinted in his hands a fraction of a second before his simultaneous attacks landed. Both guards were shoved back against the wall to either side of the door with abrupt grunts and wet, crunching sounds. Their bodies sagged, but neither fell.

Shadow had stabbed them in their throats with such force that both guards were pinned to the wall.

He vanished just as quickly as he'd appeared, and his hands settled on Alice's hips from behind immediately afterward. He turned her around and led her through the doorway, shutting the red velvet door behind them.

"Shouldn't have touched you," he muttered. "Shouldn't have put his hand on you." Growling, Shadow tightened his grip on her. He was vibrating with rage. "He *tasted* what was mine."

Alice glanced down to see Shadow's hands on her skirt. She settled her palm over his right wrist. "It's done. We just need to keep moving, because somebody must've seen that."

"None of those drug-addled revelers saw anything," Shadow replied, his voice low and thick with fury. "They'll glance over and think the two of them are still guarding the door."

She nodded. Given the state of most of the Stark Rave's patrons, she doubted anyone but the guards were lucid enough to notice anything beyond whoever it was they happened to be rubbing against at any given moment. A shudder ran through her. She could still feel the alien's touch between her legs, and it made her sick to her stomach. The only one who could make that feeling go away was Shadow.

His fingers inched a little lower, and, as though reading her thoughts, he said, "I would remove the taint of his touch myself right now, Alice, were we not in a den of enemies."

"I know." Alice turned and caught him by his collar, pulling him down and smashing her mouth against his, kissing him hard before pulling away. "I understand."

He slid his tongue out and licked his lips. For a moment, he looked as though he might take her right then and there despite everything that should've stopped him. But he simply took her hand in his and led her along the hall.

"He'd better hope he stays dead," Shadow said as they walked briskly, "because if he's not, I'm going to kill him over and over and over again for a very long time to come."

It wasn't long before they reached another red, velvet-lined door at the opposite end of the hall, identical to the one through which they'd entered but for the sign posted on it.

The sign, painted with large, messy brushstrokes, said *Guests Received by Invitation Only.*

Naturally, Shadow opened the door without hesitation and strode through.

Well, I guess we had already abandoned the whole can't be seen *plan before we made it this far.*

Alice hurried in behind him.

"My old friends!" Shadow declared, throwing his arms wide; he held a fresh knife in each hand, though Alice hadn't seen him draw either of them. "It's been far too long."

The room was surprisingly tame compared to everything else she'd seen here, containing a round table with a lacy white tablecloth, two old-fashioned wooden chairs, and a tray of sweets, pastries, and alcohol. The two individuals seated at the table were not what Alice had expected. One of them was the same species as Miraxis, though his hair was tan, his skin had a ruddy, brownish hue, and his eyes were dark. The other sat atop a stack of pillows on the chair opposite the praxian and couldn't have been more than three feet tall. He had shaggy, dark brown hair and large, drooping ears reminiscent of a donkey's. His face was startlingly human—and startlingly adult—but for his pronounced, snout-like nose and large front teeth.

Both aliens were staring at Shadow in shock, their mouths agape and eyes wide. The praxian was holding a glass of amber liquid in his trembling hand; drops of the drink splashed out to fall to the table and stain the tablecloth.

"I know you prefer sending invitations out, but I haven't received one in *so* long," Shadow continued, his voice bristling with menace rather than its usual humor. "I was beginning to wonder if you'd forgotten about me. I decided to pay you a surprise visit. What could it hurt, right?"

"Bokki and I a-always welcome you," the praxian, who must've been Grithis, said. "You do not need an-an invitation."

But Bokki's features had hardened in anger and hatred.

"We rescinded your invitation, Ghost. Indefinitely," the little alien said with surprising firmness.

"*Bokki*," Grithis warned, carefully placing his drink on the table, "The ghost is our old friend. He is *always* welcome. Remember? I-In these times, it is better to be friends than enemies."

Bokki crossed his arms over his chest and narrowed his eyes. Despite his stature, his body was proportioned similarly to that of an adult human.

"The rescinded invitation, that was just part of our...our *game*," Grithis continued, swinging his gaze to Shadow. "*The* game, right? We've all had fun, we're all friends. W-would you or your dolly like a drink?"

It was only then that Bokki looked away from Shadow, turning his attention to Alice. A crease formed between his brows. "She's the one. The one they said was with the Hatter when the Grinning Ghost killed him. The one that escaped with him."

Alice barely resisted a sudden urge to retreat.

Shadow took a step forward, sinking into an easy crouch that still left him at least a foot over Bokki's eye level. "Your bringing up the Hatter gives me the perfect opportunity to remind you that death is currently permanent. Make no mistake, my *friends*—we're not here to play a game today."

Bokki bared his teeth. "You don't come into our place and threaten—"

Shadow lunged forward, slamming one of his knives into the top of the table. Everything on the table's surface jumped and rattled, and one of the bottles tipped over, spilling a fluorescent green liquid onto the floor. "I'm sure after I stab you to death, Bokki, Grithis will be more than willing to talk."

"T-talk? What would you like to talk about?" Grithis said, his eyes flickering between Alice, Shadow, and the knife. "We would l-love to talk!"

Shadow held Bokki's hate-filled gaze. "The king. Where is he, what is he doing? I want every tidbit of information that's passed through this place concerning him."

"The king? Have we seen any kings lately?" Grithis asked.

"I can start with stabbing you if you think you're clever, Grithis," Shadow said. "There's only one king in Wonderland."

Some of the color drained from Grithis's face. "Oh, y-you must mean the *Red* King, the King of Hearts!" Grithis looked at Bokki. "Have we seen *that* king lately?"

"He was here not long ago," Bokki said, "asking about *you*, Ghost. And your dolly."

"But he didn't hurt you," Alice said. "He came here to cull the city, but you're unharmed."

"Everyone has some sort of use," Bokki replied, looking past Shadow to meet her gaze. "And some of those uses are more valuable than others. Me and Grithis, we're useful, because we keep people entertained and we keep information flowing. You're useful because you're pretty and you have a tight slit between your legs."

Alice scowled and lowered her hands to tug her skirt down farther. Without pants, she was back to feeling utterly exposed.

"The Grinning Ghost, though…" Bokki continued, "he's a liability. A problem. And now there's a permanent solution."

Shadow's posture stiffened as he bowed his head. He released his hold on the knife embedded in the table and settled his hand on Bokki's leg. Despite all his bravado, a glint of fear flashed in Bokki's eyes. He looked miniscule with Shadow's hand for comparison.

"I find that my patience has been worn quite thin, Bokki," Shadow said quietly, "so I will allow you one—and *only* one— chance to apologize to Alice for the way you just spoke about her. She's not a dolly, not an *object*, and deserves the same respect you would afford any of your peers."

Now it was Bokki's skin that paled. His nostrils flared with his suddenly ragged breaths. "Sorry," he murmured.

"To *her*," Shadow growled.

Bokki's little tongue slipped out for a moment, and his nose twitched. He looked at Alice. "I'm sorry."

"Respect, respect," Grithis muttered, then smiled big, his attention focused solely on Alice. "Of course! Would you like a drink? Perhaps a cake?" He waved a hand toward the platter on the table. "You're welcome to join us."

"No, thank you," Alice replied.

Grithis deflated, sagging in his seat as his face fell. Alice *almost* felt bad for refusing, but she wasn't going to touch so much as a drop or a crumb of whatever they had.

"We're here for answers, not refreshments," Shadow said. He patted Bokki's leg but did not remove his hand. "What did the king say? What is he doing? What's the word 'round the party?"

Bokki shook his head, and when he spoke, the prior courage in his voice had been replaced by something closer to fear. "He's going to kill you, Ghost. Kill you forever. Just like we all wished we could."

"He w-wanted to know where you w-were," said Grithis. "Asked if any word had come through. He said you're n-not an easy person to hunt."

Alice cocked her head, brows falling low, and frowned. Something seemed *off*. It was quieter now than it had been when she first entered the room. It took her a moment to realize that there was no longer music or thumping bass coming from beyond the hall.

"He came to Rosecourt to hunt us, but he also planned to cull the population. Why hasn't he?" Shadow asked.

"Why would he tell us that?" Grithis replied, lifting his palms and sinking farther back into his chair. "He d-doesn't tell his plans to the likes of us."

Shadow sighed heavily and finally removed his hand from Bokki's leg to grasp the knife stuck in the table and wrench it free. "I'm finding myself quite disappointed in the answers you're providing. I can't help but feel like you're withholding information."

Where's the music?

Alice could've sworn she'd still heard it when they'd come in here, that it had remained a muted ambience, like the heartbeat of this strange building. Or maybe she'd just *thought* she'd heard it?

No, I really was hearing it...

The unease that had lingered in Alice since they'd started their journey to Rosecourt swelled, raising the hairs on the back of her neck. Something *really* didn't feel right here.

Since when has anything *felt right in Wonderland?*

Things changed in this world in the blink of an eye. Why did this seem different?

I'm not losing my mind. I heard the music—and this seems like the kind of place where the music never *stops.*

Alice turned and stepped through the open doorway, reentering the hall. Nothing changed—no strange, ominous mist rolled in, the lights didn't flicker and go dark, she didn't find herself suddenly in a different place, and she could still hear Shadow and the aliens talking behind her.

But the door at the other end of the hallway—the door through which they'd entered—seemed far more imposing now than it had before.

"N-no! We'll talk," Grithis stammered. "We'll talk, it's just…"

She stared at the door as she continued forward, and the

silence seemed to thicken with her every step. She needed to know what was going on. There'd been hundreds of people on the other side of that door, most of them caught up in drug-addled passion. There was no way they could have just disappeared...right? If anyone had realized the guards at the red door were dead, there would've been screaming, chaos, *noise*.

"You're not going to win this time, Shadow," said Bokki. "You were *never* going to win in the long run. However powerful you think you are, he's ten times more so. Even you won't stand against him much longer."

"Where is he?" Shadow asked, voice dangerously low.

"He's already here," Bokki replied.

Alice halted at Bokki's words.

Grithis tittered fearfully, and there was a loud thump, as though a chair had fallen over.

The quiet, the stillness...was because the king was already *here*.

Before she could retreat, the door to the dance hall burst open. Her eyes widened, and her breath hitched; several of the king's dark-armored robots filled the doorway.

He's already here.

He's already here.

Alice spun around to run to Shadow, but merciless metal hands clamped over her arms and dragged her back toward the dance hall as more of the robots marched around her, their movements stiff but so *fast*.

Terror flooded her. She fought against the metal hands, but they only tightened, threatening to shatter her bones in their viselike grips.

"Shadow!" she screamed.

CHAPTER 19

It was already too late by the time Shadow turned toward Alice.

Should've known! Should've been ready.

Bokki's words, though unsettling, hadn't been surprising. The Red King had spent a lot of time hunting Shadow, had laid a great many traps, but he'd never been successful. His persistence had always struck Shadow as half-determination, half-madness. Why wouldn't the chance of killing Shadow once and for all rouse the king to action again?

And now the king's automatons had Alice.

Alice, Shadow's weakness. Shadow's *love*.

Shadow forgot about Bokki and Grithis in that moment. He had no doubt they'd communicated with the Red King, that they'd somehow alerted the king when Alice and Shadow had arrived, but they weren't important now. They were little more than messengers.

He raced into the hallway as the automatons dragged Alice through the far door. The way she screamed his name pierced Shadow to his core—she instilled those two syllables with an overwhelming amount of fear, desperation, love, and hope.

The automatons that had walked past Alice spread out in two rows of two to block the hallway. Simultaneously, they raised their guns, aiming them at Shadow.

Behind him, the door to Bokki and Grathis's room slammed shut, and a heavy lock thumped into place.

Shadow phased as the automatons opened fire. The booming of their weapons, amplified in the tight space, was powerful enough to put thunder to shame. Shadow felt the projectiles distantly; they were brief, dull pinches on his abdomen and chest that vanished in the same instant that he materialized behind the machines.

Alice and the automatons holding her were already out of sight, but he could hear her grunts and shouts from inside the dance hall. They couldn't have made it far. He wasted no time in debating whether he should chase them or eliminate the threats now behind him.

If the Red King got his hands on Alice, it wouldn't matter how many automatons were still standing.

Shadow darted through the door and into the dance hall.

The immensity of the space was apparent now that most of the revelers were gone—the handful remaining appeared to be unconscious, scattered about the room lying on the floor or slumped against the wall. Garbage—mostly cups, bottles, and discarded articles of clothing—was strewn about the checkered dance floor.

And *he* stood in the center of the chamber, flanked by at least a dozen of his machine soldiers. The automatons dragging Alice were about halfway between Shadow and the king.

"Stop," Shadow roared.

The king grinned. He lifted a hand and waved two fingers. The pair of automatons holding Alice stopped abruptly—and the weapons of all the rest turned toward Shadow. Neither the king's grin nor the wild light in his eyes wavered as he drew his pistol and aimed it at Shadow.

"You've caused a lot of trouble," the king said. "I don't know who you are, don't know *what* you are, but I'm not going to tolerate your shit anymore. Today, your luck runs out. Today, you finally face consequences for all you've done."

Shadow curled his fingers into fists. His short hairs bristled, and his tail flicked back and forth in agitation. His fury—the same overwhelming fury that had consumed him at the stream, the same fury he'd experienced when the guard had touched Alice—flared. Everything in this chamber was a threat to Alice, was an enemy to be destroyed without hesitation or mercy. The king was foremost of those threats; he controlled the automatons, and he would be the one to command them to harm Alice. But Shadow's rage was tempered by fear—Sithix might have been a killer, but the king was cruel beyond imagining, and he was *mad*.

Alice was in more danger now than ever before.

She was facing Shadow; the machines had hauled her backward out of the hallway. The same powerful, complex emotions that had shone in her eyes a few moments ago remained in place as she stared at him.

"If you could kill me, your machines would've fired the moment I emerged from the hall," Shadow said, forcing his tone to remain even. He'd never once lost a game against the king. He certainly wouldn't allow himself to lose this time—not when it was the only contest that mattered.

"You're right," the king replied. "You're some kind of anomaly. A *glitch*. But my programmers are closing in on you, and once they find you, that's the end. No more fighting. No more games. No more *you*."

Shadow tensed. His stomach felt like it was floating near his throat and like it had sunk into his groin simultaneously, and the rapid thumping of his heart had risen to replace the beat of the music that had been playing in this room only minutes ago.

All it would take was one phase and a single swing of his

knife. Two fast, easy movements, and the king would go down. Even the king couldn't come back *that* quickly. Could he?

There was no way to be certain. A few days ago, he would've dismissed the king's ramblings as the product of a tired, damaged mind, but now they held an undeniable ring of truth.

"Go ahead," the king said, grin widening. "Pull your vanishing act, and we'll fire—"

Shadow drew in a deep breath; he could endure a large amount of punishment, and he knew, somehow, that he couldn't experience true death—not in this body.

And even if he *could* die, it was worth the risk to protect Alice.

The king nonchalantly pointed at Alice. "—on *her*."

The impossible, icy cold of the void spread through Shadow, consuming him from within. The automatons, as one, trained their weapons on Alice.

Her eyes widened, and she renewed her struggles against her captors for a few seconds. Her nostrils flared with a heavy exhalation before she eased. "Do what you need to do, Shadow," she said in a calm, clear voice.

Shadow's heart nearly shattered in that moment. She was so brave, so strong, despite the odds stacked against her, despite the very real, very immediate danger to her life. Death now would mean death in *all* worlds.

He remained frozen in place, torn between two choices that offered no difference in their inevitable outcomes—act and lose her or don't act and lose her. Shadow knew the king well enough to understand that neither option would spare Alice suffering and pain.

"So, you *do* care for her," the king said. "You've never cared for a damned thing but your games. How about we play one now? Let her go."

The automatons on either side of Alice released her and, in

perfect unison, marched back to join the others in the firing line.

Shock and confusion strained her features, and she nearly stumbled as her legs were forced suddenly to support her weight.

Shadow's chest constricted, and his heart felt like it was being squeezed out of his ribcage. He knew better than to hope, knew there were no good intentions behind this, but it was a chance—a chance to save her, a chance for the king's arrogance to lead to his defeat just as it had so often in the past.

Alice ran toward Shadow, and he ran toward her. Though they were separated by no more than ten paces, he phased to her; he needed to have her in his arms *now* because that was the only way he could get her out of here fast enough.

He materialized immediately in front of her and extended his arms to draw her into his embrace. She slammed into Shadow, throwing her arms around him. A thunderous boom echoed through the chamber in the same instant—much too loud to have been caused by her impact.

Something heavy punched into Shadow's lower abdomen, followed by wet, slowly spreading heat.

Alice released a soft, startled grunt against his chest. Her hold on him tightened, and her fingers clutched at his clothing with desperate strength. She was stiff and still, so still, *too* still.

"Shadow," she breathed before she sagged against him, legs giving out. Only his embrace kept her upright.

"You finally lose one," the king said.

Shadow glanced at the king. The man's pistol was raised—aimed at Alice—and a thin, ghostly wisp of smoke curled up from its barrel.

A cold hand clamped around Shadow's heart, squeezing it until it no longer beat. His knees buckled; together, he and Alice sank to the floor. Nothing else existed as he tipped her back to examine her. Pain contorted her face. A crease formed between her eyebrows, and her skin paled but for a pair of frantic pink splashes on her cheeks. Mouth dry, Shadow lowered his gaze.

Her dress was stained crimson at her stomach, where a gaping tear in the fabric revealed a hole in *her*. Fresh blood flowed from the wound. Hand trembling, Shadow covered the wound with his palm and pressed down. More blood soaked through the arm of his jacket from the entry wound on her back. A million thoughts careened through his head, smashing into each other to burst in a chaotic, indecipherable jumble.

Her eyes—so big, blue, and beautiful—were glossy with confusion and pain as they stared into his. She drew in a labored breath, and more warm blood ran between his fingers.

"No, no, no," he whispered as her fingers curled in the fabric of his coat. "It's not real, Alice. You're okay. It's not real, remember?"

"But it hurts, Shadow," she said in a small, thin voice. "How... how can it be fake if it hurts so much?"

"I can't kill you yet," the king called, drawing Shadow's gaze briefly. The man's eyes shone with malicious glee. "But I *did* kill her. There's nothing in this world that can save her, not even you. And when the time comes, you won't be able to save yourself, either."

Shadow's fury swelled, but it was impotent; he knew the king wasn't lying, knew Alice wouldn't survive this. She'd be gone, and he'd have *nothing*—not even a name. With the one person who *saw* him gone, he would *be* nothing. As more and more of Alice's blood pumped around his hand, as her hold on him gradually lost strength, as her skin continued to pale, Shadow felt himself—or whatever unseen force it was that had always held him together—faltering.

She is mine. Mine. Mine! I won't let her go.

The shadows that always shrouded him—the shadows that had protected whatever remained of him since he'd come to Wonderland so long ago, the shadows through which only Alice had been able to see—dissipated. He felt them evaporate like mist under the bright morning sun, like smoke in a steady breeze, but he didn't care.

He didn't want the shadows, didn't want this place. Didn't want anything if he didn't have her.

"You can't go, Alice. Not without me," Shadow rasped.

The king's boots thumped across the floor as he approached, and he growled, "Look at me."

Shadow held Alice's gaze, breaking it only to lean forward and brush his lips across her forehead. She didn't have long, and he didn't want to sacrifice even a single second he could've spent staring into her eyes.

No. This isn't real. He hasn't won... There's still time!

But her blood was all over his hand, and it would always be stained, and no matter how much he'd forgotten and had yet to forget, he'd always remember Alice—and how he'd failed her. His love was tainted, and it wasn't enough. Wasn't enough to keep her safe. She wouldn't come back, couldn't come back. There was only true death in this place.

"Wake up, Shadow," Alice whispered. She covered his hand with one of hers, her features tight. "He's deathless here. Wake up and end him *beyond*. You need to *wake up*." Her eyelids fluttered, and Shadow knew she was using all her strength to keep them open and speak. "I love you."

"I said look at me," the king shouted an instant before his boot struck Shadow on the cheek.

The force of the blow knocked Shadow aside. Alice fell from his arms, crying out in startlement and pain, and Shadow's head hit the floor. He shook off the blows and pushed himself up.

"*You?*" The king snarled. "All this time, all these system scans, all that searching, and you were a fucking *sleeper* all along?"

Shadow quickly and carefully gathered Alice into his arms and covered her wounds as best he could. She curled up, burying her face against his chest, and whimpered between her ragged breaths.

Baring his teeth, Shadow finally looked up at the king, whose expression was an unsettling blend of triumph and hatred.

"Finally got you," the king said. "There's no running this time, you son of a bitch. I'm going to kill you in meat space just so I can *really* feel your blood flowing over my hands."

The king turned his left arm so his palm was facing the ceiling and tugged up his sleeve, revealing his wrist—and a strange, black device embedded in the flesh there. He tapped the device. A bright light erupted from *inside* the king, expanding and intensifying to consume him entirely. When the light faded an instant later, the king was gone.

The automatons stood in place, unmoving and unresponsive.

Wake up, Shadow.

The king was going to kill him in *meat space*. What did that mean? What was beyond Wonderland?

Was Alice's real body somewhere out there, slowly dying because of her wound here?

Yes. The answer *had* to be yes, because that meant there was a chance, that meant he could still save her. If there was no hope in this world, he would find it in another. He would *take* it.

"Wake up, wake *up*," he muttered as he carefully gathered Alice close.

She grasped his coat again; her grip was noticeably weaker than before.

Shadow stilled. He knew, suddenly, where he had to go, even if he was still uncertain of what he had to do. He couldn't wake up from Wonderland until he stopped *dreaming*.

Shadow squeezed his eyes shut and envisioned...*himself*.

The air around him wavered and cooled. Mist settled on his skin, and the uneasy silence of the dance hall was replaced by the gentle creaking of old, tired trees and the muted sound of water lapping lazily against land. His back tingled, thrumming with the energy of the presence behind him. Shadow tightened his hold on Alice and opened his eyes.

The ground was damp, covered in a layer of rotting leaves. Alice looked even paler here, and the misty air gave her skin a sickly, grayish pallor—she looked close to death.

She *was* close to death.

Shadow settled Alice on the ground and removed his coat, vest, and shirt. "This is not a place for *you* to sleep, Alice. Stay with me."

Though he'd somehow kept his voice steady, the turmoil in his mind had only intensified. His heart pounded, the sound so pervasive in his head that it might've been the heartbeat of the entire swamp—the heartbeat of Wonderland itself.

Not real. No. No! She's fine, because this isn't real. I'll kill the king, save Alice, and the only thing that's real is her, is us.

His hands trembled as he used his clothing—tearing the fabric as necessary—to bind her wounds. She grunted and groaned despite his care, pressing her nails into his forearm. His already broken heart crumbled further at the knowledge that he was causing her more pain, but he took a modicum of comfort in her grasp—it meant she still had fight left.

Alice opened her eyes and met his gaze. Despite the sheen in her eyes, despite the haze of pain that must undoubtedly have settled over her mind, there remained a piercing lucidity there. "Go, Shadow. Leave me."

"No," he begged, even though he knew he *had* to go. "I can't leave you alone. This isn't real. We're real, but this isn't. You're fine, you're—"

She pressed her trembling fingertips over his lips, silencing him. Her skin was cool and clammy. "You need to leave me. Wake up. Wake up and…and come find me. Find me beyond."

The presence behind Shadow seemed to intensify, and the tingling along his spine became a crackling heat that made his skin itch. He licked his lips with his dry, scratchy tongue and stood. After unclasping his knife belt, he tossed it aside and hurriedly tugged off his pants. He folded them, knelt, and slipped them under Alice's head. Her eyelids fluttered shut.

Not real. Not real... She's fine.

No, she's not. She's not fine, and the king is coming for me. Wake up!

Shadow pulled one of the remaining knives from its sheath on the discarded belt. He spread and curled his fingers, adjusting his grip on the weapon, as he rose. His mind—more outside his control than ever before—whispered a thousand what-ifs.

What if he was too late? What if Alice couldn't hold on? What if he couldn't wake up?

What if this *was* real?

"No," he growled. He reversed his hold on the knife, cupping one hand over the butt of its grip, and positioned the tip against his chest, just beneath his ribcage.

She's not going to die. I will not *lose her.*

The sensation on his back strengthened to the point of pain, pulsing along his spine in fiery lashes. He'd always avoided this place after he'd first discovered what currently awaited behind him. Perhaps, even back then, part of him had recognized that this swamp was a hint that Wonderland wasn't right—that it wasn't real.

Shadow plunged the blade under his ribs and forced it upward as he spun around.

The pain came only when he looked at the face of the sleeper who'd been behind him—his own face. Piercing agony set his chest ablaze. His knees wobbled, and his arms trembled, and his lungs were desperate for air, but he could not draw breath. He closed his eyes.

The entire world lurched, and the weight of Shadow's body rapidly increased, making him feel as though he were about to sink into the ground and be swallowed by Wonderland forever.

Not real, not real, not real...

"Not real."

The sound of his own voice startled Shadow. He opened his eyes to find himself face-to-face with his *other*, with his...ghost. His shadow. The ghost had blood smeared over his lips—Alice's blood—and his hands were clasped over the grip of the knife jutting from his chest.

Shadow glanced down to see his hands in the same position over the fabric of the green hospital gown he was dressed in. He moved his hands aside; there was no wound beneath, no tear in the fabric, no blood. But the scent of blood filled his nose—*her* blood. He looked up as his ghost, the body he'd inhabited during his entire stay in Wonderland, swayed. The light was gone from his ghost's eyes, and no hint of the grin he usually wore was present. The empty shell, the shadow, collapsed, barely making a sound as it hit the ground.

Shadow—he knew it wasn't his name, especially not in this body, but he couldn't remember what his name was supposed to be—shifted his gaze to Alice, who lay on the ground nearby his discarded ghost, unmoving but for the erratic rise and fall of her chest with her shallow, labored breaths.

He longed to lift her up, to soothe her, to kiss away her pain, but there was no time. He had to be quicker than the king.

"Not real, not real," he repeated. His hoarse voice cut in and out, burning in his throat. This pain felt real and immediate.

"Wake up, damn you!" Shadow pinched his arm, pushing one of his claws through his skin. Warm blood oozed from the small wound. "Wake up, wake up, wake up!" He lifted a hand and slapped his cheek hard. The sharp sting was a shock, but not enough of one to accomplish his goal.

His eyes fell on Alice again as he grasped fistfuls of his hair and tugged on the strands. Despite the cool air, pinpricks of heat danced across his skin. Each of his thundering heartbeats

268

was one closer to losing her. To losing *everything*. And if he couldn't breathe, couldn't think, how could he hope to help her?

Shadow's *other* lay beside her, lifeless and still. What if that was the real him? What if he truly was a ghost now?

"No," he growled. "I'm real. *You* aren't!"

He dropped to his knees and closed his hands around the ghost's throat.

"Not real. This...isn't...real!"

He tightened his grip and released a wordless roar. The world around him rippled, and a sudden sinking sensation made it feel like he was falling despite the solid ground beneath him—falling impossibly fast, impossibly far. He was falling into an unfathomable abyss, into a lightless void; he was falling out of existence. He turned his head to seek Alice, hoping that seeing her would ground him in reality.

No. This *isn't real.*

The darkness devoured Shadow; it didn't seem to care whether it was real or not.

CHAPTER 20

SHADOW OPENED his eyes and sucked in a wheezing breath. He tried to sit up, but there was something solid over him; fortunately, his hand struck the obstruction before his head could. The darkness receded as his eyes adjusted to the dim light. His breathing echoed around him, amplified by the tight space, as his vision wavered and spun, blurring and focusing wildly for several seconds.

When he could finally see clearly, he realized he was looking up at a small window. The soft, weak light originated from somewhere beyond the window. He shifted to get a different angle, hoping to see more than a shadowed, featureless ceiling, but a series of aches and stings cascaded through his body and halted him before he could.

He gritted his teeth and dropped his head onto the padded cushion beneath him. Everything hurt, everything felt heavy, and he had no idea where he was—apart from someplace cramped and dark.

I know this place. Alice told me about it.

And I...I remember.

Images flashed through Shadow's mind's eye—halls with dull

artificial light, men in strange uniforms, a chamber filled with long, silent pods. These images had never been wild imaginings; they were memories from when he'd been brought here—from when they'd locked him in the dark.

Lifting his head again, he looked down at his prone body. His gown—which should've been pale green—was made gray by the poor lighting, and his feet were lost entirely to the lingering darkness at the opposite end of the pod. Various tubes and wires were embedded in his body along the way. He could feel their points beneath his skin, shifting with his every tiny movement.

He willed himself out of the pod, seeking that strange energy that had allowed him to phase in Wonderland, but it was gone. It didn't exist here.

The king is hunting...and Alice needs me.

Those thoughts sliced through his confusion and fear. His heart sped as he groped in the blackness with both hands, sliding his palms and fingertips along the walls and ceiling of his pod. He stilled when his claws caught on something—a handle of some sort. He curled his fingers beneath it and yanked it down. There was a hiss of air being released, and the lid rose, allowing more light to flow in around the edges.

Shadow planted both palms against the lid and shoved up against it. He felt it strain as he pushed it faster than it was designed to move. Once it was high enough, he sat up.

Though his range of motion was limited by several of the connections embedded in his skin, his head spun, and his stomach flipped at the sudden movement. With shaky hands, he clawed at the tubes on his forearm, pulling one loose; the needle that slid out of his flesh as he tugged on the line had to be at least three inches long.

"Emergency disengagement activated," said a gentle, feminine voice from the lid overhead. "Please remain still to avoid injury."

The color of several of the tubes changed, and something icy cold flowed through his veins, washing away his lingering disorientation. A moment later, Shadow's throat constricted in panic as the remaining lines and tubes moved on their own, producing fresh, dull pain as they withdrew from his flesh. He watched them recede with wide eyes. It wouldn't take much of a leap in imagination to see them as living creatures, as writhing parasites that had been feeding off him from the inside.

After the final connection—this one at the base of his skull—had withdrawn, the voice said, "Please remain in your immersion chamber. An attendant will be with you as soon as possible." There was a brief pause before it added, "Your wait may be prolonged due to a communication error with our monitoring systems. Thank you for your patience."

Shadow raised a hand to the back of his neck. Apart from a small lump, there was no sign that anything had just been buried in his skin—in fact, the spot was now oddly numb. *All* the spots where a needle had been injected were numb but for the one from which he'd removed the first tube, which also seemed to be the only one that was bleeding.

He grasped the side of the pod and hauled himself over. His legs refused to support him when his feet first touched the floor. He collapsed, keeping his torso upright only because of his desperate grip on the edge of the pod. With a grunt, he pulled himself onto his feet. The room teetered and turned around him, and his stomach revolted, threatening to empty itself of whatever meager contents it currently held.

For a moment, he staggered backward and waved his arms to catch his balance. His tail brushed against something solid behind him, and he stiffened it, producing just enough force to push himself forward. His flailing hands swung overhead and came down, latching onto the lid of his pod. As his weight bore down upon it, it swung closed. He leaned against the pod and caught his breath. His body was too heavy, too weak—it felt like his bones were made of rubber, and, despite the numb spots everywhere, every one of his muscles ached.

How long had he been in that pod?

How long had he been in Wonderland?

Swallowing thickly, he surveyed the room. His pod was but one of many—at least thirty more stood in a row beside it, split almost evenly to the left and right, each with the same thick bundles of cords, tubes, and wires connecting it to the wall. A single door stood at the center of the wall opposite the pods with a blank screen mounted on the wall five or six feet away. The lights were turned low, leaving the glowing screens over each pod that much more vibrant in comparison. All the displays showed what appeared to be vital signs—pulse rates and oxygen levels and other things he couldn't understand— along with names and a small string of letters and numbers. The name over his pod was Kor, Vailen.

Shadow growled as pain blazed in his skull, so intense that it felt like his head would split in two. He raked his claws across the top of the pod, scraping metal. Memories flashed through his mind in rapid, violent succession, too quick and disjointed to make sense of—gunfire, explosions, screams, fire. An alien sky set aglow by the flames surrounding hundreds of dropships as they descended from orbit.

Doesn't matter now. Need to find Alice. Need to hurry.

He thrust the memories aside and stumbled toward the door on the far wall, turning to look across the screens over the other pods. No Claybourne. No Alice. His chest constricted with another surge of panic—he didn't know how big this place was, how many rooms awaited him, how many pods like these were scattered throughout the facility. There wasn't time for a prolonged search; who knew if the passage of time here even matched Wonderland's?

"Focus," he said. He turned back toward the door, and his eyes settled on the dark screen on the wall.

Shadow hurried to the screen. Each step was a little more solid, a little more confident, than the last, but his fingers were clumsy and slow as he fumbled with the screen's controls. Exhaustion pressed in around the edges of his consciousness, making his eyelids feel as heavy as the rest of his body. He fought it.

"Coming, sweet Alice. Coming." Somehow, he found his way into a program named *Patient Directory*. The touch screen display brought up the characters of the human alphabet.

Flattening a palm against the wall to keep himself steady, he entered Alice's name one letter at a time, only to realize he wasn't sure how to spell her last name. He held his extended finger in the air and struggled to recall the spelling rules of a language he doubted was his native tongue.

C-L-A…

He hesitated. What was next? *I? Y?*

The nearby door slid open before he could settle on the correct letter, allowing slightly stronger light to spill in from the hallway. Shadow pressed himself against the wall as a male human stalked into the room.

The human had long, dark hair, and was athletically built. He held something in his trembling right hand—a pistol.

He stopped three or four paces away from Shadow's pod, aimed the gun toward it, and fired six shots. The firearm went off with explosive force, each shot punctuated by the high *ping* of the projectiles punching through the metal lid.

Shadow flattened his ears, but that didn't stop them from ringing as the final gunshot's echo faded.

"Fucking nuisance," the man growled. "Now you're a *real* fucking ghost."

Shadow knew that voice. He knew it *very* well. This human was the Red King—and he was alone and vulnerable. The fires of hatred and rage reignited in Shadow, dumping adrenaline into his veins and filling his limbs with renewed strength.

The king is vulnerable beyond.

Clenching his jaw, Shadow crept toward the king, his bare feet silent on the cold floor.

The king strode up to the pod, keeping his gun raised. "You deserve to suffer, but I'll take this victory gladly. Vanish now, you—" The king leaned forward and looked through the window on the pod's lid. He released a frustrated roar which ended just as Shadow—who'd closed the distance between himself and his enemy to a single pace—brought his leading foot down.

Shadow had overstepped; in his effort to maintain balance, his toe claws tapped the floor lightly.

The king spun to face Shadow, swinging the gun around. Shadow lunged forward, one hand darting out to catch the king's wrist before the gun's barrel came to bear. But the king closed the distance between himself and Shadow quickly, eliminating the reach advantage afforded by Shadow's longer limbs.

The human's fist connected with Shadow's jaw, and Shadow's head snapped aside. His knees wobbled, and the king pressed his advantage, throwing more strength and weight behind his gun arm.

Shadow's eyes rounded as the trembling weapon turned toward him one degree at a time, its barrel yawning like a black hole, ready to snuff out light and life. He grasped the king's jacket with his free hand and pulled the human closer still, driving his knee into the king's gut.

Grunting, the king doubled over, but he wasn't long deterred. He hammered his fist into Shadow's defenseless ribs over and over, each blow producing more pain than the last. Shadow refused to relinquish his hold; to do so would mean death. He curled his fingers tighter. The tips of his claws pressed into the flesh of the king's wrist. The human's pained growl became a shout as Shadow twisted his hand, forcing the claws deeper.

The gun fell from the king's hold and struck the floor with a dull thud. The king punched Shadow's ribs again, and something crunched under the force.

Shadow staggered aside as the breath fled his lungs, forced out by the immense pain clutching his chest. Instinctively, he willed himself to phase, to escape, to reappear anywhere other than right here, but this wasn't a simulation, wasn't a game; this was reality. Whether it was the aftereffects of being in the pod or not, right now, when it mattered most, Shadow was slower, weaker, and more unsteady than ever in memory.

Pain was real here. And death was forever.

The king took advantage of Shadow's imbalance, wrapping his arm around Shadow's torso and tackling him to the floor. Shadow fought without conscious thought, clawing, swinging his arms, and writhing, desperate to escape as the king tried to pin him. The human's hands clutched at Shadow's throat, but Shadow twisted his head and bit down on a few of the groping fingers, sinking his fangs deep. The coppery tang of human blood danced across Shadow's tongue.

"You fucking rodent, just die!" The king rained blows upon Shadow, who threw his arms up in defense; it wasn't enough to spare him from several heavy strikes, all of which landed with dull, meaty *thwaps*.

Alice's face formed in Shadow's mind's eye, so beautiful, so happy.

Happy. That wasn't how Alice looked now. If she yet lived— *she's alive, has to be,* must *be*—her features were drawn in agony, her skin deathly pale, her dress stained with her own blood. And this human—this mortal man, whose eyes were madder than anyone's in Wonderland—was the one who'd done it to her.

A second wave of fury rose from deep inside Shadow, blasting fire into his limbs. It didn't matter how many people had suffered at the king's hands, didn't matter how many hearts he'd torn from his victims' chests, didn't matter how much blood was on his hands—he'd harmed Alice.

There could be no forgiveness for that. No mercy.

Shadow raked his claws across the king's face, opening the flesh in a set of cuts from the man's left cheekbone to the right side of his chin. The king reeled backward, and a spray of blood flew from the cuts to splatter Shadow's face.

The king lunged again after an instant. Shadow bent his leg, managing to plant his knee against the king's sternum and halt the human's forward momentum. When the king lashed out with both arms, Shadow caught the king's hands in his own, curled his fingers to bury his claws in their backs, and growled as he twisted his hips, heaving the king aside with his knee.

Shadow rolled with the king and came down with his knee atop the king's gut, driving his weight down on that point of impact.

The ensuing struggle was desperate and chaotic, occurring in a flurry of swinging arms and grasping fingers. The king landed several more solid blows, but Shadow gave back twice as many, unfazed by the punishment he'd received; his pain was dulled and distant now, and what did it matter anyway?

Finally, Shadow closed a hand around the king's throat and leaned forward, using his other arm to fend off as many of his foe's flailing attacks as he could. The king clamped a hand around Shadow's wrist and pulled desperately while his face darkened, shifting gradually from bright red to purple. His eyes, though bulging from their sockets, remained locked with Shadow's, their bright, hateful gleam stronger than ever.

The king drove his other fist into Shadow's ribs.

The pain was immediate and explosive. Shadow gritted his teeth and grunted, struggling to maintain his hold, but a second blow to the same spot proved to be too much. His hand loosened, and the king pried it away, sucked in a harsh breath, and shoved Shadow aside.

Catching himself on an elbow, Shadow tucked his other arm against his throbbing side in a vain attempt to relieve the agony. His tail whipped restlessly across the floor until it bumped into something solid lying nearby.

The gun.

He curled his tail around the weapon.

"You don't get to win this time," the king growled, voice raw, as he moved onto his knees. His face was still red—as was his throat—and his shoulders heaved with his heavy breaths. Blood ran from the cuts on his face and dripped off his chin, making soft but distinct pattering sounds as they struck the floor. "I'm in charge here. This is *my* place. *Wonderland* is my place!"

Shadow swung his free hand down to meet his tail as the king lunged. The human's momentum knocked Shadow onto his back. He caught the king's throat in one hand, but his arm didn't have the strength to hold back the man's weight. The king leaned forward and wrapped both hands around Shadow's neck, squeezing.

Dark spots danced across Shadow's vision. He slipped a finger behind the gun's trigger guard and bent his arm to position the weapon between his body and the king's. Pressure was building rapidly in his face due to his cut-off circulation, his throat was raw, and his lungs burned.

My Alice. You can't take her away.

He squeezed the trigger six times; the first four produced deafening bangs, the last two only the clicks of an empty chamber.

The king jolted with each shot. His eyes flared somehow wider, and he released a startled, choked grunt, spraying bloody spittle from his lips. The stench of singed flesh joined the blood scent on the air. His eyes took on a glassy sheen as he released Shadow's throat, leaned back onto his knees, and dropped his chin to look down.

Faint wisps of smoke drifted from the four scorch-ringed

holes in his chest. He parted his lips as though to speak but managed only a rattling exhalation. For a moment, his face reddened further, and then all the color drained from his skin. He swayed; Shadow shoved him aside, and the human hit the floor in a heap.

Keeping the gun raised, Shadow sagged down and drew in a deep breath. Both his throat and his chest cried out in agony. His whole body hurt, and he wasn't sure if he could move—but he knew he *had* to. It didn't matter if an alarm had been triggered, didn't matter if a dozen armed men waited beyond the chamber door, didn't matter how large this place was or how many pods it housed.

Alice *needed* Shadow. That was all, that was everything.

With his jaw clenched, he rolled onto his side, sat up, and searched the king's body. He found a spare, fully loaded magazine and reloaded the pistol. The process came to him with surprising ease, though he couldn't recall having ever handled a gun in that fashion. He also found a thin, rectangular device that had been hooked to the king's belt.

Shadow pressed a button on the device, and its screen came on. His eyes widened; there seemed to be no security on the device, and the icons on its screen indicated countless documents. A small alert message, highlighted in red along the top of the screen, announced that the security and reporting systems had been deactivated by administrator override. But it was the icon at the top that immediately caught Shadow's eye.

Claybourne, Alice.

He touched the icon with his finger.

Shadow's heart leapt when Alice's picture appeared on the screen. It was accompanied by droves of information about her, including her height, weight, measurements, and several tabs of notes—including one marked *Director's Notes.*

Terror, at once cold and fiery, spread outward from a pit in

Shadow's stomach to suffuse his entire body. Beneath her picture was a list of vital signs—all of which were blank.

"No, no, no," he rasped, lifting a hand and pressing the textured side of the pistol's grip to his forehead as he raked the tips of his claws through his hair. "No. She's not gone. Not gone."

The reporting system is deactivated. There's still time. I'm not too late.

Breath shallow and ragged, he scanned the information frantically until he discovered what he needed—*Patient Location: CA-17-49B*. The designation meant nothing to him, but there was an option beside it that he pressed immediately—*Navigate to Patient*.

The device's display changed to a map; the pulsing dot at the center must've been him. Shadow staggered to his feet. He bent his arm, keeping the device facing toward him, and straightened his gun arm, settling it atop the other to ease the tremors coursing through his limbs and provide his weapon with some stability. Despite the unsteadiness in his legs—his knees felt as though they might buckle at any moment—the throbbing ache in his head, and the sharp pain in his ribs, he hurried into the hallway.

The corridor stretched on in either direction for what must've been hundreds of feet; Shadow couldn't judge the distance while his vision kept bending and blurring. He shook his head sharply, but it only gave him temporary clarity. There were no guards in sight, and dozens of doors, each with letters and numbers printed on their faces, lined either side of the hallway. A small vehicle sat only a few paces away. It was some sort of cart with six wheels, two seats up front, and a long bed on the rear—long enough to fit a person who was lying down.

Shadow moved to the vehicle, leaning his hip against its side for balance as he studied the controls—a wheel positioned above the level of the seat and two pedals on the floor. He didn't understand why it looked so...*normal,* so familiar, when he'd never seen anything like this in Wonderland.

Because I am from this world—Alice's world—whether I consciously remember it or not.

A soft chiming sound called his attention to the device in his hand. A message had appeared on the screen—*Enable auto-navigation for current route in vehicle CZCX97?*

Shadow tapped *YES* with his thumb. The next message instructed him to enter the vehicle's operator seat and activate the auto-navigation on the control screen. He twisted to check the hall behind him; it remained deserted, but he'd moved too fast. A sudden bout of dizziness made it feel like the corridor was tilting and spinning around him, and his body pitched to the side—away from the cart.

He thrust himself back toward the vehicle, inadvertently over-correcting. Fortunately, the cart had no doors, and—after a couple more bumps that were insignificant compared to what he'd suffered at the king's hands—he found himself sprawled across the front seats. He adjusted his hold on the pistol, grasped the steering wheel, and hauled himself into a sitting position. His ribs screamed in protest, but he didn't have time to be slowed by them. Once his legs were in the cart, bent at ridiculous angles to fit, he pressed the prompt to engage the auto-navigation.

The cart lurched forward with a barely perceptible hum. Its wheels rolled silently over the floor as it drove down the hall. Though it moved faster than he could have on foot in his current state, impatience—intensified by worry—sparked in Shadow. He leaned back and glanced down at the pedals. One of them would make the vehicle move faster; he knew it instinctually, though he had no idea which one was correct.

Leaving himself no time to debate the matter, he lowered his foot onto one of the pedals. The vehicle darted forward, gaining enough speed to force Shadow back against the seat.

Doors passed on either side with soft whooshes of air, and the cart's control panel lit up with an alert about the speed, but Shadow paid no attention to any of it. His focus remained on the device in his hand; he watched as the dot representing his location sped along the map's corridors. When the vehicle took its first turn, the whole thing tipped on two wheels, threatening to roll over. Shadow threw his weight in the opposite direction. The cart slammed back down and regained the speed it had lost in the turn.

All the while, Shadow muttered under his breath, feeling the words more than hearing them with his own ears.

"She's all right, she's alive, it's not too late, she's okay..."

He pressed the pedal down harder and used the map to anticipate upcoming turns, easing his foot off the accelerator and shifting his weight to keep the vehicle from tipping each time he reached one.

This facility was more unsettling than the swamp full of sleepers in Wonderland—because this place was so silent, so unnatural, and the fact that these sleepers were hidden in pods, out of sight, only made it somehow worse. There were so many, many more sleepers here. Shadow had already passed what must've been hundreds of them, if not more. Each was unaware of their state, unaware they were immersed in a false reality, unaware of *this* world.

Where were the guards, the attendants? Even if the king had disabled the security system, shouldn't there have been *someone* around? Did they really leave all these patients, all these *prisoners*, unattended?

The device in Shadow's hand chimed again. The message on its screen said *Destination Ahead*.

He lifted his foot off the pedal. The vehicle continued forward another hundred feet or so before bringing itself to a smooth stop in front of a door that had *CA-17-49* stamped on its face. Shadow leapt out of the cart and rushed to the door, allowing his legs no time to falter, offering the pain wracking his body not a single thought more than he already had. He slapped the button on the wall. The door slid open, and Shadow rushed through.

Alice's pod—CA-17-49B—was the second from the left. Shadow charged to it, stopping himself by throwing his arms over the lid. Ragged breaths burned his throat as he peered through the little view window.

It was *her*—small, delicate, pale, and unmoving. Her eyes were closed, her face strained as though she were in the grips of a nightmare. And she *was* in a nightmare—Wonderland.

He flicked his gaze to the wall mounted screen over her pod. It displayed her vital signs, all of them in red with little alarm signals flashing beside them; she was alive, but she wasn't well.

Heart pounding hard enough to cause twinges of pain in his damaged ribs, Shadow hurried to the foot of the pod, where a small control panel was positioned. He scanned through the options; none of it seemed right, and much of it was meaningless to his conscious mind. Perhaps if he had time to think, to remember...

He selected an option. It opened a submenu which included one command that caught his attention—*Emergency Awakening*.

"Stay with me," Shadow said, stretching an arm along the top of the pod. He laid the pistol down and flattened his palm atop the pod's lid as though he could touch her through the metal. He pressed the *Emergency Awakening* command.

Supervisor clearance required to proceed.

Shadow tapped the screen over and over with increasing franticness, but it didn't change.

"What does that *mean*? No. No, no, no, no!" He banged his fist on the pod. "Alice, wake up!"

Swinging his hand up to grasp his hair, he stepped back. This wasn't real. Couldn't be real. He couldn't get this close to her only to fail, only to lose her anyway.

The king's device!

He raised the device and reactivated the screen. A message appeared—*Approve emergency awakening CA-17-49B? Vital signs critical.* Shadow pressed *YES* before he'd even finished reading.

The pod beeped, and there was a loud hiss of releasing air as the lid jolted up a fraction of an inch. Shadow quickly snatched the gun off the top of the pod, stepped back, and watched with his breath caught in his throat. Unseen machinery rumbled before the lid, which was hinged near the wall, swung upward.

Alice was revealed to Shadow a little at a time—first her dainty toes and feet, then her ankles, shins, and knees, followed by the bits of her thighs that were visible below the hem of her gown, which was identical to Shadow's. The fabric covering her pelvis and torso was run through with little bulges and bumps created by the wires and tubes beneath it. Slowly, those tubes and wires disconnected themselves, sliding out of her flesh and leaving no blood behind.

No blood...what if she's not real? What if she's a ghost here, like I was there?

Shadow shook his head, dropped the king's device and the pistol onto the padded bed inside the pod, and grasped the pod wall to hold himself steady as a fresh wave of dizziness washed over him. The needles that had pulled themselves out of him hadn't left any blood behind either. Only the one he'd torn out of himself had bled at all.

This *was* Alice. He could sense it, could *smell* her—her honey and vanilla fragrance was even more pronounced here, was even more *hers*, and he forced in another deep breath through his nose just to draw in more of it.

His gaze settled on Alice's face, which was sorrowfully beautiful in that moment—the pain in her expression would tear his heart to shreds if he stared too long, but he couldn't look away from her.

The last of the visible lines disconnected from her.

Alice's eyes snapped open. Her back arched sharply, and she clawed at the padding beneath her, mouth agape in a soundless cry. For several seconds, she remained in that position—every muscle tense, the cords of her neck standing out, and bluish veins visible beneath her pale skin. Then she sucked in a wheezing, agonized breath and collapsed onto the padding, chest rising and falling rapidly as she panted.

"Shadow," she whispered.

CHAPTER 21

ALICE LAY STILL, too disoriented and scared to move. She'd just woken from a nightmare—but the nightmare had been so vivid, had felt so real, that she wasn't entirely certain she was truly awake.

The immense pain that she'd felt in that nightmare lingered, but it was merely a phantom of itself; the oddly cool sensation flowing through her veins was chasing it away. Swallowing thickly, she struggled to ease her breathing and slowly ran her hand along her abdomen to where she'd been shot. There was no blood, no wound, no pain as she applied pressure.

I was dying.

She'd *felt* it. She'd felt her heartbeat slowing, fading; she'd felt her lungs burning as she battled to draw in her final, desperate breaths; she'd felt ice creeping up her limbs toward her chest and had known it would steal whatever life remained in her when it reached her heart. And she'd stared at Shadow, who lay motionless beside her, his eyes empty and blank, throughout— she'd stared until he disappeared.

Over and over, Alice had repeated the words in her head.

This isn't real. Shadow's not gone, he's awake. Shadow's alive.

Before long, all she'd been able to do was whisper his name as she bled out.

There was movement in her peripheral vision; suddenly, Shadow was above her. Except...his face was thinner, sharper, and he was splattered with blood—a lot of blood. At least some of it appeared to be his own, trickling from a cut over his right eye and his swollen, split lower lip.

"Shadow, wh—"

He slipped his arms beneath Alice and lifted her as he brought his mouth down on hers. His kiss was both familiar and foreign, reminiscent of the kisses they'd shared in the simulation while somehow being wholly new and unique. The sensation felt stronger, more powerful, more...*real*.

They were real.

We made it!

Joy surged within Alice, and she forced her heavy arms up to loop them around his neck. This was Shadow. *Her* Shadow. The one who'd been there for her from the beginning, who'd helped her, believed in her, and *loved* her even when he'd thought her mad. And he was here with her, in the real world, in the flesh.

He'd saved her.

Alice curled her fingers in his long, black and gray hair, parted her lips, and returned the kiss. She tasted his salty, metallic blood—along with something more undefinable, something entirely *him*.

"Alice," Shadow rasped against her mouth before deepening the kiss and holding her tighter against him.

This kiss wasn't about seduction or blazing desire—it was a grounding kiss, confirming that they were real, that they were alive, that they were together. They'd never kissed one another with such desperation and relief; no other kiss had ever been so comforting.

When they finally pulled away from one another, Alice searched his face, frowning at the cuts and swelling, at the first hints of bruising on his gray skin. Easing down on the cushion beneath her, Alice lightly touched the side of his mouth near the split.

"What happened?" she asked.

"The king and I found one another," he replied, voice hoarse.

Alice's eyes flared. The *king*? She tore her gaze away from Shadow to take in her surroundings. Though she and Shadow were no longer in the simulation, they were still in Wonderland —or at least the asylum that *housed* Wonderland. "Where is he now?"

"Showed him true death."

Perhaps it was wrong to feel relief over someone's death, but she couldn't help it now. Though she'd recently dealt with death when she'd lost her father, Wonderland had given Alice her first experiences with violence and bloodshed—the worst of which had been perpetrated by the Red King.

"We need to leave," Alice said, gently brushing her fingertips over his cheek.

Shadow nodded and removed one arm from around her, leaning away to pick up a small black tablet from the foot of the pod—a gun lay beside it on the padded bed. He winced and held the device to her. "This has a map on it. Could you use it to find a way? I...my head is too fuzzy, and I can't...I can't remember enough."

Pushing herself up with her hands, Alice took the tablet, but she didn't remove her eyes from Shadow. "How hurt are you?"

He glanced down at himself for a few seconds before returning his gaze to hers. "I'm sure I've had worse. I just can't remember it."

Frowning, Alice settled her hand just over his hip and slowly ran it up over his hospital gown. He stiffened and sucked in a sharp breath through his teeth when she reached his ribs.

"Just a little tender," he said in a strained voice.

"I barely touched it... Oh, Shadow."

How badly was he hurt?

"I'll be fine," he said. "Barely felt it, thanks to all the drugs they must've pumped into me."

Alice's frown deepened, but she chose not to press him on the obvious lie. Despite the concern eating away at her from within, there wasn't much she could do to help him while they were in this place.

She carefully pulled away from him and climbed out of the pod, keeping the tablet in hand as she moved. Her legs were unsteady at first, feeling terribly weak, but Shadow—holding onto the pod to anchor himself—offered her his arm in support. She was suddenly aware of every spot on her body where a needle had been embedded; they were highlighted by patches of numbness beneath which that strange, cold sensation lingered.

Alice looked around the room. She'd been drugged when they first dragged her in here, and her vision had been too blurred to see much of it. The pod had looked like a coffin to her at first glance; it might as well have been one, in the end, had Shadow not saved her in time. There was one pod to the right of hers, and at least twenty-five more to the left—meaning that, just in this room alone, there were nearly thirty people trapped in Wonderland.

How many of them actually belonged here? How many people in this facility were like Alice, imprisoned unjustly and against their will?

How many of them desperately needed treatment, *real* treatment, but instead were subjected to that surreal, chaotic, dangerous simulation?

She turned her face back toward Shadow. Why was *he* here?

Whatever the reason, Alice didn't care, and she wouldn't allow them to keep him here. Shadow was *hers*.

"Were there other guards or workers out there?" Alice asked, turning the tablet in her hands.

"I didn't see anyone on my way here. The device said the security and reporting systems were deactivated. I think the king turned them off before he came for me."

"This was *his*?"

Shadow nodded. "And it's totally unsecured. I was able to use it to override your pod and force you awake."

An unsecured tablet that could override systems in this facility? Alice leaned forward and pressed a kiss on the corner of his mouth as elation warmed her, fighting back the chill that had settled into her body since waking. This tablet, so plain and unimportant at a glance, was their way out. "Good. I'll figure out a way to lock the door so we can have a few minutes to think."

She swiped her finger over the screen. It came on to display Alice's picture—her file was open. Brows lowering, she skimmed the document.

Patient suffers from intermittent explosive disorder, depression, delusions, and paranoia. Family has reported violent outbursts and threats, and patient exhibited those tendencies while being transported to facility.

Alice tightened her grip on the tablet as disbelief, horror, and anger flooded her.

Family has reported…

Lies!

Tabitha and Jonathon *had* done this? *Why?* Why would they have sent her here?

She pressed one of the tabs in the file marked *Director's Notes.* Her eyes widened as she read.

High marks for attractiveness, but patient is too spirited. Will need to be broken in before suitable for play. Recommend time with patient Edward Winters (alias: the Hatter) for reconditioning.

Family unconcerned with wellbeing; would prefer loose ends tied up.

Candidate for cleaning program—family will not question patient death.

Alice's anger and disbelief warred with one another. She didn't want to believe she'd been betrayed, that her *father* had been betrayed. She was supposed to have been able to trust Tabitha—Alice's father had meant for Tabitha to be a mother to her, had hoped Tabitha would one day care for Alice as though she were the woman's own daughter.

Though Alice and Tabitha had never been able to build such a bond, Alice had never thought her stepmother capable of *this*.

Shadow placed a hand on her arm; it was only then that she realized she was trembling.

"Whatever that says, Alice, we can deal with it later. We need to go now, right?"

She would've agreed with him were it not for the links included at the bottom of the document—communication logs marked *CLAYBOURNE T.* Alice clenched her jaw and opened the logs. Stinging heat built beneath her skin as she read the communications, and her rage swelled to new, titanic proportions.

"*She* did it," Alice said in a low voice, "and she wasn't even subtle about it."

"Who did what, Alice?" Shadow asked, his hand tightening slightly.

"Tabitha. My stepmother. She bribed the director of this place—the *king*—to have me committed here. To make me disappear. My father left almost everything to me, and his will superseded what she would've inherited otherwise, which meant I would either have to die or be deemed incompetent to subvert his wishes. And it's all right here."

He frowned deeply; even here in the real world, even now, it was strange to see him without that grin.

"So, what do we do with this information, then?" he asked. "We still need to go, don't we?"

"No, Shadow. We don't need to go anywhere. We can stay right here. This"—she lifted the tablet—"is our escape route. We can contact the authorities and wait for them to come to us. This is all the evidence we need of the wrong-doings going on here."

Shadow's brow was creased with worry. "But I *killed* him, Alice. And killing someone...that's not okay here, is it?"

Alice reached up and cupped his jaw. "He shot at you, didn't he? That's why you have the gun?"

He nodded. "I was out of the pod when he came in. He fired into the pod before he knew where I was."

A fresh wave of relief swept through her; she'd come so close to losing him. They'd come so close to losing each other. If he'd taken any longer to wake himself up, they both would've been dead by now.

"It was self-defense, Shadow. You were protecting yourself. And no matter what, *I* will not let anything happen to you."

She would fight for him in any way possible.

His nostrils flared as he took in a deep breath. He covered her hand with his own and brushed the pad of his thumb over her skin. "This is the only way?"

"It's the *right* way." She leaned forward and gently pressed her forehead to his. "Everything will be okay. I promise."

He closed his eyes and slipped his arms around her. "I trust you. I *love* you."

A different kind of warmth coursed through her; it soothed her, lifted her spirit, and made her heart race. "I love you, too."

She embraced him, careful not to squeeze because of his ribs. The feel of him only reminded her how much thinner he was out here. He'd been just as tall in the simulation, and had been leanly muscled, but this...he seemed to have wasted away in reality. How long had he been imprisoned here?

When she finally—reluctantly—pulled back from him, she returned her attention to the tablet and navigated to the main menu. Within a few moments, she'd managed to discern their location—the Liddell Psychiatric Hospital, only twenty miles outside Apex Reach, the city in which she'd spent most of her life.

That discovery settled her even further; her father had been well-connected in Apex Reach, and she'd met many of his friends and acquaintances over the years—including the chief of police.

A search on the net turned up the contact information for the police headquarters. She didn't waste a moment in making the call.

"I need to speak with Chief Farland," she said to the operator who answered.

"I'm sorry, ma'am, but the Chief is very busy. I can take a message—"

"Tell him it's Alice Claybourne, Daniel Claybourne's daughter. And it's an emergency."

"Claybourne?" the operator asked. There was a muted conversation in the background, none of which Alice could make out, before the operator said, "I'm transferring the call now. Please hold for just a moment."

The line went silent; Alice counted her heartbeats as she waited.

There was a faint crackling sound on the other end of the call.

"Alice?" Chief Farland said in a raised, worried voice.

She could've just called the police, could've just called emergency services, but their best chance was with the chief—with anyone else, they risked being mistaken as a couple of disturbed patients who'd broken out of their pods and killed the facility's director, and that had too much of a chance of going bad before they could tell their story. But she knew Chief Farland; he'd been one of her father's closest friends and had been like family to Alice while she was growing up.

"Uncle Sean, I need your help."

"Alice, what's going on? Tabitha wouldn't tell me a damned thing. Where *are* you?"

Alice met Shadow's eyes and smiled. "The Liddell Psychiatric Hospital."

CHAPTER 22

Blue-white energy bursts pulsed through the thick gray clouds surrounding Shadow's dropship, occasionally silhouetting one of the other ships in his wing. Apart from those flashes, he couldn't see anything—he had to rely upon the scanner alone to avoid collision.

The ship jolted and rattled as a nearby blast disrupted the air, but the shields held.

"The fleet was supposed to soften them up before we made entry," said the lieutenant over the comm system.

Their pre-mission briefing had mentioned an orbital bombardment of the landing zone; had the fleet screwed up, or had the strike simply been ineffective? Shadow had made dozens of drops on almost as many planets during his career, most of which had been under enemy fire, but he'd never seen the sky so lit by anti-aircraft bursts. His heart beat steadily but loudly; he felt as though he were teetering on the edge of a precipice, and he'd be plunged into mindless terror if he fell.

The ship broke through the cloud cover, and Shadow's eyes widened as the world opened up below—a world that was all wrong.

Massive trees, each at least two hundred feet tall, surrounded a large clearing which was crisscrossed with purple pathways that

followed winding, nonsensical courses and intersected one another at random without any discernable reason or pattern. A large building stood in the center of that clearing, none of its angles or parts quite matching the rest.

"This is all wrong, sir," Shadow called. "Wrong landing zone, wrong planet."

"Get us on the ground," the lieutenant replied.

Shadow turned his head to look at his co-pilot, but—despite the light of energy bursts in the air all around and the glow of the instrument panels in front of him—the other seat was shrouded in an impenetrable patch of darkness.

An explosion shook the ship violently. Alarms blared and beeped, and the ship pitched to the right. One of the engines died, and the stabilizer failed. The ship whipped into a rapid spin.

Shadow's muscles strained as he wrestled the controls. The world below spun wildly, but one focal point remained oddly, impossibly stationary—the building at the center of the clearing.

And the dropship was hurtling toward that building.

The cacophony around him—soldiers shouting, the dropship shaking, alarms blaring—made it difficult to hear his own thoughts. All he could do was fight his losing battle against the controls.

With a deafening crash, the drop ship hit the building. Wood snapped, splintered, and shattered against the hull, and metal groaned and whined. The initial strike was followed by an immense impact so powerful that Shadow's world went black.

He opened his eyes sometime later—it could've been seconds or hours, he couldn't guess—to find himself still strapped into his seat, bathed in the glow and heat of a nearby fire. Dazed but feeling no pain, he unbuckled his harness and stumbled to his feet, placing a hand on the control console to balance himself against the drastic tilt of the floor. He looked to his co-pilot first, and froze as terror—sudden, confusing, and consuming—spread outward from his gut to ice his veins.

There was another him, another Shadow, in the co-pilot's seat, slumped back and dressed in a pale green hospital gown. The holes on the front of the gown—bullet holes—were ringed with glistening blood.

"I never made it out of the pod," the other-him rasped without moving his mouth.

"No." Shadow backed away. His foot slipped off the edge of the floor and he stumbled, landing on his backside partly on broken wood planks and partly on dirt. He swept his gaze around, only then realizing what should've been obvious from the start—the crash had torn both the building and the ship apart. He turned toward the rest of the craft as he regained his feet.

Dead soldiers were strewn everywhere. One row of transport seats had separated from the rest of the ship, and its passengers were scattered amidst the wreckage and debris.

The lieutenant lay closest to Shadow. He'd been impaled through the chest by a signpost, the sign for which was on the ground nearby. The hand-painted letters on the sign were still legible despite the blood spattered across them—Hatter's Tea Party.

The lieutenant's dark, lifeless eyes turned toward Shadow. The name plate on the human's uniform said WINTERS, and Shadow recognized his face.

Edward Winters. The Hatter.

This is wrong, all wrong. The Hatter…he didn't serve with me. I never knew him before… The lieutenant was someone else…

"Death is real," the Hatter said in a dried-out whisper. "Death is in Wonderland, Wonderland is death." His head turned with a slow, jerky motion to face Shadow fully. "You are dead."

"No. This isn't real. You're not real." Shadow hurried away from the Hatter and turned around.

He found himself suddenly surrounded by mist, the ship wreckage nowhere to be seen. He stepped forward. His foot landed in cold water. Dread lodged itself in his throat.

"I left this place. I woke up. I woke up."

"Shadow..." Alice's voice drifted to him, made ethereal by the fog.

He scanned his surroundings, searching for her among the indistinct trees, vines, and too-still water. His gaze stopped on a distant, shadowy figure—a figure in a short-skirted dress.

Shadow ran toward it, plunging into frigid, waist-deep water. The muddy bottom sucked at his feet. With each step, he sank a little deeper, his pace slowed a little more, and his heartbeat gained speed and volume.

"Shadow," Alice called again; she sounded no clearer, seemed no closer.

He strained against the mud, sputtering and coughing when his head dipped below the surface, pushing himself harder and harder, willing himself toward Alice. But the muck only thickened and grabbed at him ravenously. His head went under again, and he couldn't straighten enough to get it above the surface. He clawed at the bottom, dragging himself forward, and growled in anger and panic.

His claws dug into more solid ground. Lungs burning, he hauled himself forward and up a sharp incline until his head finally emerged. Shadow sucked in a harsh breath; the air was like fire as it flowed into his lungs, but it was so sweet.

Shadow pulled himself onto land fully, tugging his legs out of the mud's lingering grasp, and looked forward. Alice's form was still obscured by the mist, but she was much closer, standing amidst a jumble of vines and gnarled branches. He staggered to his feet and hurried forward, catching himself with his hands when he stumbled; his legs felt so light now, after his war with the mud.

"Alice," he called. *"Alice, I'm here! I'm coming."*

She didn't move, didn't respond; he ran faster, heart pounding.

He pushed through the branches and vines, breaking and snapping them to clear a path, and ignored the way they scratched and clawed at his skin and clothing. He was close. He needed Alice—only she could ground him, only she could remind him of what was real.

Though she stood only a few feet away, her form remained indistinct, like a phantom in the mist.

"Alice!" Shadow extended his arm, reaching for her.

His fingers caught the fabric of her skirt, and the dress simply fell away to dangle his hand. Shadow's heartbeat intensified, his chest constricted, and his throat tightened. The dress had been dangling from a cluster of branches with a vaguely humanoid shape.

"No, no, no," he muttered, lifting the dress in both hands. There was a hole in its abdomen, surrounded by bloodstained cloth.

"Not real, not real, this isn't real!"

"Yes, it is," the king whispered from behind him. "And you're dead."

Shadow spun around, but instead of finding the king, he found... himself. He was looking into his own face, his own eyes. The other him grinned wickedly and thrust a knife into Shadow's chest.

Shadow woke with a gasp and sat up, one hand pressed to his chest—where a hot, tingling sensation was slowly fading. His palms and feet were cold and clammy, his heart was racing, and tremors coursed along his limbs.

Soft, soothing hands slid across his shoulder, back, and chest. "Shh. It's okay, Shadow," Alice said, leaning close to brush her nose in his hair. "It was only a nightmare. You're here. You're awake now."

He glanced around the room. It was dark, but not so dark that he couldn't make out the hotel room's furnishings—the long mirror behind the desk, the wide, currently blank entertainment screen, the low, six-drawered dresser. A simple as the room was, Shadow was grateful for it; he preferred this place over anywhere he'd stayed in Wonderland.

He would've preferred *anywhere* over Wonderland, so long as Alice was with him.

Shadow slipped his arm around Alice and held her close, pressing his lips to the top of her head and inhaling her scent. This was real; she was real; *they* were alive. He wanted to tell her that he knew he was awake, that he knew he was with her, that he was all right, but he couldn't find his voice. His throat was tight, and his chest felt hollow. No words would come out.

He had dealt with nightmares almost every night since they'd left the psychiatric hospital. It had been jarring; in Wonderland, his sleep had always been dreamless. Most of the nightmares had been flashbacks—memories he didn't seem to possess during the day surfacing by night, while his mind was most vulnerable. Chaotic, terrifying battles; his ship crashing; the torture he'd suffered afterward—none of it seemed to happen in order, and little of it stayed with him after waking, but they were always vivid. They also, at times, mixed with his experiences in Wonderland.

Thanks to Chief Farland, Shadow had an identity to put with his legal name—Vailen Kor had been a Warrant Officer in the Intergalactic Union Defense Forces, a dropship pilot. He'd flown a great many combat missions and had suffered several injuries along the way, but it was his last mission that had eventually resulted in him being committed at Liddell Psychiatric Hospital. It had been that last mission that broke a mind that must already have been battered.

His ship had crashed, and almost everyone on board had died. Shadow—then Warrant Officer Kor—and a few of the other survivors had been taken prisoner by the enemy and tortured for nearly a year before being rescued by friendly forces.

The events following Shadow's rescue had been what Chief Farland called *a sadly typical story*. Despite his service, Shadow had simply not received the care he'd required; his government had failed him. The trauma he'd suffered had impeded his ability to function normally. Eventually someone—there was no record of who—had brought him to Liddell Psychiatric Hospital and had him committed, where Shadow simply became another sleeper in the system, forgotten.

The information he'd received about himself hadn't been a magic key—it hadn't suddenly unlocked his memories, hadn't changed who he was. Though he now knew his given name, Alice had fallen in love with *Shadow*, not Vailen Kor, and he didn't want to be anyone but *hers*. She'd told him he could be whoever he wanted, that she loved him no matter what name he'd gone by —and he wanted to embrace the life he'd already begun to build with her, wanted to look toward the future. He was Shadow, and when that name came from her lips, it meant so much more than it ever had before. She'd made it something special.

But it was nice to know he was *someone* and not just a ghost from a simulated world, all the same.

"I'm okay," he said once his breathing had eased and his heart had slowed. "Sorry I woke you again."

She pressed closer against him; the silk of her nightgown was soft and cool on his skin. Her fingers rubbed back and forth across his chest, petting him, letting him know she was there. "You have nothing to be sorry about."

"I know, it's just..." he sighed and shook his head. "It's been four weeks and they're just as bad. And when they're like this one... I was back there again. Back in Wonderland. And it was so real, and everything was *wrong*, and..." Shadow tightened his hold on her.

"It was only a dream." She lifted her head and looked up at him. Her eyes shifted as she searched his face, her pupils wide and unfocused; her eyesight wasn't nearly as good as his in the dark. "Your doctor said it's normal, especially after spending so many years in a simulation. It's a process, Shadow, but you're not going through it alone. I'm here with you." Raising her hand, she brushed her fingers over his brow, tucking his hair to the side. "Your mind just needs time to heal."

He settled his hand over hers, pressing his cheek into her palm. Her touch had been exquisite in Wonderland, but here in the real world, it was so much more powerful, and he *craved* it. They'd been restricted to largely innocent interactions over the last few weeks—his doctors had ordered it.

For the first week of his recovery, Shadow hadn't had much choice other than comply—his injuries had been even more tender during that time than they'd been immediately after his fight with Victor Koenig—the Red King—and his body had been weak. Despite the chemicals and processes the asylum had used to fight muscle atrophy and other problems caused by being immobile for long periods, Shadow's body had worn down over the seven years he'd been under.

But he'd seen the difference in the mirror lately—he was filling out. Every day, his aches diminished a little more, and he felt a little stronger. He knew he would never feel as fast or strong as he had in Wonderland, and that was still disorienting, but he would adjust.

With Alice at his side, he could overcome anything.

Despite his injuries, despite everything that had been going on regarding the investigations into Koenig, the Liddell Psychiatric Hospital, and Alice's stepmother and stepbrother, despite frequent trips to doctors and repeated psychiatric evaluations, despite numerous interviews with the police—or perhaps *because* of all that—Shadow was desperate to have her.

They hadn't mated once since leaving Wonderland. Between his healing injuries and the stress and exhaustion caused by their ordeal, there'd been neither the time nor the energy on either of their parts.

It'd been a *long* time since they'd joined.

Too long.

He dropped his hands to Alice's hips and lifted her, dragging her onto his lap so that she straddled him. She released a startled breath, and her hands fell to his shoulders.

"Shadow, what are you doing?" she asked.

He kicked away the blankets covering them and moved his hands to her thighs, sliding his palms up beneath the silky material of her nightgown to feel *her*. "It should be obvious, sweet, sweet Alice."

"But you're still healing. The doctor said—"

His mouth swooped down and captured hers. "Don't care," he said against her lips. Her heat radiated into him, so inviting, so maddening. The pads of his thumbs brushed over her pelvis. "I need you. The rest doesn't matter."

She remained tense for a moment; he knew she was worried about hurting him, but the flush on her skin told him she was just as desperate for this as he was. Her lips parted, and her tongue slipped out to dance with his. She eased her muscles and smoothed her palms down his chest. He growled when she curled her fingers to trail her nails over his skin, scraping them down his abdomen.

Alice tore her mouth from his to kiss along his jaw. "I need you, too," she rasped. "So much."

Hearing her voice—hearing her *need*—fanned the desirous flames within Shadow to new heights.

Under her touch, everything else faded away—neither this world nor any other mattered. Neither this world nor any other existed. Reality was only Shadow and Alice; she was his universe.

He slid his hands up, palms gliding over her soft skin as he drew her nightgown off over her head. He tossed the garment aside; it may as well have fallen into the void for all he cared about it in that moment. Once she was bared to him, he pulled away, taking a moment to bask in her beauty, letting his eyes devour her a little at a time. Her hair fell around her naked shoulders and curled around her breasts, and those soft globes and their hardened peaks made his mouth water and drew him in. He wrapped an arm around her, tipped her back, and sucked one of her nipples into his mouth.

Alice gasped. Her back arched, and her fingers delved into Shadow's hair, holding him to her breast. When he sucked harder and twirled his tongue around her nipple, she moaned. It was amongst the sweetest sounds he'd ever heard. He nipped the hard bud before moving his mouth to her other breast, lavishing it with the same attention as he caressed the first with his free hand.

She undulated her hips on his thighs. Inhaling deeply, Shadow took in the sweet, heady scent of Alice's desire. A deep, low sound rose from his chest—part groan, part purr, part growl—and his cock grew so stiff it hurt, throbbing against the flat of her stomach. A bead of seed—*his seed!*—trickled from its tip and rolled down his shaft.

He moved his tail around Alice and trailed it down her back toward her ass, tickling her cleft before slipping it between her legs to stroke up her sex to her clit. She bucked and moaned, and within moments, she was gyrating against his tail, her breath coming in soft pants.

"Now," Alice said, gripping his hair to pull his mouth away from her breast. Her nipples were a lovely red after his attentions. "I need you inside me *now*, Shadow. No more waiting."

The desire on her face—run through with deep, undeniable love—made her more beautiful in that moment than ever before, a feat he would've thought impossible a moment ago.

"I love that you're willing to play," he said, withdrawing his tail and curling it possessively around her waist. "But I love it even more when you're done with the games."

Shadow settled his hands on her hips as she rose on her knees. Even if he hadn't recovered, he was more than strong enough to do what was required of him—and would've found the strength regardless. He lifted her up, drew her forward, and pressed the head of his cock against her entrance.

She bore down on him.

The head of his shaft slipped into her tight, wet channel. She pushed down upon him farther, her nails digging into his shoulders as she stretched around him, rising slightly only to press down again, easing her passage. She panted, her brows creased in concentration, impatience, and need.

Shadow flexed his fingers on her hips, careful not to curl his claws into her tender flesh. Everything within him, every instinct, demanded he take over, demanded he savagely thrust inside her, but he held himself still; he didn't want to hurt her.

Alice didn't seem to share in his concern.

She grasped his face between her hands and met his eyes. "Do it," she commanded before her mouth reclaimed his in a desperate, hungry kiss.

His restraint shattered into a million tiny pieces and drifted away on the winds of his desire; he did not mourn their loss.

Tightening his hold on Alice, he lifted her and thrust his cock into her while simultaneously slamming her down atop him. Alice cried out but didn't break the kiss. Her body tensed, and her sex clenched around his cock as tremors swept through her. His fingers curled, grazing her skin with his claws. She was dripping for him, so hot, so tight, and for a moment he couldn't breathe—the pleasure was too much.

What they'd shared in Wonderland hadn't prepared Shadow for the way this felt—the simulation hadn't come close to how *good* it was, to how perfectly they fit together. It hadn't been able to account for the way every tiny movement in her body sent a thrill along his shaft to crackle outward in electric currents all the way to the tips of his fingers and toes. It hadn't been able to account for the reality of Alice, for the truth of Alice.

He knew, without a doubt, that she was all for him. She was forever.

Alice broke the kiss and pressed her forehead to his. "Don't stop. Oh please, don't stop, Shadow."

He forced his hips into motion, lips parting with a gasp at the overwhelming sensation of it, of *her*. His movements gradu-

TIFFANY ROBERTS

ally gained speed and power, pushing faster and deeper with each thrust. "I'll never stop. Never."

Shadow smoothed a hand up her back, following the curve of her spine, and slid his fingers into her hair to cup the back of her head. He held her against him as he pumped in and out of her welcoming body. He didn't know how long he could last; he was enfolded in her heat, enveloped in pleasure, and it was consuming him—*she* was consuming him—until there'd be nothing left but the way this felt. Nothing left but ecstasy. He didn't want it to end.

"You're too perfect to be real," he said, "but you're mine, Alice. My sweet, my dearest, my Alice."

"Shadow," she whispered, her breath fanning his lips.

Suddenly, her body stiffened, and her tempo faltered. A rush of liquid heat flooded her, bathing him in her essence as her sex contracted around his cock, her inner walls pulsing with her release. She gasped, hands clutching him desperately as she was lost in her pleasure.

And Shadow did not delay in joining her. For a few seconds, he pushed harder and faster than should've been possible. Alice's body shuddered as she cried out in rapture; Shadow came undone in that moment.

The pressure that had built in him—not just tonight, but over the last few weeks, over the last *seven years*, waiting for *her* all along—finally became too much. His toes and tail curled as he climaxed, and every muscle in his body seized at once. His head reared back, forcing his back to arch—which only pushed him deeper into her, allow her hungry sex to squeeze out every ounce of his searing hot seed.

Even after he was spent, her sex pulsed and clenched around his throbbing shaft in aftershocks. He made no effort to withdraw from her body; he clung to her, panting.

As the pleasure slowly ebbed, Shadow's awareness of the world around him returned—but the worry and stress that

usually accompanied that awareness didn't come back. For the
first time in memory, Shadow felt…at peace.

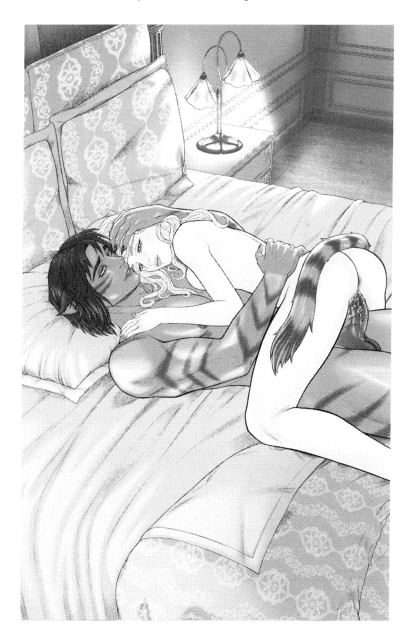

This was real. He and Alice were real. And what they shared was more real than *anything*. Whatever challenges lay ahead—and he wasn't so foolish or far-gone to believe they'd be without difficulties—they would overcome one by one. Together.

EPILOGUE

ALICE DREW in a deep breath as the car pulled around the circular driveway. Shadow squeezed her hand, and she looked up at him. He wore a soft, reassuring smile, the sort of smile that said *I'm here, don't worry*. She was grateful for that smile, was grateful for him. Nothing about the last six weeks had been easy—well, up until about two weeks ago, anyway, when they'd started making love again—but his presence had made it all bearable. Even though he was struggling, too, he'd made every effort to support her. That meant the world to her.

The driver brought the car to a stop. "Here we are, miss."

"Thank you," Alice said.

Shadow opened the door, slipped out, and turned to offer her his hand. She took a moment to admire him; he was dressed in a dark, tailored suit that enhanced the elegance of his long limbs. Though they'd had it designed with modern sensibilities, she and Shadow had been in agreement when it came to adding a few old-fashioned touches—particularly in his long overcoat and its collar. His silk vest was a deep maroon, offering just enough color to offset the black fabric dominating the rest of the outfit.

Alice placed her hand in his and stepped out of the vehicle. He closed the door behind her. The driver walked around to the trunk and removed their bags, which Shadow accepted—one in each hand. His health and physique had made immense improvement, especially during the last couple weeks.

He'd said it was because of their lovemaking. Though Alice remained skeptical of that, she couldn't deny the results.

"Anything else I can do for you, Miss Claybourne?" the driver asked.

"No, we'll be fine. Thank you," Alice replied with a smile.

He nodded and returned to the driver's seat. Once Alice and Shadow were a few steps away from the vehicle, the driver departed.

Alice turned her attention to the building in front of them— the only home she'd known for her entire life. Coming home wasn't the final step in their current journey, but it felt like a milestone on the path, albeit a bittersweet one.

They'd spent the last month and a half dealing with Shadow's frequent medical and psychiatric appointments, cooperating with the police investigations into the asylum and Tabitha and Jonathon, and sorting through the legal process of solidifying Alice's claim on her inheritance and ensuring that everything her father left her was rightfully recognized as hers.

And she couldn't forget the media. She'd managed to shield Shadow from the constant stream of reporters that had hounded them over the last six weeks, and had only given a few public statements herself, but it had proven an unexpectedly stressful aspect of this whole situation.

The public knew all about Director Victor Koenig and the Liddell Psychiatric Hospital now. Chief Farland had kept the information quiet for as long as he'd been able, but it was impossible to keep the secret for long. The tablet Shadow had taken from Koenig had provided droves of evidence to prove the abuse and neglect on display in the asylum, and several of the staff members had been charged with a plethora of crimes as a result—including Doctor Miranda Kade.

She and several of the other staff members were even facing murder charges. The sudden appearance of true death in Wonderland—which had apparently caused feedback in the physical bodies of victims so strong it had induced cardiac arrest—had been the result of a deliberate programming change made under Koenig's orders. As if that wasn't enough, the director's tablet had also revealed the reason for that programming change.

The facility had been operating at near-maximum capacity, which meant it was unable to bring in new patients regularly. Koenig had seen that as a problem, considering each new patient brought along a hefty governmental subsidy. He'd decided to clear some room to simultaneously make way for new patients and indulge his sadistic urges.

The Intergalactic Union had taken control of the facility and was currently in the process of carefully reviewing both the methods used there—the simulation—and the cases of each and every patient. There were rumors that Alice hadn't been the only person committed there under false pretenses, and she wouldn't have been surprised if those rumors eventually proved true. She just hoped that Jor'calla was the last patient at Liddell Psychiatric Hospital who'd suffered unduly.

Tabitha and Jonathon were facing charges of their own. As though the conversations between Tabitha and Koenig found on the tablet weren't evidence enough, Jonathon had confessed to everything when the police arrested him, corroborating the evidence on the tablet and providing new details in the process.

Daniel Claybourne had left ninety-five percent of his wealth to Alice in his will, with the rest split between Tabitha and Jonathon. Alice had spent her rare moments alone wondering what her father's motivations had been in drafting that will; had he known, deep in his heart, the kind of person Tabitha was?

Had he suspected something? Or, perhaps, had it been some way for him to assuage potential guilt he'd carried for so often being absent to deal with business matters?

She wished she could've had just a few more seconds with him. Just long enough to say she loved him, that she didn't blame him for working. That she understood how hard things had been for him after what her mother had done.

Whatever his reasons, she knew he never would've imagined the hatred and contempt with which Tabitha had reacted to his will.

Intergalactic Union law gave precedence to the will of the deceased over the default inheritance laws save in particular circumstances—such as when the benefactor of said will was proven to be mentally incompetent or unstable. Hence Tabitha's contacts with Victor.

Alice still felt the hurt of their betrayal when she stopped to think about it. But she was far more than hurt; she was *angry*. Tabitha had been in Alice's life for seventeen years, since Alice was eight years old. Even though Alice had never really liked the woman, had never fully trusted Tabitha's intentions with her father, she never would've guessed Tabitha was capable of anything like this. Capable of having Alice falsely committed to an asylum where she was meant to die alone, silenced, and forgotten.

But Tabitha and Jonathon would face justice. They would pay for what they'd done. And Alice had more important things to turn her attention toward—more important people.

She glanced at Shadow, offering him another smile, as they walked toward the front entrance.

This was the place she'd been brought to after she was born. The place where she'd played with her toys, where she'd had piano lessons, the place where her father had bandaged her scraped knees and read her bedtime stories. This place, until recently, had contained almost all her happy memories.

But it was also the place where her mother, screaming and swearing, had abandoned Alice and left her father. It was the place where her father had passed away a few months ago. And this was the place where her stepmother and stepbrother had conspired against her, had plotted to have her imprisoned and murdered.

She opened the front door, and Shadow followed her into the foyer. She stopped in the center of the space and, as she stared up at the double staircase leading to the second floor, knew what she'd suspected during the drive over.

This wasn't home anymore. Even if her memories of this place balanced out between the positive and the negative, without her father around, it meant *nothing* to her. She could bring her dad with her wherever she went—he'd always be in her heart, in her memory, and that was *good*. She didn't want the bad that went along with this house anymore.

"Home sweet home," Alice said quietly. She twisted to look at Shadow, who stood just behind her. "What do you think?"

He frowned, and a small crease formed between his brows. "Seems a bit...*much*, doesn't it?"

"A bit much?"

"It's nice—I'm not saying it isn't—but it's so...big. And it feels *empty*."

"You got all that from walking into the foyer?"

Shadow shrugged. "I can't imagine how it must've seemed to you when you were even smaller than you are now."

Alice chuckled and turned toward him fully. "How can you not imagine it after spending so long walking through a giant forest with flowers as big as houses?" She poked his chest. "And I'm not *that* small."

Shadow arched a brow and glanced down at her, having to dip his chin to do so. His gaze dropped, trailing over her body before rising to meet hers again. "You *are* small, sweet Alice, and I rather like you just as you are."

Alice smiled and reached for him. He crouched, setting their bags on the floor, and she took his hands. She turned around and tucked her back against his chest, guiding his arms around her. She stared at the chamber as he rested his chin atop her hair.

"It does seem a bit much, doesn't it?" she asked.

"Especially for just the two of us. And all these angles and colors…they're so *plain*. Where's the style, the flair, the *chaos*?"

Alice felt her smile stretch. "Oh? And what sort of place would you prefer to live?"

"This sort of home might do, but it'd take a lot of work. It's entirely too orderly, for starters. We'd need a bucket of paint in every color—perhaps two." He extended a hand and swept it from side to side, as though indicating the entire room. "Just pop off the lids and splash it around. The best thing about it is we could always get new paint if we want to change it. The flooring is rather humdrum, too. We'd need to vary that up in much the same way. And doors! Clearly, there need to be more doors. They don't have to go anywhere so long as they're unique."

Alice laughed; her entire body quaked with it. And that laughter felt cathartic, like it expelled some of her stress. "I don't think we're going to do any of that here."

Shadow dropped his arm, and she could almost *feel* his disappointed frown. "Why not? Think of the fun we'd have, dearest Alice."

"Because…I think I want to sell this place. And if I let you loose on it, nobody will want to buy it. At least, not in this world." She rested her head against him, her smile persisting even as her laughter faded. "We can build a home of our own. Together."

Shadow tipped his head forward to peck a kiss atop her hair. "As long as you're with me, I'll live anywhere."

Alice released one of his hands to reach up and cup the side of his face. "I'll always be with you, Shadow." A warmth flooded her. "Also, who says it will always be just the two of us?"

There was a pause before he spoke next. "What do you mean?"

She turned in his arms to face him, head tilted back so she could meet his eyes as her hands settled over his heart. "I want to have a family with you, Shadow, when the time is right. A home, children. I want everything…with you."

He stared down at her, cat-like ears perked, his teal eyes softening with emotion so raw and pure that it seemed on the verge of overwhelming him. He answered her by dipping his head and pressing his lips against hers. The kiss was slow, sensual, lingering; it ignited a spark deep in Alice's core and left her breathless and wanting.

She never would've thought a kiss could drive a person mad before meeting Shadow, but madness was a small price to pay in exchange for his love.

AUTHOR'S NOTE

Hello everyone!

We hope you all enjoyed *Escaping Wonderland*! While this book wasn't always the easiest to write, and we had a few (okay, maybe a lot) of disagreements at times (haha!), we still absolutely loved writing it.

I adored Shadow, the embodiment of chaos, which is exactly what the Cheshire Cat was. He was such a lost, lonely soul who just needed someone to give him the support and love he so needed. We were originally going to have the Mad Hatter as the hero, but immediately decided against it. We know he is a popular character, but we wanted to show the Cheshire Cat some love. We hope you all loved Shadow as much as we did.

Also, if you would be so kind, please leave a review! I'm sure you've heard it many times, but reviews are vital in helping authors gain visibility, and we would appreciate it dearly. <3

To keep up on current news from us, be sure to join our newsletter. We always share monthly updates on what we're working on as well as art, book recommendations, and more. Also consider joining our Facebook Reader Group!

ALSO BY TIFFANY ROBERTS

THE INFINITE CITY

Entwined Fates

Silent Lucidity

Shielded Heart

Vengeful Heart

Untamed Hunger

Savage Desire

Tethered Souls

THE KRAKEN

Treasure of the Abyss

Jewel of the Sea

Hunter of the Tide

Heart of the Deep

Rising from the Depths

Fallen from the Stars

Lover from the Waves

THE SPIDER'S MATE TRILOGY

Ensnared

Enthralled

Bound

THE VRIX

The Weaver

The Delver

The Hunter

THE CURSED ONES

His Darkest Craving

His Darkest Desire

ALIENS AMONG US

Taken by the Alien Next Door

Stalked by the Alien Assassin

Claimed by the Alien Bodyguard

Saved by the Alien Crime Boss

STANDALONE TITLES

Claimed by an Alien Warrior

Dustwalker

Escaping Wonderland

Yearning For Her

The Warlock's Kiss

Ice Bound: Short Story

ISLE OF THE FORGOTTEN

Make Me Burn

Make Me Hunger

Make Me Whole

Make Me Yours

VALOS OF SONHADRA COLLABORATION

Tiffany Roberts - Undying

Tiffany Roberts - Unleashed

VENYS NEEDS MEN COLLABORATION

Tiffany Roberts - To Tame a Dragon

Tiffany Roberts – To Love a Dragon

ABOUT THE AUTHOR

Tiffany Roberts is the pseudonym for Tiffany and Robert Freund, a husband and wife writing duo. The two have always shared a passion for reading and writing, and it was their dream to combine their mighty powers to create the sorts of books they want to read. They write character driven sci-fi and fantasy romance, creating happily-ever-afters for the alien and unknown.

Sign up for our Newsletter!
Check out our social media sites and more!
http://www.authortiffanyroberts.com

Printed in Great Britain
by Amazon

4637a429-9812-43e1-9eba-5147fec641a0R01